INSPECTOR WITHERSPOON ALWAYS TRIUMPHS . . .
HOW DOES HE DO IT?

Even the inspector himself doesn't know—because his secret weapon is as ladylike as she is clever. She's Mrs. Jeffries—the determined, delightful detective who stars in this unique Victorian mystery series! Be sure to read them all . . .

The Inspector and Mrs. Jeffries
A doctor is found dead in his own office—and Mrs. Jeffries must scour the premises to find the prescription for murder!

Mrs. Jeffries Dusts for Clues
One case is solved and another is opened when the inspector finds a missing brooch—pinned to a dead woman's gown. But Mrs. Jeffries never cleans a room without dusting under the bed—and never gives up on a case before every loose end is tightly tied . . .

The Ghost and Mrs. Jeffries
Death is unpredictable . . . but the murder of Mrs. Hodges was foreseen at a spooky seance. The practical-minded housekeeper may not be able to see the future—but she can look into the past and put things in order to solve this haunting crime!

D0842060

Mrs. Jeffries and the Missing Alibi
When Inspector Witherspoon becomes the main suspect in a murder, Scotland Yard refuses to let him investigate. But no one said anything about Mrs. Jeffries . . .

Mrs. Jeffries Stands Corrected
When a local publican is murdered, and Inspector Witherspoon botches the investigation, trouble starts to brew for Mrs. Jeffries . . .

Mrs. Jeffries Takes the Stage
After a theatre critic is murdered, Mrs. Jeffries uncovers the victim's secret past: a real-life drama more compelling than any stage play . . .

Mrs. Jeffries Questions the Answer
Hannah Cameron was not well-liked. But were her friends or family the sort to stab her in the back? Mrs. Jeffries must really tiptoe around this time—or it could be a matter of life and death . . .

Mrs. Jeffries Reveals her Art
Mrs. Jeffries has to work double-time to find a missing model *and* a killer. She'll have to get her whole staff involved—before someone else becomes the next subject . . .

MRS. JEFFRIES
TAKES THE CAKE

EMILY BRIGHTWELL

BERKLEY PRIME CRIME, NEW YORK

MRS. JEFFRIES TAKES THE CAKE

A Berkley Prime Crime Book / published by arrangement with the author

PRINTING HISTORY
Berkley Prime Crime edition / October 1998
All rights reserved.
Copyright © 1998 by The Berkley Publishing Group.
This book may not be reproduced in whole or in part, by mimeograph or any other means, without permission.
For information address: The Berkley Publishing Group,
a member of Penguin Putnam Inc.,
375 Hudson Street, New York, NY 10014.

The Putnam Berkley Inc. World Wide Web site address is
http://www.penguinputnam.com

ISBN: 0-425-16569-8

Berkley Prime Crime Books are published
by The Berkley Publishing Group,
a member of Penguin Putnam Inc.,
375 Hudson Street, New York, NY 10014.

The name BERKLEY PRIME CRIME and the BERKLEY PRIME CRIME
design are trademarks belonging to Berkley Publishing Corporation.

PRINTED IN THE UNITED STATES OF AMERICA

10 9 8 7 6 5 4 3 2 1

MRS. JEFFRIES
TAKES THE CAKE

CHAPTER 1

Maisie Donovan pulled the heavy trunk up the last two stairs and heaved a sigh of relief that she'd got the ruddy box this far. She gave the thing a vicious kick and then plopped down on the top of the flat lid to catch her breath. Only one more flight to go, she told herself. Too bad that wretched boy had taken it into his head to run off; by rights this should have been his job, lugging the mistress's trunk up to her room. But the household had awoken this morning to find Boyd gone and she'd got stuck with the job. Sighing, Maisie rose to her feet. She'd better push on. They'd be here any minute now and she didn't want to get caught sitting on the landing.

In the fading evening light, the landing was so dark as to be almost black. Perhaps that's what caught Maisie's eye—the streak of light seeping out of Mr. Ashbury's door. Blast. She swore softly and fluently to herself. Now, why was he home? ''What's that old tattletale doin' here?'' she muttered. She wondered if he'd heard her kicking the truck.

Maisie didn't think she'd get the sack, not after Boyd's runnin' off like that. But she wasn't sure. Mr. Frommer could be a right old tartar. Breaking the silliest rule could find you out on the street, she thought, remembering what had happened to Emma only a few days before the household had gone to Ascot. Poor girl had been sacked over a ruddy flowerpot. Blast. It'd be just like that old Ashbury to pretend he wasn't here and then tell the master he'd heard her kickin' their precious trunk. Well, she wasn't having it. She wasn't going to spend the next few hours or even days wondering if the ax was going to fall. She glared at the doorway and then, when she heard nothing, boldly decided to take matters into her own hands. Maybe Mr. Ashbury hadn't come in yet.

''Mr. Ashbury?'' she said softly as she pushed the door open. ''Are you in here, sir?''

There was no answer.

She stepped inside and gazed sharply around the spacious sitting room. Empty. But he'd been here.

The heavy curtains were wide open, letting in the last rays of the fading sun. A fully loaded tea trolley stood next to his favorite balloon-backed chair. Bloomin' odd, she thought stepping farther into the room. She could see that the door to the connecting bedroom stood open and the top of the spread was rumpled. ''Mr. Ashbury, sir. Are ya here?''

No one replied.

The hair on the back of Maisie's neck stood up. Something was wrong. Very wrong. Tentatively she took a step closer to the tea trolley. ''Mr. Ashbury?''

Silence.

''Oh, this is stupid,'' she muttered, more to give herself

courage than for anything else. The back of Mr. Ashbury's chair faced the door. Maisie walked over to it and peeked around the edge. She gasped in surprise. The old man himself was sitting there, staring straight at her.

"Oh, I'm sorry sir," she began as she backed away. "I didn't realize you was in here."

He said nothing; he merely gazed at her out of his pale, washed-out hazel eyes.

"I thought there might be something amiss, sir," she explained, "when I saw the door open a crack, sir. I mean, we didn't think you were due home till tonight, sir."

He continued to stare at her.

Maisie stopped. She realized he hadn't so much as blinked. She walked back across the room and knelt right in front of him.

He didn't move a muscle.

She waved her hand in front of his eyes.

He didn't blink.

Relieved, she sighed. At least he wouldn't be running to Mr. Frommer telling tales now. "Old blighter's kicked off," she murmured. Death was no stranger to Maisie. She'd buried both her parents and three brothers by the time she was fourteen. Matter-of-factly she reached over to close Mr. Ashbury's eyes. Not because she liked him, but out of respect for the dead in general. As she touched him he toppled to one side.

It was only then that Maisie saw the blood on the back of the chair and the gaping hole in the side of the man's skull.

"Looks like the poor bloke didn't know what hit him," Constable Barnes said to Inspector Witherspoon. "Shot directly in the side of the head." He clucked his tongue sympathetically. The constable was a tall, craggy-faced man with iron-gray hair beneath his policeman's helmet.

Inspector Gerald Witherspoon suppressed a shudder. If he could have managed it, he'd have avoided examining the body altogether. But as it was a necessary part of the investigation, he steeled himself to do his duty. "It doesn't appear as if the man put up a struggle," he replied. He swallowed heavily as he gently moved the victim's head to one side. Witherspoon was no expert on gunshot wounds, but even he could see that the weapon had been fired at close range. Very close range.

"No," Barnes agreed, "he didn't struggle. Just sat here like a lamb to the slaughter and let the killer do his worst."

"Perhaps he didn't see it coming," Witherspoon suggested.

Barnes nodded in agreement. "Could be the killer come up on his blind side, sir. With these kind of chairs"—he tapped the heavy side padding—"you can't see a ruddy thing unless you stick your head out."

"Yes, I expect the killer was counting on that." Gerald Witherspoon was a tall, robust man with thinning dark brown hair and a neatly trimmed mustache. He had a long angular face with a sharp, rather pointed nose and, behind his spectacles, clear, blue-gray eyes. "Most people don't generally sit calmly and wait for someone to put a bullet in their head. Not if they see it first, that is. Do you think in might possibly have been suicide?"

Barnes shook his head. "I shouldn't think so, sir. For starters, if he'd done himself in, the gun should be somewhere right here." He pointed to the area around the body. "And we've looked, sir. It's not."

"I see what you mean. Suicides don't generally hide the gun after they've used it." Witherspoon pursed his lips and stepped back to survey the scene. The walls were decorated with nice but unimaginative paintings of hunting scenes and wildlife. There was a decent but well-worn camel-colored Turkey carpet on the floor and terra-cotta-colored muslin summer curtains hung at the windows overlooking the back garden. To one side of the chair where the victim reclined was a settee upholstered in thick, navy-blue cloth. A fully loaded tea trolley stood at the far end of the settee. A dark-colored cake with a large sliver missing was next to a pink-and-white-rose teapot. Two dessert plates, both used, two forks and two cups and saucers testified to the presence of two people.

Barnes grimaced. "Seems wrong, doesn't it, sir? Sitting down and havin' tea with someone you're plannin' on killin'."

"Breaking bread with a murderer," Witherspoon replied, shaking his head sadly, "seems somehow so very, very, awful. More awful, really, than just getting murdered in the course of one's day."

Barnes's gaze dropped to the two dessert plates, one scrapped clean and the other spotted with several tiny rocklike mounds. "One of them didn't like walnuts." He sighed and straightened his spine. "Well, sir, do you want to begin taking statements now?"

"We might as well get cracking. The police surgeon's on his way and we've had a good look at the victim. Do we know the poor fellow's name?"

"It's Ashbury, sir." Barnes flipped open his notebook. "According to the maid, Miss Maisie Donovan; she's the one who found the body. The victim is one Roland Arthur Ashbury."

"He owns the house?"

Barnes shook his head. "He lives here, sir, with his daughter and son-in-law, Andrew Frommer. They are at their country house in Ascot; they're due back later this evening."

"Frommer," Witherspoon repeated with a frown. "Now, why does that name sound so familiar?"

"He's an MP, sir." Barnes sighed again. "So that means this case'll probably get sticky. I expect we'll have the home secretary and half of Westminster puttin' their oars in on this one."

"Oh dear," Witherspoon groaned. "I'm afraid you're right, Barnes. Unless, of course, we get very lucky and this turns out to be a simple case."

"Simple, sir?" Barnes snorted in disbelief. "I don't see that happening. They never are, sir. I expect that's why the chief sent you out on this one. He's got a nose, he does, our chief inspector. A call comes in and he can tell by the smell if it's goin' to be a clean one or a right old tangle to sort out. But you're right good at it, sir. If I do say so myself."

Witherspoon's narrow chest swelled with pride. "Thank you, Barnes, but I don't solve cases alone. You're just as important as I am." He sighed, thinking of the tremendous responsibility he would have to shoulder. "All right then, complex or not, let's get this sorted out." He darted a glance at the door to the hall. The maid who'd discovered the body and the other servants had been asked to remain in the kitchen. "We'll search the room thoroughly and then get on with taking statements. I suppose I ought to send a message home, telling them not to wait up for me."

"I've already taken care of that," Barnes said as he hurried toward the bedroom door. "As soon as we got the call, I sent a street arab off to both your home and my missus. No sense in worryin' people when we don't get home on time, is there?"

• • •

The street arab, one Jeremy Slaven, age eight, stared at the coin the pretty blonde maid had just dropped into his dirty palm. A whole shilling. He couldn't believe it. Fearing she'd made a mistake and might snatch it back, he quickly closed his fingers on it and stepped out of reach.

"Thanks for bringing us the message," Betsy, housemaid to Inspector Gerald Witherspoon, said as she smiled brightly at the filthy, spindly-legged lad on the backdoor stoop. She was aware of exactly what was going on in his head. Having been poor herself, she knew precisely how suspicious one could be of unexpected generosity. The boy looked as though he'd not had a decent meal in days. "Don't worry," she said reassuringly, "I'm not going to take it back. You've earned it. If you've a mind to, you can come in. There's a bit of pudding left from supper. You're welcome to it."

For a moment Jeremy studied her, and then shrugged as though the matter was of no importance. "All right, seein' as you've asked."

Betsy turned and started down the back hall, the boy following right at her heels. As they came into the kitchen Jeremy had second thoughts. A whole ruddy bunch of people was sitting at the table. Everyone stopped talking and stared at him.

"The lad's just come in to finish up that bit of pudding," Betsy said brightly, ushering him toward the table where the others sat. "As he's come all the way from Charing Cross with a message from the inspector, I thought he might be a bit peckish."

"Is the inspector going to be in for dinner?" Mrs. Goodge, the cook, asked. She studied the street lad over the top of her spectacles. He was filthy enough to make her squirm. But she held her tongue. Something was happening, she was sure of that.

"No, he's been called out to a possible murder." Betsy said the words carefully, not wanting to indicate any excitement whatsoever in the presence of a stranger. Even one who was only a youngster. The household's investigations on behalf of Inspector Witherspoon were a secret.

"I see," Mrs. Goodge replied, with equal care. Her round face broke into a welcoming smile at the lad. What did a bit of dirt being tracked into her kitchen matter? There was plenty of carbolic in the washroom. "Do sit down, then," she said briskly, getting up and heading toward the larder, "and I'll get the pudding."

Jeremy stopped a few feet from the table as everyone in the kitchen broke into broad, welcoming smiles. These were an odd lot, that was for sure. But he was hungry, so he'd take his chances. He'd not had a bite all day and only half a slice of stale bread the day before.

" 'Ere." Wiggins, the inspector's young footman, pointed to an empty chair next to him. "This is a nice seat. Come on, now, don't be shy."

Jeremy hesitated for a moment and then plopped down in the seat. "Ta," he muttered.

Wiggins smiled brightly, his round apple cheeks flushed with excitement. He was barely out of his teens and not as good at hiding his feelings as the others.

"I understand you brought a message to the house?" Mrs. Jeffries, the inspector's housekeeper, asked.

Jeremy looked at her and decided she was all right. He couldn't say why he thought that way; it was something you just knew. He'd gotten good at sussin' out people. She reminded him of someone he used to know, but he couldn't say who. He only knew he'd decided she could be trusted. Her eyes were a bright brown, kindly-like. She had red-brown hair streaked with gray at the sides and a ready smile that made him glad to be sitting at this table.

"Here you are, boy." Mrs. Goodge popped a plate heaped with food under his nose. "You might as well help us get shut of this food, seein' as how you've come so far."

His eyes widened in disbelief. He'd been expectin' a bit of puddin', but this was a feast fit for a king. He stared at the slab of chicken pie, the mashed potatoes and the peas, and his mouth watered.

The cook handed him a fork and knife. "They'll be treacle pudding for afters," she said lightly. Brushing a bit of flour off the apron covering her ample girth, she sat down next to the housekeeper.

Jeremy wasn't one to look a gift horse in the mouth. He snatched up the fork and tucked right in.

"As the young man's been taken care of"—Mrs. Jeffries flashed a quick smile at Betsy—"why don't you tell us the rest of the inspector's message."

"Oh it's not much," Betsy replied airily. "Just that the inspector's been called out on a case and won't be home until late."

"I wonder what kind of a case?" Wiggins mused. "I mean did he know fer sure it were a murder, or were it an accident of some kind?"

"It were a murder," Jeremy volunteered. "The copper that sent me told me so. Seems some old fellow got himself shot in the 'ead."

Mrs. Goodge clucked her tongue. "Shocking. Absolutely shocking. You didn't by any chance happen to hear the name of the poor man, did you?"

"Nah." The lad shook his head. "But I heard the old bas—copper tellin' another copper the address. It were on

Argyle Street. Number twenty-one. That's over near the Midland Railway Terminus.''

Using various indirect means, they questioned the lad closely. But it was soon evident he'd told them everything he knew.

"Blimey," he finally said, scraping the bowl and spooning the last of the pudding into his mouth. "I'd best get movin'. I've got to tell that old copper's missus he's not comin' home till late too."

Betsy walked him to the back door. Reaching into the pocket of her lavender broadcloth skirt, she pulled out another shilling. "Here," she said, handing it to the boy, "hang on to this. You might need it for a rainy day."

'' 'Ow come you're bein' so nice to me?'' Jeremy was no longer suspicious; now he was just plain curious. These were a strange lot of people, they were. He'd never in his life had so many grown-ups listening to every word he said.

Betsy shrugged. She wasn't sure she could explain it properly, even to herself. But she'd been young and poor herself once. "No reason not to be, is there? Besides, I've been skint myself a time or two," she said, yanking open the back door. "You look like you could use a bit of coin in your pocket. Go on, now. Get off with you. Constable Barnes's missus is probably getting worried."

With a jaunty wave he hurried across the small terrace toward the side of the house. "Thanks for everything," he called over his shoulder as he disappeared around the corner.

When Betsy got back to the dining room, the others were already discussing what needed to be done.

"I think I ought to get over to Argyle Street and suss out what's up," Wiggins volunteered.

Mrs. Jeffries thought about it for a moment. The staff

had been helping their dear inspector with his cases for several years now, but, as always, it was imperative they be discreet. Inspector Witherspoon wasn't aware that he was getting any help in his investigations.

"I think you ought to wait for Smythe," Betsy said before the housekeeper could reply to Wiggins's query. "He should be back any minute now."

Smythe was the household's coachman. He'd gone the station to collect their neighbor Lady Cannonberry.

"But it might take ages for him to get back 'ere," Wiggins protested. "And you know what Mrs. Jeffries always says; the trail goes cold if you don't get right on it."

"It doesn't go that cold," Betsy told him. "Besides, you know we're not supposed to go off snooping about on our own. It's not fair, is it? Especially at the beginning, everybody should have a chance."

Mrs. Jeffries listened carefully, hoping to be able to nip any incipient rivalry in the bud. Over the course of their investigations, they'd all become just a tad competitive with one another. Everyone, it seemed, wanted to be the one who discovered the clue that solved the case. To that end, they'd informally agreed to a set of rules. Everyone was to have a chance to hear all the pertinent information about the case as it was gathered. Yet the housekeeper could understand the footman's eagerness to get started. They had an address. They had a body. It did chafe a bit to have to wait. Then she realized there might be a way to accommmodate both points of view.

"You're both right," she said briskly. "On the one hand, it's only fair to wait for Smythe to get here before we leap into action, so to speak."

"Are we goin' to wait for Luty and Hatchet as well?" Wiggins asked.

"I'm getting to that," the housekeeper replied. "Actually, what I was going to suggest is that you escort Betsy down to the high street and put her in a hansom. She can go get Luty and Hatchet. You can nip over to the murdered man's house and try and pick up a bit more information, and by the time everyone gets back here, Smythe ought to have returned."

"The killer left us a present, sir," Barnes muttered. He was on his knees in front of the tea trolley, his nose to the carpet. "Looks like there's a gun here." The constable carefully reached behind the wheel and slowly pulled the weapon out. Getting a grip on the handle, he straightened up and held it out to Witherspoon. "A revolver, sir. An Enfield."

Grimacing, Witherspoon took it and held it to his nose. He wasn't certain what, exactly, it was supposed to smell like. As far as he could tell, the only scent was a slightly smoky metallic one. But he'd seen other policemen put a gun barrel to their nose and then pronounce on whether it had or hadn't been fired. The inspector supposed that if it hadn't been fired, there wouldn't be a scent at all. "It's been fired," he concluded. "Here, have a whiff and see if you don't think I'm right."

Barnes took the gun and gave it a good long sniff. "Right, sir," he agreed, "it has been fired. I'd say this is our murder weapon. Odd that the killer left it here and didn't take it with him."

Witherspoon almost sagged in relief. "Well, then, that would rule out suicide."

"Right, again, sir. That trolley is a good ten feet from the victim." Barnes pointed at the expanse of carpet between the chair and trolley. "Ashbury wouldn't have shot himself in the head and then heaved it under that far."

"Agreed. And it certainly wasn't an accident." The inspector shook his head. "But why leave the weapon at all?"

"Maybe the killer panicked sir," the constable suggested. He'd been a policeman a lot longer than the inspector, and in his day, he'd seen some pretty stupid criminals.

Just then another constable appeared in the doorway. "The police surgeon's just here, sir," he said to Witherspoon, "and the mistress of the house, a Mrs. Frommer, has arrived. She's getting upset. What do you want me to do?"

"Send the police surgeon in here, but make sure Mrs. Frommer is kept downstairs. I don't think she ought to see her father this way. It would be most shocking, most shocking, indeed. We'll be down in a few moments to have a word with her." Witherspoon handed the gun to Barnes. "Would you take charge of this?" The constable was far more experienced with firearms than himself, and frankly he didn't want to risk shooting off his big toe by carrying the gun himself.

"Yes, sir." Barnes took the gun, opened the thing up and peered into the cylinder. "There's only five bullets here, sir. That mean's that one's been fired." He popped the bullets out of the gun and put them into his pocket. "We'll place it in evidence when we get back to the station."

"Er, ah, yes, Constable, that's a good idea," Witherspoon muttered. He wished he'd thought to open the gun himself, but the truth was, he was a bit frightened of them.

The two men went down the stairs to the ground floor. As they neared the front door Barnes veered off and gave the weapon to the constable who was stationed there. Witherspoon went on into the drawing room.

The lady of the house was a plump, middle-aged woman with light auburn hair peeking out of an ornate bonnet and pale blue eyes. Dressed in a dark green traveling dress, she leapt up from the settee when the inspector stepped through the door.

"Who are you?" she demanded. Her voice was thin, reedy and edged with hysteria. "Why are all these police here? What's happened? Where's my father? Where are the servants?"

"I'm Inspector Gerald Witherspoon, madam," he replied sympathetically. "I take it you're Mrs. Frommer."

She clasped her hands in front of her. When she spoke, her voice shook. "Yes, I'm MaryAnne Frommer. Mrs. Andrew Frommer. What's happened? Where's my maid?"

The inspector could tell by her demeanor that the woman was well aware that something awful had happened. One doesn't come home to find one's house full of police without realizing that something terrible has occurred. But even with that, he wanted to break the bad news to her in as kindly a way as possible. "Your maid and the rest of the servants are in the kitchen, madam," he said gently. "I'm afraid I've bad news. Very bad news. Was your father expected here today?"

"Yes." She paled even further. "We've all been out at our country house. Father came home on an earlier train today. He should be here. Where is he? For God's sake, has there been an accident?"

"I'm afraid he's dead, ma'am." The inspector hated this part of his job. Watching someone learn of the death of a loved one was heartbreaking.

MaryAnne Frommer stared at him for a long moment. Her mouth parted slightly and she cocked her head to one side, as though she hadn't heard correctly. "Dead?" she finally whispered. "But that can't be. He was fine at luncheon . . . he ate two apple tarts for dessert. How can he be dead? How did it happen? Was it his heart? A stroke?"

"He was shot, madam." Witherspoon dearly wished the lady's husband would get here. He wasn't sure what to do if she had hysterics.

"Shot?" She shook her head in disbelief. "No, I don't believe it. Father? But who . . . how . . . ? I don't understand. But he didn't keep firearms in his room. All the hunting rifles are kept at the country house. How could he have been shot?"

"He wasn't shot with a rifle, ma'am. He was shot with a revolver," the inspector replied. "And it doesn't appear as if it was an accident of any kind. It appears to have been done quite deliberately." Witherspoon generally didn't like to use the word *murder* until he absolutely had to.

Her eyes widened to size of scones. "Are you saying he was murdered?"

"I'm afraid so, ma'am," Witherspoon replied. Drat. He noticed that Barnes hadn't come in to take notes.

She swayed on her feet and, before the inspector could reach her, sat down heavily on the settee. "I don't believe this," she whispered as her eyes filled with tears. "Father dead. Shot."

"What's all this, then?" A booming voice sliced into the quiet drawing room.

Witherspoon looked up just as a short, rather stout, dark-haired man in thick spectacles strode into the room. "Now, see here," he began, as soon as he spotted the inspector. "I demand to know what's going on? That blockhead of a constable wouldn't say anything. I demand to know why my house is swarming with policemen."

• • •

Wiggins mingled with the small crowd that had gathered on the pavement in front of number twenty-one. The huge, pale gray-brick house was at the end of the fashionable street and set back behind tall, spear-pointed black fencing. A police constable stood guard at the front gate. Two more stood like sentinels on the wide doorstoop of the house. Wiggins thought the one on the left looked familiar. So he quickly darted behind two tall women, both servants from the look of their clothes. No reason to stick his face out where he might be spotted.

Staying to the center of the crowd, well behind the women, he kept a sharp eye out, hoping that none of the police constables coming and going would notice him. Too many of them knew who he was and that he worked for Inspector Witherspoon.

"What's 'appened?" Wiggins asked the youngest of the women.

"The old bloke wot lives here 'as got done in," she replied excitedly. "Shot he was, while he was havin' his tea."

"Now, Vera. You don't know that fer sure," the other, older woman cautioned.

"Do too," the one called Vera replied. "Heard it from our Agnes, who got it directly from that young police constable that's sweet on her. She spotted him comin' back from raisin' the alarm and he told her that old man Ashbury 'ad been shot in the 'ead. So don't tell me I don't know what's what." She folded her arms over her chest and glared at her companion.

"Your Agnes was wrong about that robbery over at that Yank's house, wasn't she?" the other woman shot back. "And she'd supposedly got that from the constable too. If you ask me, he don't know what's what."

"He does too," Vera countered hotly. "Anyone could have made a mistake on that other one. The door and the window was wide open."

"But nothing was taken, was it?" her companion said triumphantly. "So there weren't no robbery."

"Does this Mr. Ashbury live on 'is own?" Wiggins asked quickly, before the two women could get into a full-blown argument.

"'Course he don't live on his own," Vera snapped. "Lives with his daughter and her husband. Mr. and Mrs. Frommer. He's an MP. He just went inside a few minutes ago. Stopped and had a right old dustup with that constable on the door." She giggled. "Mind you, I expect by the time the night's over, the police'll be wishin' it were Andrew Frommer that'd been shot. He's a nasty one, he is."

"Nasty fellow, is 'e?" Wiggins knew he couldn't stay much longer, but he wanted to learn as much as he could before going back to the others.

"Won't give ya the time of day," Vera said flatly, "and treats the help like they was dirt." She jerked her head toward the house. "Most of the staff there is untrained. They can't keep proper servants. They've even got a footman that's a half-wit."

"Really?" Wiggins edged away. He wanted information about the murder. About what had gone on this evening, not about what kind of employer Frommer was. That could come later. He worked the crowd, keeping up a discreet but steady stream of questions. By the time he left, he'd found out enough to get the household started.

"Lady Cannonberry's train was late," Smythe the coachman explained. "And by the time I got 'em loaded up and on the way, it was later than I'd thought." He was a tall, muscular, dark-haired man with brutally heavy features. Were it not for the kindness in his brown eyes and the good-natured set of his mouth, he could easily be mistaken for a ruffian. But nothing was further from the truth. The coachman was as kindhearted as he was strong.

"Them?" Mrs. Goodge queried. "I thought it was just Lady Cannonberry you were bringing home."

"She's brung a houseguest with 'er." Smythe took a quick sip of tea and glanced at the clock. "Some sort of distant cousin of her late 'usband. Fellow's name is Pilchard. Morris Pilchard. Bit of a toff. I could tell it niggled 'im that she were so friendly to me."

"How foolish of him," Mrs. Jeffries murmured. "We are all Lady Cannonberry's friends." Ruth Cannonberry was the wife of a late peer of the realm. She was also the conscience-driven daughter of a clergyman, a bit of a political radical and halfway in love with their dear Inspector Witherspoon.

"She didn't pay any mind to 'im," Smythe replied. "She were just 'er usual nice self." He shot a fast glance at the clock. "Blimey, it's gettin' late. What's takin' 'em so long?" He hated for Betsy to be out in the evening on her own. "By rights, Betsy's had plenty of time to get Luty and Hatchet back here."

"There are dozens of valid reasons why they might have been detained. Luty may have had guests or they might have been in the midst of something," Mrs. Jeffries replied. "She's not been gone all that long. Just a little over an hour. Besides, we can't start until Wiggins gets back. So far the only thing we know is that someone's been murdered. We don't even have the victim's name."

"But we've got their address," Mrs. Goodge said brightly. "And believe me, in that neighborhood I know

I can find out who the victim is pretty quick. You know my sources; they cover this whole city.''

The cook wasn't simply bragging. From her own cozy kitchen here at Upper Edmonton Gardens, she had a veritable army of people to call upon. Deliverymen, milkmen, butcher's boys, chimney sweeps, costermongers, rag-and-bones men and fruit vendors to name but a few. She did her bit in the investigations in her own way, but she never left her kitchen. She could also call upon a circle of acquaintances that included cooks from some of the wealthiest houses in all of England. She could find out any scrap of gossip, any breath of a scandal about anyone in the city.

Mrs. Jeffries gave an understanding smile. She too was eager to begin, but as she had told Wiggins earlier, it wouldn't be fair not to wait for the others.

Their patience was soon rewarded. Smythe heard the carriage first. ''That's them,'' he said, rising to his feet and heading for the back door. ''Now let's just hope that Wiggins gets himself back here quick.''

A few moments later Betsy and two others hurried into the kitchen. Leading the charge was an elderly, white-haired woman with sharp dark eyes. Her frame was small and her body frail looking, yet she marched into the kitchen like a general leading her troops. Wealthy, American and some would say eccentric, Luty Belle Crookshank loved investigating murders more than anything.

Directly behind her was her butler and archrival in the game of gathering clues. Hatchet too had white hair, but he was a vigorous fellow in late middle age. Proper and proud, he was devoted to his plain-speaking and blunt mistress. ''I trust we haven't kept you waiting too long,'' he said by way of a hello.

''We got here as quick as we could,'' Luty said as she

took the chair next to Mrs. Jeffries. "But wouldn't you know it, Myrtle and some of her friends had dropped by and we couldn't get rid of 'em without bein' rude."

"I believe that suggesting they take their 'fat little fannies' elsewhere could constitute being rude, madam," Hatchet corrected her.

"Fiddle." Luty waved her hand dismissively, unmindful of the way the diamond and sapphire rings she wore caught the light. "They knew I was just funnin' with 'em. Besides, they'd been there long enough. If I'd had to listen to Myrtle much longer, I might have run screamin' from the room." She flashed an impish grin at the others around the table. "What kind of a killin' we got here?"

"A man has been shot," Mrs. Jeffries replied. "That's really all we know. We're fairly certain Inspector Witherspoon has the case. Wiggins is at the scene of the crime now, trying unobtrusively to find out more information. He ought to be back any moment."

"Do we have a name?" Hatchet inquired.

"No, only an address," Mrs. Goodge replied. She sighed and reached for the teapot. "Though if that boy doesn't get back soon, I've a mind to box his ears. This waitin's awful."

"It shouldn't be much longer," Smythe said easily. He'd cocked his head to one side. "I fancy there's a 'ansom pullin' up outside."

Within minutes a breathless Wiggins rushed into the kitchen. "Sorry it took so long," he said, "but there was ever so much gossip goin' on I couldn't tear myself away. You'll not believe what all I've learned." He yanked out a chair and plopped down. Fred, the household mongrel, bounced up and down next to the chair, deliriously happy to see his friend. Wiggins absently patted his head.

"Take a moment to compose yourself," Mrs. Jeffries

instructed as she poured him a cup of tea, ''and then tell us everything you heard.''

''What's the victim's name?'' Betsy asked eagerly. It niggled her that Wiggins had got to go the scene of the crime and she'd been sent to fetch people. But that was a woman's lot in life, gettin' stuck with the borin' bits.

''His name was Roland Ashbury,'' Wiggins replied. ''He lived with his daughter and son-in-law. You'll never guess who his son-in-law is, either.'' He paused dramatically. ''Andrew Frommer. Member of Parliament.''

CHAPTER 2

"Have you gone deaf, man?" Frommer snapped. "I said why are policeman swarming all over my house? There's an ungodly crowd outside. I demand to know what is going on?"

Witherspoon glanced at Mrs. Frommer. He'd kept quiet, thinking that bad news might be less shocking coming from a member of the family. But apparently his was a minority opinion.

MaryAnne Frommer didn't say a word to her husband. She ignored him and huddled in one corner of the settee. She seemed to have visibly shrunk in size.

The inspector silently chided himself for being so insensitive. Why, the poor woman was probably so overwrought, she wasn't capable of saying anything. How could he have been so impolite? Mrs. Frommer was in shock. It would be his duty to relay the terrible news. He took a quick step toward the angry man striding impatiently through the doorway.

"I'm sorry, sir," he said quickly. "I'm Inspector Gerald Witherspoon. I'm afraid I've very bad news for you."

Frommer stopped abruptly. He tilted his head in a gesture which had the unfortunate result of fattening his face by adding another chin. "Bad news? What sort of bad news? Has there been a robbery?"

"I'm afraid it's worse than that, sir," the inspector said. "Your father-in-law is dead. He's been shot."

"Shot? Roland? But that's ridiculous. He was a bit of a windbag and a fool, but I can't see why anyone would want to shoot him." Frommer didn't so much as glance at his wife as he spoke. "When did it happen?"

"We're not sure," Barnes interjected softly. "We think it was sometime late this afternoon."

"I can't believe this." Frommer began to pace the room, the thud of his footsteps masked by the thick carpet of the drawing room. "It couldn't happen at a worse time. The party doesn't need this sort of thing. I'll have to make some sort of statement. Good Lord, this isn't going to look good at all. A murder in an MP's home." Without so much as a glance at any of the others in the room, he whirled on his heel and stalked back toward the hallway.

"Excuse me, sir," the inspector called just as Frommer reached the door, "but I do need to ask you some questions." Witherspoon was appalled by the callous way the man treated his wife. Good gracious, the poor woman had only just learned her father had been murdered, and here her husband couldn't be bothered to offer one word of comfort.

"Questions? Me?" Frommer looked outraged. "Whatever for? I haven't seen Roland since breakfast this morning."

"That's not true," Mrs. Frommer said. "I saw you talking to him in the garden before he left." She straightened from her slumped position and stared at her husband speculatively. "It looked to me as if you were having quite an argument about something."

Clearly stunned, Frommer gaped at his wife. "Don't be absurd," he said. "I merely stopped to tell the old fellow to be careful and to say good-bye."

"You two were arguing," she countered, pointing a finger at him. "Papa was all puffed up like a bullfrog and your face was as red as a cherry. So don't tell me you weren't having words." She smiled maliciously at her spouse. "And you've never told my father to be careful in your entire life."

Witherspoon felt some of his sympathy for Mrs. Frommer evaporate. What on earth was wrong with these people? He stifled a sigh. Unfortunately, as a policeman, he'd seen all too often that many families not only weren't happy, but positively loathed one another. He was beginning to think that might be the case here.

He looked at Mrs. Frommer. "What time did your father leave the country house?" he asked.

"It must have been around two o'clock," she replied. "He took the two-fifteen train. I believe he was planning on going by his office."

"His office?" Barnes asked. "And where would that be?"

"On Russell Street near the East India Docks," she replied. "He wanted to have a word with—"

"Look, Inspector," Andrew Frommer interrupted, "if you need to ask me questions, please do so now. You can question *her*"—he jerked his head toward his wife—"later. Considering that old Ashbury's managed to get himself murdered in my house, I've a number of things to take care of, so please get on with it.''

MaryAnne Frommer stared at her husband with undisguised loathing. Then she giggled, apparently delighted that her husband was so annoyed.

Frommer's jaw dropped. His mouth opened and closed rapidly, as though he were trying to say something but couldn't quite find the right words. Mrs. Frommer, seeing her husband silenced—perhaps for the first time in their marriage, Witherspoon caught himself thinking—giggled again and said, ''Dear, dear, Andrew, don't you think you ought to wait before you answer any questions? Unless, of course, you have a perfect alibi for where you've been this afternoon.''

''Why . . . you . . . how dare you . . .'' Frommer sputtered as he finally found his voice.

''Oh, now that dear old Papa is dead,'' she hissed, ''you'll find I dare quite a bit.''

Whatever was going on, the inspector thought, enough is enough. ''All right, Mr. Frommer,'' he said firmly. ''If you'll please sit down, we'll take your statement.'' He turned his attention to Mrs. Frommer. ''Madam, you have my deepest sympathies. If you don't mind, we'd like to take your husband's statement now.''

She gazed at him curiously. ''Does that mean you want me to leave?''

''Just for a little while,'' Witherspoon said.

She nodded regally and then, completely ignoring her husband, rose to her feet and left the room. The inspector wondered what had happened to change her so completely and so quickly. When Mr. Frommer had first entered the room, she'd cringed like a kicked pup. But within minutes she was baiting the man and virtually accusing him of being a liar.

Frommer sat down on the settee his wife had just vacated. He tapped his fingers restlessly against his knee. "Well, get on with it, man. I don't have all evening."

The inspector glanced at Barnes, making sure the constable's notebook was out and ready before beginning. This was one statement he wanted taken down word for word. Having not been invited to sit, he stood next to the ornate marble fireplace. "When was the last time you saw your father-in-law?"

"As my wife said, it was in the garden after lunch." He shrugged his shoulders casually. "I'd quite forgotten seeing Roland then."

"Your wife was quite sure you were having an argument with her father," Barnes said.

"She was mistaken," Frommer returned disdainfully. "To be perfectly truthful, my wife tends to imagine things. I saw Roland leaving and stopped to say good-bye and to wish him a safe journey."

"What were you doing in the garden, sir?" Witherspoon asked. It sounded a bit like a silly question, but the inspector was amazed at the number of times seemingly stupid questions had led to the arrest of a murderer.

"I was getting some fresh air," Frommer replied. "We'd had a rather heavy lunch and I had a lot of work to do. I'd gone to the garden to get some air, hoping to refresh myself so I could take care of a number of important matters."

"Your servants have said that the entire household was coming back this evening. Is that correct?"

"That's right."

"Did everyone in your household come back to the city separately?"

"I don't understand the question?" Frommer wrinkled his nose in distaste. "What do you mean?"

"Exactly what I said, sir," Witherspoon explained. "Apparently the victim, Mr. Ashbury, came up early, as did the other servants. It was your 'tweeny, Maisie Donovan, who discovered the body," the inspector continued. "Then your wife came home and you arrived a good fifteen minutes after she did. I was merely curious as to what your traveling arrangements had been."

"I don't see how my household's movements can have any bearing on Roland's death, but if you must know, the servants came back with our cases by coach."

"How many servants do you have?"

Frommer thought about it for a moment. "Well, let's see, there's the butler and the cook, of course. Then there's a housemaid and an upstairs maid and a 'tweeny . . . oh yes, and we've a scullery maid and a footman as well." He was counting on his fingers as he spoke. "That makes seven servants, Inspector. Though I fail to see how the number of people I have in my employ has anything to do with Roland's death."

"You'd be surprised, sir," Witherspoon muttered. In his experience, the more staff there was the more opportunity there might be for a good policeman to find out a great deal about a household. So many people, he had observed, tended to think their servants were like pieces of furniture. Deaf, dumb and existing only to serve. He strongly suspected that Andrew Frommer was this kind of person. No doubt Mr. Frommer would be absolutely stunned to know that amongst his own staff there were people of keen intelligence and perception. "What time did your staff leave Ascot for London?"

"Right after lunch."

"At the same time that Mr. Ashbury left for the train station?" Barnes asked.

Witherspoon nodded approvingly. That might indeed be useful information to have.

"Yes, the servants were packing up the coach when Roland and I were chatting in the front garden." Frommer stroked his chin.

"When did you and your wife return to London?" Witherspoon asked. "Apparently, from what Mrs. Frommer said to you, you weren't together."

"She was correct about that," he admitted. "We did come back to town separately. Mrs. Frommer went to visit the vicarage and I came on ahead on the four o'clock. MaryAnne was supposed to take the five o'clock."

"You've been in the city since late this afternoon?" The inspector mentally calculated how long it took to get from Ascot to London. "Since about four forty-five." He pulled out his pocketwatch and noted the time. "It's well after seven, sir. Where have you been?"

"That's none of your business"—Frommer blustered—"but you can't possibly think I had anything to do with Ashbury's death. I'd no reason to dislike Roland."

"I've no doubt that's true, sir. In which case you can have no objection to telling me where you've been since four forty-five. It doesn't take two hours to get here from the station."

"Actually"—Frommer cleared his throat—"I did a bit of shopping. That's why I came on early; I wanted to stop off on Bond Street and see my tailor. Trouble was, fellow wasn't in, so it was a wasted trip."

"What's the name of your tailor, sir?" Barnes asked.

Frommer's eyebrows shot up. "Are you implying you don't believe me?"

"It's merely routine, sir," Witherspoon put in hastily. "We have to confirm everyone's whereabouts."

"That's absurd." Frommer's eyes snapped angrily and

a crimson flush spread up his neck. "I'm a respected member of the community, Inspector. A member of Parliament. I'll not be questioned like some common criminal. Now, if you don't mind, sir, I'll say good day." With that, he turned on his heel and strode from the room.

Barnes looked at the inspector. "What do you make of that, sir?"

"Difficult to say, Constable." Witherspoon sighed. "He might be one of those people who feel they're so important they're above the rules that govern ordinary people."

"Or he might be scared."

"Yes, that's definitely a possibility as well." Witherspoon shrugged. "It doesn't really matter, though, does it? We'll have to confirm his alibi."

"How can we do that, sir? He never told us the name of his tailor."

"I daresay his wife will," the inspector replied. "I don't think she likes him all that much."

A wide smile flashed across Barnes's craggy face, making him appear years younger. "Right, sir, I should have thought of that. Do you think he'll cause us a bit of bother, bein' an MP and all? He could go running to the home secretary."

"I expect he will," Witherspoon replied. "But it won't make any difference in our investigation. We must find out the truth; it's our duty."

Barnes nodded somberly. Sometimes he wasn't sure whether his superior was a saint or a fool. Politicians could cause no end of bother. But either way, the constable was firmly in the inspector's corner. "Shall I go and get Mrs. Frommer?"

"Yes, please. I'll be very interested in hearing what she has to say."

• • •

"An MP, cor blimey." Smythe shook his head. "That's a bit of 'ard luck for our inspector."

"Why?" Wiggins asked.

" 'Cause politicians got friends in high places," Luty said darkly, "and the right kind of friends can make life awfully miserable for an honest policeman tryin' to find a killer."

"Let's not jump to any conclusions as yet," Mrs. Jeffries put in quickly, though she too was a bit worried about this latest turn of events. "Wiggins still has to tell us the rest of what he found out this evening."

"It were dead easy, Mrs. Jeffries," Wiggins continued eagerly. "A whole crowd had gathered in front of the 'ouse. There were police everywhere."

"You made sure that none of them saw you?" Hatchet asked. They were all aware that one slip and the whole game could come down around their ears. The inspector was a dear man, quite naive and innocent, but he wasn't a fool. Seeing a member of the household staff at the scene of all his crimes would not be a wise thing.

" 'Course I did, I kept a right sharp eye out; there was two women as tall as pine trees standin' in front of me. One of 'em was fairly wide too. I kept well behind 'em." He waved a hand in dismissal. "I know what's what."

"Of course you do," Mrs. Jeffries said, "but Hatchet has a valid point. It's imperative we keep firmly in the background on the inspector's cases." The last few cases had thrust one or more of them firmly in the forefront of an investigation, and this time the housekeeper wanted to nip that sort of thing in the bud.

"We understand, Mrs. J." Smythe answered for all of them. "Believe me, everyone knows we've shaved it fairly close in the last year. Now go on, lad"—he encouraged the footman—"tell us the rest."

"Well, like I said, the victim's name was Ashbury," Wiggins continued. "'E's an older gent, probably up in his late seventies. He's lived in the Frommer 'ouse for a good number of years, moved in after his wife passed on." He leaned forward eagerly. "And you'll never guess what else I 'eard. Seems 'e's a bit of a snob and there's some dark 'ints that 'e's done 'is daughter wrong."

"Are you sure of this information?" Mrs. Goodge asked. Sometimes, she thought, the lad could get ahead of himself and say things he only thought were true instead of knowing for sure. As she'd been guilty of that herself a time or two, she was especially sensitive to it in others.

"'Course I'm sure," Wiggins said defensively. "I 'ad a nice natter with two 'ousemaids from the place right next to the Frommer 'ouse, and after I'd gotten everythin' I could out of them, I found a talkative footman. He actually works for the Frommers."

"No one's doubting your truthfulness, Wiggins," Mrs. Jeffries soothed, "it's simply that in the heat of the moment people will say anything. After all, you were in a crowd just outside the victim's house. I remember my late husband once telling me there was a near riot in York when a suspected child killer was rumored to be hiding out in the attic of a boardinghouse."

Mrs. Jeffries's late husband had been a constable in Yorkshire for over twenty years. She often thought it was through him that she first got her love of snooping.

"The truth was," she continued, "it was only a man who merely had had a drink with the felon who was actually in the house. But by the time the story made the rounds of the crowd, they became so enraged it took several dozen policemen to hold them back.''

Wiggins nodded in understanding. ''Don't worry, Mrs. Jeffries, I was right careful about 'ow I put things. I'm pretty sure what I 'eard is true.''

''How had he done his daughter wrong?'' Betsy asked curiously.

''Neither of the maids 'ad any details,'' he replied. ''They just said they'd 'eard some gossip from the Frommer servants that Mr. Ashbury had a right old dustup with 'is daughter a while back, and even though they live in the same 'ouse, she's barely spoken to 'im since.''

''How long ago was the alleged altercation?'' Hatchet asked.

''I'm not sure of the actual date—they couldn't remember—but it were after the new year, they knew that much,'' Wiggins answered.

''That was months ago,'' Betsy said. ''That's a long time to go without speaking to someone.''

''Did you ask the footman about it?'' Mrs. Goodge asked. ''You know, just to suss out if what the maid told you was the truth and not just some talk she made up to make herself look important?''

''I were goin' to''—Wiggins shook his head—''but all of a sudden the lad took off like the 'ounds of hell were on 'is 'eels.''

''Ya followed him, didn't ya?'' Luty asked eagerly.

''Almost,'' Wiggins admitted, ''but then I decided not to. I knew everyone was waitin' fer me, so I came on 'ome.''

There was a collective groan around the table. Wiggins looked crestfallen.

''That's enough,'' Mrs. Jeffries chided them. ''Wiggins did just as he ought. The first thing we must do is to get started on the this case, not go haring off after someone who may or may not know anything pertinent about it." She too was a bit disappointed, but she wouldn't let it show. She'd not have the lad starting off on this hunt thinking himself a failure. "Now, I suggest we decide what we're all going to be doing."

"I'll nip out tomorrow morning and have a go at the shopkeepers in the area," Betsy said. She was quite good at that; she'd done it enough times that she knew exactly how to poke and prod until she found someone who had information.

"You'd best be back by eleven o'clock," Mrs. Goodge told her bluntly. "If you'll recall, Lady Cannonberry is comin' round for morning tea."

There was another collective groan. This time Mrs. Jeffries didn't try to silence them. Ruth Cannonberry was their neighbor and a delightful friend, but all of them hated postponing their snooping for a social occasion.

"Can't we put 'er off?" Smythe asked. "I'm itchin' to get out. I want to 'ave a go at the cabbies and the pubs in the area."

"I'm afraid we can't get out of it." Mrs. Jeffries sighed. "Ruth's been gone for over two weeks; she'll be very hurt if everyone isn't there."

"Well, at least Madam and I can make a good start," Hatchet stated conversationally.

" 'Fraid not," Luty said. She looked a bit shamefaced. "We were invited too, and I accepted. Ruth's expectin' us."

"Really, madam." Hatchet's eyes narrowed. "I do wish you'd let me know when you've accepted a social invitation."

"Cor blimey," Wiggins whined. "We'll be ages gettin' started if we 'ave to 'ave tea."

"You're not goin' to tell 'er what's goin' on?" Smythe asked anxiously. His concern was quite valid. Lady Cannonberry had been involved in several of their other cases. She considered herself an excellent detective. As a matter of fact, she frequently hinted that she'd love nothing more than to be asked to join all the cases.

"Of course I'm not going to mention it," Mrs. Jeffries replied. "In any case, as she has a houseguest, I don't think she'd want to become involved."

Luty snorted. "Fiddlesticks. She'd dump her guest in two seconds flat if you'd let her into the case. She loves to snoop more'n I do."

Hatchet raised his eyebrows. "I hardly think that's possible, madam."

"I suggest that we all meet here at ten o'clock," Mrs. Jeffries said firmly. "That will give us plenty of time to have our meeting before we have tea with Ruth. It will also give the early birds who want to get out and about a few hours to do so before the meeting. Is that agreeable to everyone?"

"Sounds fine to me." Wiggins nodded. "It'll give me time to get over to the Frommer 'ouse and see if I can find that footman. Maybe I can get 'im to talk."

"If you haven't any luck with the footman," Mrs. Jeffries suggested, "try making contact with another servant from the house. Try and find out as much as you can about the events leading up to the murder."

"I'll get onto my sources down at the bank," Luty said. Her connections into the heart of the British financial community were legion. When she said "down at the bank" she was referring to the Bank of England. "If this Frommer is an MP, there ought to be plenty I can dig up on 'im."

"But if you'll recall, madam . . ." Hatchet sniffed.

"Mr. Frommer isn't the victim. His father-in-law was."

"I know that," Luty shot back. "I'll find out what I can about the victim and the rest of the household too."

"Very well," he replied, unperturbed. "I, of course, will be using my own rather extensive network of resources for information."

Luty glared at him. She and Hatchet were fiercely competitive when it came to hunting clues.

"What are you going to do?" Mrs. Goodge asked Mrs. Jeffries. Everyone already knew that the cook was going to bake up a storm so she'd be able to feed the army of people she'd have trooping through her kitchen.

Mrs. Jeffries thought for a moment. "I'm not really sure. I think I'll hear what the inspector has to say before I decide what I need to do."

"Do you think Dr. Bosworth will be doing the post-mortem?" the cook asked. "He comes in handy every now and again."

"He most certainly does," Hatchet agreed.

Dr. Bosworth was a young physician who'd helped them on several of their cases. As he'd practiced the healing arts for several years in San Francisco, he knew an awful lot about gunshot wounds. Americans, Mrs. Jeffries thought wistfully, had so many more murders than the English. Accordingly Dr. Bosworth had developed some very interesting theories. She found them most fascinating. "Dr. Bosworth is the police surgeon for the Westminster area. I don't know if the victim's home is in his district," Mrs. Jeffries replied. "But it would certainly be convenient if it werc."

MaryAnne Frommer smiled wearily as she sat back down on the settee she'd vacated only half an hour earlier. "You wanted to question me, Inspector?" she said.

"Only if you feel up to it," Witherspoon replied. Her earlier bravado was gone; now she merely looked like a very weary, very tired middle-aged woman doing her best to cope with bad news.

"You've a lot of questions, Inspector," she said, shrugging her shoulders, "and I'd like to answer them now and get it over with. I still can't believe he's gone."

Witherspoon couldn't make head or tails of the woman. She certainly didn't seem cold or callous, yet he had the sense that she was more shocked than grieved by her father's demise. Interesting and also very sad. "I'm sure it's most difficult for you," he began, "and I appreciate your cooperation. I'm sure you're as eager as I am to get to the bottom of this."

"I'd like to know who did it," she replied softly, her attention focused on the window across the room. "And why."

Witherspoon cleared his throat and glanced at Barnes. The constable had his trusty notebook open and his pencil at the ready. "Mrs. Frommer, who's your husband's tailor?"

She started in surprise. "Pardon? Did I hear you correctly? Did you ask who was my husband's tailor?"

"That's correct." He hesitated for a moment. "Your husband claims he's been on Bond Street shopping since four forty-five this afternoon. He says he went by his tailor's. Unfortunately he neglected to give us the man's name."

She smiled broadly. "He goes to Barkham's."

"Thank you." Witherspoon suddenly went blank. Now that he'd asked the one quesion on his mind, he found he simply couldn't think of another one. Oh dear, this wouldn't do. It wouldn't do at all. "Er . . . Mrs. Frommer . . . er . . . uh, can you tell me what you think your husband and your father might have been arguing about when you saw them in the garden today?'' Yes, he thought, that was a good one.

"I've no idea," she answered. "Neither of them took me into their confidence."

"But you're certain they were arguing?" he prompted. What if she were merely guessing or, even worse, simply making things up so her husband would look guilty? From what he'd seen of both the Frommers, there was no love lost between them.

"As certain as I can be without having actually heard what they were saying." She shrugged. "But as I told you earlier, they looked like they were quarreling fiercely."

"How long has your father lived here?" Barnes asked.

"Since my mother died sixteen years ago." She clasped her hands together in her lap.

"Yes, I understand, your poor father probably couldn't stand to be alone after losing your mother," Witherspoon murmured sympathetically. He'd often found that a small dose of understanding went quite a long way and got one a great deal of information.

"Oh no, that wasn't it at all," she explained. "He came here because after Mama died, he'd nowhere else to live."

Witherspoon frowned. "You mean he'd no home of his own?"

"That's right. You see, he'd lived in my mother's house all of their married life. Mama was a Sheridan," she said proudly, dropping the name of one of England's oldest and wealthiest families. "I was already married and living here, so when she passed away, he had to leave. The house naturally went to one of my mother's cousins. He was most put out about it too. He'd always thought Mama had left the house to him, but she couldn't, could she? I mean, it belonged to her family, not to her. I don't think Mama was always truthful with Papa, but then again, why should she be? He certainly wasn't truthful with her.''

''I see.'' Witherspoon nodded encouragingly. ''So your father couldn't afford a home of his own—''

''Oh he could afford it,'' she interrupted. ''He just didn't want to live on his own. Not when he could live in an MP's home.''

''I see,'' the inspector said. ''Do you know if your father had any enemies?'' That was always a good, straightforward question. Generally, though, it always got the same response. The victim was universally loved and hadn't an enemy in the world.

''Oh, lots of them, I should imagine,'' she replied airily.

''Oh, and who would these enemies be?'' the inspector said quickly. Goodness, he hadn't expected that reply.

''I expect most of the neighbors disliked him,'' she replied. ''He was quite a nosy sort, my father. And he loved the sound of his own voice. He monopolized conversations and had opinions about everything. It didn't matter to him whether his opinions were informed or intelligent, either. He wasn't at all shy about sharing them. The neighbors used to run when they saw him coming down the street.''

''That must have been difficult for him,'' Witherspoon suggested.

''Not at all,'' she answered. ''He never noticed. Honestly I've no idea how the man lived so long without realizing that he was so disliked. He could clear a room faster than a bad smell. People would make their excuses the moment he walked in.''

"Other than the neighbors, who else disliked him?" Witherspoon asked.

"None of the servants were fond of him," she said. "He was such a tattletale. One small infraction and he'd go running to Andrew." She held up her hand and ticked off her fingers as she spoke. "Let's see, the neighbors and the servants. Then there are his business colleagues. He wasn't terribly popular with any of them. Not that he does much work these days; he simply sticks his head in his office every once in a while to annoy poor Henry."

"Henry?" Witherspoon queried.

"Henry Alladyce. The son of my father's late business partner," she replied. "Oh yes, of course, I almost forgot. I loathed the man." She looked up at Witherspoon and Barnes and smiled brightly. "I thought I might as well tell you myself rather than have you learn it from the servants. I didn't like my father. I've barely spoken to him for months."

Witherspoon was so scandalized he could barely speak. He knew he oughtn't to be so shocked; as a policemen, he'd seen enough horror to convince him that human beings were capable of anything. Yet still, he was stunned by the cheerful way she spoke of hating her own father, her own flesh and blood. "I see," he finally said.

Barnes asked, "Why did your father come into town early?"

"He wanted to stop by his office and check on things." She smiled. "At least that's what he told us. But it was obviously just a ruse to get away early."

The inspector regarded her quizzically. "Why do you say that? From the manner in which you describe your father and your relationship with him, why would he need a ruse to get away?"

"Oh, he wouldn't care about offending me." She

laughed. "Not one whit. But he walks on eggs not to offend Andrew. Andrew's important, you see. He'd walk over burning coals rather than offend my husband. So he needed a ruse, you see. That's why he came up with that sad tale of going to his office."

The inspector's head started to ache and he found himself wishing he wasn't getting all this information quite so quickly. He could barely take it all in. "I'm not sure I understand." He shook his head, almost to try and clear it. "What makes you think there was a ruse . . . I mean—"

"What the inspector means," Barnes interrupted, "is why did your father want to come home early in the first place? Why not just wait and come with either you or Mr. Frommer."

"I should think that's obvious," she declared. "He was meeting someone. Someone he didn't want the rest of us to know about."

"You think he planned to meet someone here?" Witherspoon said. "Why? What makes you think so?"

"Because he was having tea with whoever killed him," she replied proudly. "I overheard one of the constables talking when I was waiting for you to question me. Plus I saw the tea trolley being taken out of the room. So it must have been planned, mustn't it?"

Witherspoon hazarded a guess. "He could have met someone when he was at his office and invited them back for tea?" He'd have a quiet word with the constables later. It was easy to slip and talk about the circumstances of the murder, he could understand that, but he would warn them to be a bit more careful when there was a possible suspect in the area.

Mrs. Frommer shook her head. "He wouldn't have done that. He was neither generous nor kind and he never ever did anything impulsively. Every aspect of his life was planned out to the last detail. Believe me. I know the man. He came back early to meet someone. Furthermore, the house had been empty for two weeks.''

''Yes, we know that,'' the inspector said.

''But you don't understand the significance of it,'' she insisted. She pointed in the direction of her father's quarters. ''The man was shot while having tea. But the house had been empty, which means there wasn't a scrap of food to be had. Yet someone had bought milk for tea and stopped at a bakery to buy a cake. That someone could be only one person. My father. So you see, he planned to be here this afternoon, and whoever he planned to meet killed him.''

Witherspoon forced himself to speak with the servants. His head pounded and he'd heard more information than he could possibly understand in a very short time, but he felt it imperative he question the servants himself.

He smiled at Maisie Donovan. She was a tall, buxom young lady with dark blonde hair and a wide, intelligent-looking face. ''Now, Miss Donovan. Could you tell me again how it was that you went into Mr. Ashbury's quarters and discovered his body?''

Maisie nodded vigorously. ''I might not have noticed if I'd not stopped on the landing to rest. That trunk of Mrs. Frommer's weighs ever so much. If that bloomin' Boyd hadn't run off, I'da not been stuck draggin' the ruddy thing up to the attic, but it's a good thing it were me and not him, if you know what I mean. A bit slow is our Boyd. He'd have not noticed the light comin' out of Mr. Ashbury's door.'' She paused to take a breath.

''I'm afraid I don't quite understand.'' Witherspoon frowned. ''Are you saying a member of your staff has gone missing?'' This was rather important news.

"Oh yes. We woke up this morning and Boyd had scarpered," she said cheerily. "His clothes were gone too, so we knew he'd gone, you see. Mind you, everyone was quite shocked seein' as how attached to Mrs. Frommer Boyd was. Loved her, he did. But maybe he got tired of bearin' the brunt of Mr. Frommer's temper all the time. He used to always say he was fixin' to go off to Australia someday. Claimed he had a cousin in Adelaide."

Witherspoon thought about this statement. "So the lad was gone before anyone, including Mr. Ashbury, left the Ascot house? Is that correct?"

She nodded. "That's right. And Boyd wouldn't 'ave killed anyone, 'specially not Mr. Ashbury. He's simple, you see. That's why it were a good thing it were me on the landin' and not him. Boyd wouldn't have gone into Mr. Ashbury's quarters under any circumstances. Dead scared of Mr. Ashbury he was. Used to run and hide every time the old man came through the kitchen."

Witherspoon didn't see how a footman who'd gone off hours before the murder could have anything to do with its commission, but one never knew. "But you did go into Mr. Ashbury's quarters, correct?"

"That's right."

"Did you hear anyone else in there?" Barnes asked.

She shook her head. "No, I didn't hear anything."

"Did you see anything odd or unusual?" Witherspoon asked. "You know, when you first arrived back at the house. Was there any sign that someone had been in here? Any doors left open? Any windows?"

"Nothing like that," she replied firmly. "The back door was locked tighter than the vault at the Bank of England."

"How about the front door?" Barnes asked. "Was it locked?"

"I think so." Maisie seemed less sure now. "I mean, I didn't go to the front of the house and look. That would be the butler's job. Not mine. But I'll tell you one thing; whoever left, didn't go out by the back door. Not unless they had a key."

CHAPTER 3

"You didn't need to wait up for me, Mrs. Jeffries." Witherspoon handed her his hat. "But I'm very grateful that you did."

"I was curious about your new case, sir," she replied, hanging the bowler on the coat tree and then starting down the hall. "Do come and have a sit-down, Inspector. I've made a fresh pot of tea."

He followed her into the drawing room and sat down in his favorite chair while she poured tea for the both of them. He closed his eyes for a moment, trying to clear some of the muddle out of his mind. But everything about this evening was a jumble. The dead body, the gun being left on the scene, the apparent hatred between the Frommers, Maisie Donovan's interview and the missing footman. It was no good. He couldn't make heads or tails of anything. The only thing which would do any good at all was having a nice long chat with his housekeeper.

"Here you are, sir," she said, handing him his cup. She sat down on the chair opposite him and waited patiently for him to begin. Mrs. Jeffries had no doubt he'd tell her everything. He always did.

"It's very good of you to have tea waiting for me," he began after he'd taken a nice long sip. "I'm going to become spoiled and expect it."

"You deserve it, sir," she said truthfully. He was the best of employers. He'd inherited this house and his fortune from a rather eccentric aunt, and having not been born to wealth, he'd never learned to treat servants badly. Unlike most men of his position, he actually treated the staff like human beings and not objects put on this earth for his pleasure and amusement. Even if he hadn't been a police inspector and hadn't given Mrs. Jeffries a chance to do what she most loved doing, solving mysteries, she thought she still might wait up for him when he came in late. "Now, sir, do tell me all about this case of yours."

"It's going to be one of those dreadful ones, Mrs. Jeffries." He sighed. "I just know it. Why, already I've learned so much that I can't quite keep everything straight in my mind. Does that ever happen to you?"

"Of course," she answered promptly. "It happens to everyone, but I'm sure it must be especially difficult for you, sir. After all, your mind is quite different from the rest of us. Your mind, sir, is always on the hunt, so to speak."

He gazed at her blankly, as though he couldn't quite decide whether she was complimenting him or insulting him. "Yes," he said slowly, "I suppose it is . . . I mean, I suppose I am a bit different. Well, I must be, mustn't I?"

"But of course, sir," she said briskly. She realized he needed a bit of a confidence boost here. The dear man sometimes took it into his head that he wasn't up to the task at hand. "I'm sure that even as we speak there's a corner of your mind that's sorting through everything you've learned today. Why, you're sure to be cataloging and analyzing all of it, sir. Now, what happened, sir?"

Her words made him smile. She was, of course, correct. Even though he couldn't sort things out yet, he was certain his "inner voice" was doing its job properly. Eventually he'd clear the muddle up. He always did. "A fellow named Roland Ashbury was shot this afternoon," he replied. "While he was having tea, of all things."

"How awful, sir." She didn't have to force the note of disgust in her voice. Mrs. Jeffries thought murder was the worst of all crimes. "When did it happen?"

"As near as we can tell, it must have been around half-past three," he continued.

"Do you have a witness that heard the shot?" she asked hopefully. To be able to pinpoint the time precisely would give them an excellent starting point.

"Unfortunately, no. That's actually quite a puzzle too. No one seems to have heard the shot at all. It must have been quite loud too."

"Then how do you know what time it happened?"

"One of the neighbors saw him going into his house at about ten minutes to three. Maisie Donovan, the maid, discovered the body at around four o'clock. If you factor in the time it must have taken him to make tea and exchange some pleasantries with his guest, we venture to assume the shooting probably took place around three forty-five," he said proudly. He and Barnes had worked out that particular timetable. He was quite pleased with it.

"Why do you think he entertained his guest?" she asked curiously. "Maybe the killer murdered him as soon as he arrived at the house."

"He couldn't have." Witherspoon smiled with pride. "He ate the cake. Both of them did. We found their empty plates right next to the empty teacups. One of them hates walnuts and the other cleaned his plate of every last crumb."

"I see," she murmured. "And from that you've deduced that he not only knew his killer, he trusted him enough to have tea with him?"

"Right," Witherspoon said enthusiastically. "It's obvious they spent some time talking and enjoying their tea before the killer pulled out the gun and shot him in the head. Besides, from the position of the body, it doesn't look as if the victim knew what hit him. His posture wasn't in the least defensive." The inspector continued on, telling her every detail that he could remember from the crime scene. Talking to her helped him; now that he'd shared the horror of the hole in that poor man's skull, he sincerely hoped he'd be spared nightmares.

"He was shot in the head, sir?" she asked. She already knew some of these particulars, but she couldn't let on that she did. Mrs. Jeffries didn't want the inspector to become suspicious at her lack of curiosity.

"Oh yes." He took a sip from his cup. "At very close range too."

"And no one heard the shot?" she pressed again. That was an important fact; she wanted to make sure it was absolutely correct.

"Not so far," Witherspoon replied. "But we've still got lads doing house-to-house interviews. Something may turn up tomorrow. The whole situation is very odd. Except for the killer, Ashbury was apparently alone in the house. Quite deliberately so, it seems. The rest of the household was in the country and they didn't come home till later this afternoon. According to the evidence and statements made by the victim's family, Ashbury connived to get to the house early so that he could meet the person who probably killed him.''

"So you're assuming he knew his killer and had actually invited him to tea, is that it, sir?'' Mrs. Jeffries was beginning to get a tad confused herself.

"That's the assumption we're working on.'' He sighed again and continued specifying the other details of the investigation. Carefully he gave her a moment-by-moment account. As he spoke he felt as though a huge weight were being lifted off his shoulders. By the time he'd finished his narrative, he felt positively cheerful.

"So you can see why I thought this might be a difficult one to solve,'' he said. "After all, this is going to be one of those cases where the victim wasn't well liked by anyone but doesn't seem to have done anything bad enough to actually make someone want to shoot him. Yet someone did shoot the poor chap, and it's my job to find out who. Most puzzling.''

"But you're very good at solving puzzles, sir,'' she reminded him. "I must say, his daughter's behavior seemed rather odd.''

"Very odd, indeed,'' he replied, then took another sip from his cup. "As was her husband's behavior. About the only behavior that wasn't odd was the servants'. They were all just frightened, of course. Except for the one that found the body; she didn't seem to be scared. Mind you, I'm going to have another chat with the staff. It was so late by the time I got to them that everyone was tired.''

"Are you going to look for the missing footman?'' Mrs. Jeffries sipped her tea.

Witherspoon considered this. "I'm not sure. The lad left hours before the killing happened. I don't see what it could have to do with the murder, but then again, I'm not sure I quite believe it was a coincidence. But yes, I'll try to find the boy. He may know something.''

Mrs. Jeffries nodded and went on to her next question. ''Are you sure the gun you found under the tea trolley was the same one used to kill the victim?'' She'd learned never to take anything for granted.

''We won't know more until after the postmortem's been done,'' he replied. ''The revolver had been recently fired.''

''Did anyone in the household recognize the gun?''

Witherspoon stared at her blankly. ''Pardon?''

''Oh, how silly of me.'' She waved her hand dismissively. ''Please, forget I asked that question. Of course you won't show the gun to the servants until after you find out whether or not it's likely to be the murder weapon.''

The inspector gazed at her for a moment and then broke into a wide smile. ''You're never silly, Mrs. Jeffries. But you are right in that I wouldn't show it about until after I have the results of the postmortem. Of course, even a good autospy can't tell us precisely if it is the murder weapon, but if the bullet is retrieved, it can narrow it down quite a bit. And, at that point, I'll try and find out if anyone recognizes it.''

They talked for a good half hour more. Mrs. Jeffries listened carefully and occasionally asked a pertinent question or two. By the time a yawning Inspector Witherspoon took his leave and headed for the stairway, she was sure she'd learned all the details of the case. She knew the names of the two suspects, the number of servants in the household and the time everyone claimed they arrived at the Frommer house. She knew how many cups were on the trolley, that walnut cake had been served and the name of Andrew Frommer's tailor. What she didn't know yet was how many more people would turn up who had the motive, means and opportunity to murder one Roland Arthur Ashbury.

"The police'll have a hard time findin' out what's what," Nat Hopkins said as he plunged his hand into the soapy water and grabbed the washrag. "Not with Frommer bein' a bloomin' politician. Thinks he's above the law, he does."

"Why do ya say that?" Wiggins asked. He glanced up the street, hoping that the inspector or, even worse, Betsy didn't see him chatting up this shopkeeper. Of the two, he'd rather face his employer. At least the inspector wouldn't tear him off a strip for poaching on his territory. When it came to shopkeepers, Betsy thought they were hers by right. "I mean, wouldn't a member of Parliament want to find out who murdered his father-in-law?"

Nat slapped the washrag against the window and energetically stroked it from side to side. "Frommer'll make like he does, but take my word fer it, he's not losin' any sleep over the old man's death."

"I guess 'e musta not liked 'im much," Wiggins said casually. " 'Course, seems to me it were pretty decent of 'im to let the bloke live with 'im, seein' as 'ow 'e didn't like him."

Nat slopped the rag across the bottom of the window and then dropped it back in the bucket. "Don't be daft, boy. Frommer only let the old man stay on because he had to. That one"—he jerked his dark head in the direction of the Frommer house—"doesn't do anything out of the kindness of his heart. If he'd tried to toss him out, Ashbury would have blabbed to everyone who stood still for thirty seconds about Frommer's mistress. That'd not done his career any good."

"Cor blimey," Wiggins exclaimed, "you know a lot."

"Sure I do," Nat said conversationally. He reached into the bucket of rinse water and grabbed a clean rag. Wringing the water out, he started mopping the suds off the top of the pane. "My niece Emma used to work for the Frommers. She was the upstairs maid. Treated her like dirt, they did. A couple of weeks ago the old bastard sacked her because she broke a flowerpot. Can you believe it? Sackin' someone over a trifle like that. Well, I can tell you, we've no reason to keep quiet about Mr. Holier-Than-Thou Frommer. Not now. We kept our peace even though Emma used to come home tellin' these bloomin' awful tales about the rows the mister and missus'd have, but now we're tellin' the whole neighborhood, we are. They wouldn't even give the girl a bloody reference."

"Cor blimey," Wiggins said sympathetically. "That's a bit of 'ard luck. It's tough to get a position without a reference."

Nat shrugged. "Yeah, but what can you do? Poor girl'll just have to do the best she can. She's a right pretty girl; it's just as well she's not livin' in that house. I'd not trust a man like Frommer to keep his hands to himself." He sighed. "Still, it's one extra mouth to feed. The shop's doin' all right, but well, you know how it is. I only wish one of them coppers would come along and ask our Emma a few questions. She could set 'em straight."

That could be arranged, Wiggins thought. "Did she ever see Mr. Frommer's mistress?" He could feel himself blush as he asked the question, but he wanted to have as much information as possible before this morning's meeting.

"That she did." Nat grinned broadly and dropped the rag into the water. A few drops shot up and splattered over the apron spread across his wide belly. "Twice."

Wiggins nodded encouragingly. He'd come out this morning to try to find that footman who'd scarpered off the previous night. Failing that, he'd hoped to make contact with a servant from the Frommer house. But no one had so much as stuck their head out the door this morning, and rather than go back to Upper Edmonton Gardens empty-handed, he'd come along to see if any of the tradespeople could give him any clues about the footman's whereabouts. He'd only had to mention the murder to the dark-haired grocer and Nat Hopkins gave him an earful. "Cor blimey, then she actually saw him with his fancy woman." He shook his head in pretended amazement. "That wasn't too smart of the fellow, lettin' himself be seen that way."

"Frommer's not too smart." Nat picked the bucket up and started for the edge of the pavement. "He's arrogant and stupid. Probably didn't even realize that Emma was in the house when he had his woman there." He dumped the dirty water into the street and looked up at Wiggins speculatively. "You're a curious one, aren't you?"

Like a bolt from the blue, Wiggins was suddenly inspired. There was a way to kill two birds with one stone. "'Course I'm curious," he admitted. "Murder always makes a body ask questions like. Especially if they work for Inspector Gerald Witherspoon. He's in charge of this killin' and I'll bet my next quarter's salary 'e'd be right interested in anythin' your Emma 'ad to say."

"Here we are, Constable." The inspector stopped in front of a door upon which a faded sign reading ASHBURY AND ALLADYCE, SHIPPING AGENTS was attached. They stood in front of a tall, rather scruffy-looking office building on a small, narrow street just off the East India Docks. On one side of the building was a long, fully occupied warehouse;

its front doors stood wide open, and despite the narrowness of the street, vans, carts and freight wagons were lining up to pick up and deliver goods. On the other side was a smaller but equally busy goods depot. In the bright morning sunshine, the blue-black Thames glittered through the spaces between the buildings.

Witherspoon knocked once, opened the door and they stepped inside. They found themselves in a small, rather dim room. The inspector blinked, trying to adjust his eyes to the gloom. What light there was crept in through the rather dirty transom over the front door.

"May I help you gentlemen?"

Witherspoon jumped and turned to see a tall, cranelike man stepping out of a door on the other side of the room. "Er, we'd like to speak to Mr. Roland Ashbury's clerk," he said, squinting so that he could see the fellow better. "I say, it's awfully dark in here."

"I haven't drawn the curtain yet," the man replied. He sounded rather petulant. His hair was dark blond and curly, his face bony and his mouth a thin line slashed across a jutting chin. "I've only just unlocked the door and come inside." He swept a heavy curtain down the entire wall, revealing a set of windows and letting the sun inside the gloomy room. At once the place was brighter, but not much else.

The furniture, such as it was, consisted of two huge desks overflowing with papers and cluttered with boxes, bags and baskets along the top. The floor was gray linoleum. A straight-backed chair sat before each desk. Along the wall was a row of cabinets, their tops cluttered as well with all manner of things. Above the cabinets was a chalkboard covered with rows of names and dates.

"Are those references to ships?" Witherspoon asked curiously as he pointed to the chalkboard.

"Yes, and their estimated departure dates. We are a shipping company." He waved them toward him. "I suppose I'm the person you need to see, but I'm not Roland Ashbury's clerk."

"I'm sorry," Witherspoon said sincerely. "No offense was intended. I'm Inspector Witherspoon and this is Constable Barnes. We were told that Mr. Ashbury had a clerk and that it was this clerk he stopped to see yesterday—" He broke off as he realized he wasn't making a great deal of sense.

"What's your name, sir?" Barnes asked quickly.

"Henry Alladyce." He sat down on one of the chairs. He was dressed neatly in a crisp white shirt, black tie and yellow waistcoat. His outer coat, the same pearl-gray color as his trousers, was hung neatly on the coat tree by the door. "I'm the only one here. As I said, I'm not a clerk; I own half of this company."

Witherspoon hesitated for a moment. He did so hate telling people bad news, but there was nothing he could do to soften the blow. "I'm afraid I've some bad news Mr. Alladyce—" he began.

"Yes, yes, I know," Alladyce interrupted impatiently. "Old Roland's got himself murdered. It was in this morning's papers. Well, it's too bad, I suppose, but let's be frank, Inspector. Roland was quite old and not particularly well liked. I shouldn't think he'll be missed."

"Apparently not," the inspector murmured. "Er, Mr. Alladyce, when was the last time you saw Mr. Ashbury?"

Alladyce leaned back in the chair, steepled his fingers together and stared up at the ceiling. "Let me see, I suppose it must have been over a fortnight ago. Yes, that's right. It was the day before Roland went off to the Ascot house with his daughter and her husband."

"You didn't see Mr. Ashbury yesterday?" Barnes

asked. "He didn't call here in the afternoon?"

"No," Alladyce replied. "As I said, I haven't seen him since before he left for Ascot."

"Were you here all afternoon?" Witherspoon asked.

Henry spread his hands. "Where else would I be? I'm the only one here and I've a business to run."

"You don't have a clerk, sir?" Barnes asked.

"Roland claimed we didn't need one." Henry pursed his lips. "But of course we did, and do."

"Did you see anyone yesterday afternoon, sir?" Barnes pressed. "Anyone who can verify you were here all day?"

Henry's expression didn't change. "No, I didn't. I spent the afternoon going over the accounts. I didn't leave until almost seven last night. I saw no one and no one saw me."

"You're sure Mr. Ashbury didn't come here?" Witherspoon asked.

"Quite sure," Alladyce replied. "If he were coming here, he'd have sent a message or a telegram. He did neither."

The inspector nodded. "Did Mr. Ashbury have any enemies?"

"No more than any other businessman." Alladyce shrugged casually. "You mustn't judge the firm by the appearance of our office." He waved his hand around the room. "This is quite a successful venture, sir. It's a bit untidy just at the moment, but that's only because Roland was ridiculously cheap and absolutely refused to spend a penny on proper furniture and fittings."

"So you're saying that Mr. Ashbury had made enemies in the course of running his business?" Barnes clarified.

"Not exactly." Alladyce sighed. "What I meant was that it was entirely possible that Roland had made enemies. When he and my father were building this business, Roland wasn't above undercutting someone else's rates.''

"I see," Witherspoon replied. This interview wasn't getting them much information. But at least they'd confirmed that Ashbury hadn't called here before going to the Frommer home. "Well, thank you, Mr. Alladyce. You've been most helpful. Do get in touch with us if you can think of anyone who might have had a reason to want to harm Mr. Ashbury."

"Oh." Alladyce brightened immediately. "Then you'd best sit down, Inspector. I can think of lots of people who would have loved to harm Roland."

"I do hope you don't mind my bringing Morris with me." Ruth Cannonberry whispered the words to Mrs. Jeffries as they walked across the small terrace behind Upper Edmonton Gardens. They headed toward the oak table which sat invitingly underneath the shade of a large tree. Her houseguest, who'd been introduced to them as Morris Pilchard, was at the far end of the gardens. He stood beneath a yew tree, staring fixedly at the trunk.

"Of course we don't mind," Mrs. Jeffries assured her. The others were already at the table, which was set for a splendid morning tea. "Your guests are always welcome."

"Thank you." Ruth smiled brightly and her pale, middle-aged face was transformed. "I really didn't know what else to do with him. He's not terribly interested in seeing the sights of London." She sighed and turned her head, seeking her houseguest. "He must be watching ants," she muttered when she spotted him.

"Is he a naturalist, then?" Mrs. Jeffries tried to move Lady Cannonberry along a bit faster. The others were

champing at the bit to get started, and if the truth were
known, she was rather in a hurry herself.

"Oh no." Ruth shrugged. "He simply likes watching
bugs. Oh, this looks lovely," she exclaimed as they finally
reached the table. "Mrs. Goodge"—she beamed at the
cook—"you've outdone yourself. It looks wonderful."

The table was loaded with food. There was a large
brown pot of tea, a plain seedcake, scones, cream, jam, a
Victoria sponge and a bowl of quince sprinkled with
sugar.

"Thank you," the cook replied briskly. Naturally the
reason she'd baked so much was to feed her sources when
they came trooping into her kitchen. But it didn't do any
harm for Lady Cannonberry to think the display had all
been laid out for her. "We wanted to welcome you home
right and proper."

Mrs. Jeffries took her seat. "Wiggins, please go and
fetch Mr. Pilchard while I pour the tea."

Wiggins was off like a shot. For a few moments they
made small talk and filled their plates. The footman returned with the errant houseguest, who blushed when he
realized none of the others had touched their food and
were waiting for him.

"I'm so sorry," he apologized quickly as he took the
seat next to Lady Cannonberry. "Sometimes I do get carried away. Nature is so very fascinating."

Morris Pilchard looked to be in his fifties. Tall and thin,
he had a long, melancholy face with deep-set hazel eyes
and a rather protruding nose. His complexion was pale,
his hair a nondescript beige blond streaked with gray.

"Please don't apologize, Mr. Pilchard," Mrs. Jeffries
said briskly. "We all quite understand. The garden is a
fascinating place." She was determined to get this tea
moving right along so they could finish their meeting and

get back on the hunt. Unfortunately they'd been in the middle of Wiggins's report when Lady Cannonberry and her houseguest had turned up.

"Has the inspector any interesting new cases?" Ruth asked brightly.

They all looked at the housekeeper, waiting to follow her lead before opening their mouths and risk giving the game away. Everyone liked Ruth Cannonberry and no one wanted to lie. She was too good a friend for that.

Mrs. Jeffries smiled, delicately reached for a scone and laid it on her plate. She was desperately trying to think of how to answer. "Actually, he's been rather busy lately."

"Oh goody." Ruth leaned forward eagerly. "Has he a good murder?"

"Lady Cannonberry!" Pilchard stared at his hostess in utter shock. "Surely you're jesting. You can't possibly have meant what you just said."

"Of course I did," she declared. "I don't condone the taking of life, Morris. But let's do be honest here: murder is fascinating."

Morris pursed his lips and shook his head. "I think it's quite distasteful."

"Here's your tea, Mr. Pilchard." Her eyes twinkling behind her spectacles, Mrs. Goodge handed him his cup. "Would you care for a scone or a slice of cake, sir?"

Momentarily distracted, he turned away from his hostess to study the offerings. "A small slice of sponge, please." He whipped his head back around, apparently ready to take up the argument again, but Ruth was a step ahead of him.

"It's only distasteful if you think it's right that killers can take life with impunity," she charged.

"It's very . . . common. Yes, that's right, murder is

common and almost always done by the lower classes." As soon as he said the words, a bright blush crept up his cheeks as he realized whom he was having tea with. "Oh dear, I don't mean to imply that any of you would ever do such a thing—"

"Hello, hello." The inspector's cheerful voice interrupted the terribly embarrassed Mr. Pilchard. "I was just on my way to the Magistrates' Court and thought I'd pop in and welcome our dear neighbor home." He smiled happily at Ruth Cannonberry as he approached the table. "I do hope I'm not interrupting, but when Mrs. Jeffries mentioned this morning that you were coming around for morning tea, I just had to stop in and see you."

"Gerald, I'm delighted to see you as well," Ruth said quickly. Her eyes suddenly sparkled with pleasure, a flush crept up her cheeks and her mouth curved in a wide smile. "I'm so happy you came. It seems as if it's been far more than a fortnight since we've seen one another."

"Uh . . . uh." Morris Pilchard cleared his throat loudly. The indelicate sound grated loudly in the quiet garden. Ruth dragged her gaze away from Witherspoon's and made the introductions.

Mrs. Jeffries looked at the others. Luty, Smythe and Hatchet seemed to be amused. Betsy and Mrs. Goodge looked impatient, and Wiggins was too busy stuffing his face with seed cake to notice anything.

"Wiggins," she ordered gently, "could you go and fetch the inspector a chair?" The lad nodded and leapt to his feet.

Mrs. Jeffries hoped the inspector wouldn't say anything about the murder. If Ruth found out they were "on the hunt," she'd want to help, and as she had a houseguest in residence, that wouldn't be a wise course of action. "Would you care for tea, Inspector?" she asked.

"Thank you, that would be lovely. I've not got long. Constable Barnes is meeting me here in a few minutes." His smile was strained as he spoke and his eyes seemed to dart between Morris Pilchard and Ruth. "Oh, thank you, Wiggins," he said as the lad returned and shoved a chair under him.

He took the tea his housekeeper handed him and then reached for a plate. Witherspoon put a scone and a slice of seedcake on it and then slapped on a huge dollop of heavy, clotted cream. "Are you staying long, Mr. Pilchard?" he asked. He forked a quarter of the cake into his mouth.

"I'm not really sure," Pilchard replied. He glanced at his hostess and smiled. "It all depends."

"On what?" the inspector asked. He reached for a knife and slathered the cream across the top of the scone.

Morris shrugged. "Oh, this and that."

"This and that, you say?" Witherspoon nodded encouragingly. His smile was quite strained by now. When Mr. Pilchard remained silent and merely kept smiling at Lady Cannonberry, the inspector stuffed the remainder of the cake into his mouth and then took a huge bite of the scone.

Luty's eyebrows shot up and she gave Mrs. Jeffries and Mrs. Goodge a knowing grin. Seeing the glance that passed between the two women, Hatchet poked his employer in the ribs.

Betsy, a surprised expression on her pretty face, glanced at Smythe, who shrugged ever so faintly. Wiggins finally looked up from his plate, with a puzzled expression. " 'Ow come it's gone all quiet?" he asked.

Mrs. Jeffries decided she'd best do something. The situation was getting more and more awkward by the minute. "We're all enjoying the nice sunshine," she explained brightly. "Would anyone care for a slice of sponge?"

"I would," Witherspoon said, handing his plate to Mrs. Jeffries. He glanced at Lady Cannonberry. "Er, I'm rather tied up at the moment, but I would so like to take you for ride in the country soon. We want to take advantage of the weather while we can."

"I should love that, Gerald," she began enthusiastically.

"That would indeed be nice," Morris interrupted. "Do let us know when you're free." He smiled and rose to his feet. "Now, if you'll excuse us, Lady Cannonberry and I are off to the Natural History Museum." He reached over and helped her to her feet.

"Thank you for the tea," Ruth said, her expression uneasy. "It was lovely." She gave the inspector one long, meaningful look and then allowed Morris to lead her off toward her own home at the far end of the communal gardens.

Witherspoon didn't take his eyes off them. But even with his attention firmly diverted, his fingers managed to grab the plate full of sponge cake that the housekeeper handed him. He forked the cake in his mouth without blinking, his attention completely focused on the retreating man and woman. Finally he sighed. "I'm so glad she's come home," he said.

"We are too," Mrs. Jeffries said stoutly. "And we're so glad you found the time to join us for tea this morning. Now, sir, do tell, what have you been up to today? You know how fascinated all of us are by your investigations."

Witherspoon nodded absently. His gaze was still fixed on the huge four-story brick home at the far end of the garden. *Her* home. "Yes, thank you," he muttered. "I'd love another scone."

Mrs. Jeffries smiled softly. She felt rather sorry for her dear inspector. The poor man was so obviously wrestling with the demons of jealousy he wasn't even listening. "Right, sir. Another scone."

Mrs. Goodge looked outraged, but she managed to reach for his plate without smacking his fingers. She'd never seen anyone stuff himself so full of food. What was wrong with the man? If he kept eating at this rate, she'd not have enough provisions to feed her sources this afternoon.

"Me too." Wiggins started to take a scone but stayed his hand when the cook glared at him. "Uh, maybe I'll not."

"Inspector." Luty raised her voice quite a bit to get his attention.

Blinking, he came out of his daze and turned to look at the American woman. "I'm sorry, were you speaking to me?"

"Yes, sir, I was," Luty said. "I was jes' wonderin' if you wouldn't mind tellin' me a bit about this here murder you've got. You know how Hatchet and I like hearin' about all your investigations."

"Oh well, of course." He smiled proudly. "Uh, let me see, I suppose Mrs. Jeffries has told you some of the details." He picked the scone up in his fingers and took a bite.

"She sure did." Luty leaned toward him and dropped her voice. "What I want to know is what were ya up to this morning? Did ya catch the killer yet?"

"Not quite," the inspector replied. "Actually, I've only just got started. But we're making progress. We confirmed this morning that the victim didn't go to his office yesterday afternoon. We spoke to his partner. Fellow named Henry Alladyce. Alladyce claimed that Roland Ashbury had no intention of going to his office. If he had, he'd have sent Alladyce either a message or a telegram. He sent neither.''

Smythe opened his mouth to speak, thought better of it and leaned back in his chair. Betsy noticed. But then she noticed most everything about the coachman. She cocked her head and looked at him speculatively.

''Do you think he planned on going back to the Frommer house all along, sir?'' Mrs. Jeffries asked. ''And that his telling the family he had to go to his office was only a ruse to leave Ascot earlier than the others?''

Again Smythe seemed to lean forward, his expression clearly indicating that he wanted to say something, and again he thought better of it.

''I don't know,'' Witherspoon replied. Absently he plopped another dollop of cream on the small sliver of seedcake left on his plate. ''Yet his daughter is convinced he lied about needing to go to his office. She's sure it was a ruse to get away without offending Andrew Frommer. But if what Mrs. Frommer thinks is true, that means he'd planned to meet his killer there all along. . . .'' His voice trailed off as he tried to think of the best way to say what he was thinking. But he couldn't seem to find the right words. ''I mean, it seems to me that—''

''Of course, sir,'' Mrs. Jeffries said quickly. She knew exactly what he was trying to articulate. ''What you're saying is that he planned to meet his killer and he kept that plan a secret. As a matter of fact, he connived to get the privacy he needed for the meeting. Therefore, the meeting must have either been with someone he didn't want his family to know about or it must have been about something he didn't want made public. Is that what you're trying to tell us, sir?''

Witherspoon brightened immediately. ''Yes, that's it

precisely. Well, you can see what that would imply, can't you?''

"I can't," Wiggins said honestly.

"It would imply that the victim might have something to conceal," Hatchet said softly. "Secret meetings usually mean both parties have a vested interested in hiding something."

"Do you think Ashbury was being blackmailed?" Luty asked.

Witherspoon licked the last of the cream off his fork. "I'm definitely leaning in that direction," he answered. "But, of course, if he were being blackmailed, why would the killer murder him?"

"Maybe *he* was the blackmailer?" Betsy guessed.

"That's possible too," the inspector replied. "But we've no evidence either way. Oh dear, I'm getting way ahead of myself. The only thing we know for certain is that he's dead. We don't know for certain that he didn't go to his office. I mean, we only have Henry Alladyce's word, and from what I understand, he benefits from Ashbury's death."

"You think this Alladyce feller is lyin', then?" Luty asked eagerly.

Witherspoon shook his head. "Not really. I mean, I suppose it's possible. But it didn't strike me as likely. He was actually quite candid with us. He gave me a long list of people who didn't like the victim. Of course, if he's the killer, that could have been a ruse as well. What better way to throw the police off the scent than by giving them false information."

"He gave you a list of people, sir?" Mrs. Jeffries clarified.

"Oh yes." Witherspoon eyed the bowl of sugared quince. "According to Alladyce, there were quite a number of people who disliked the victim rather intensely.''

At hearing this, everyone at the table went to full attention. Even Wiggins. They all gave the inspector their complete concentration.

''Really, sir?'' Mrs. Jeffries encouraged. ''A whole list? That might make your task much more complicated. But then again, perhaps it will make it easier.'' She desperately wanted to get the names out of him, and the only way to do that was to keep him talking.

''Yes, that's just what I was thinking,'' he agreed. He licked his lips, picked a crumb off his plate and popped it into his mouth.

''Are the people on this list going to be easy to . . . uh—'' She broke off deliberately, hoping he'd jump right in.

''Investigate.'' He smiled. ''Why, yes, indeed they are. As a matter of fact—''

''Hello, Inspector,'' Barnes called from the side of the house. ''If you don't mind, sir''—he pointed toward the street—''I've got a hansom waiting.''

''Oh dear.'' Witherspoon leapt to his feet. ''I must go. Thank you ever so much for the lovely tea. Don't wait dinner on me,'' he called over his shoulder. ''I expect I'll be quite late.''

CHAPTER 4

———◦◦◦◦◦———

"Bloomin' Ada," Smythe muttered as the inspector and Barnes scampered out of sight. " 'Ow'd we let him get away without spillin' the beans?"

"A list of the victim's enemies would have been most useful," Hatchet agreed.

"Useful, hmmph," Mrs. Goodge snapped. "Necessary, if you ask me. We need a few more suspects. I can't question anyone unless'n I have names. Not that they'd do me any good now." She gestured furiously at the table. "Just look at this, it's practically all gone. What am I goin' to feed my sources? The man sits here and stuffs himself fatter than a Christmas goose then has the nerve to scarper off without being any help at all."

"I don't think he meant to eat so much," Mrs. Jeffries murmured. She too was a tad annoyed at their dear employer. Not so much that he'd made a pig of himself— after all, it was his food—but at the way he'd dashed off without giving them the information they so desperately needed. "I think seeing Lady Cannonberry with her houseguest must have made him a bit anxious."

"He was as jealous as an old tom," Betsy declared. "But it's his own fault; he should have paid more attention to Ruth."

"He gives her lots of attention," Smythe countered. "She's the one that's always going off to the country."

"She's got relatives to visit," Betsy said, defending her friend. "Her own and her late husband's. She got stuck with that lot too, you know. What do you want her to do, ignore them?"

"She could stay home for a change and give a fellow time to court 'er properly." The coachman frowned darkly, an expression that was known to clear a path in the roughest of pubs, but Betsy wasn't in the least intimidated.

"She's given him plenty of chances," she shot back. "But like most men, he's not got the sense to see what's right under his nose. He just assumes she'll be sittin' there waiting for him when he decides he's got time for her."

Smythe's jaw dropped in outrage, but before he could form the words to protest, Mrs. Jeffries interrupted.

"Smythe, quickly, follow them."

"Huh?" Confused, he still got to his feet. "Follow the inspector?"

"Yes, now. Hurry; if you run you might be able to catch their hansom up at the corner. There's always a dreadful traffic jam there."

"What do you want me to do?" he called over his shoulder as he raced toward the side of the house.

"See where they go," she called back to him. "And then get back here this afternoon."

Without another word, the coachman disappeared around the corner.

Mrs. Jeffries turned and smiled at the others. "Let's hope he can catch the inspector's hansom." She'd sent Smythe on the errand to halt the squabble that was developing between him and Betsy. The maid hadn't really been complain about Witherspoon's shortcomings in the courtship department; she was sending Smythe a message. Had she not sent the coachman off, the argument might have become very heated and very personal. A fact that both the parties involved would soon regret once they'd calmed down.

"You want poor Smythe to hotfoot it after the inspector's 'ansom all day?" Wiggins asked incredulously.

"Of course not," she replied. "I'm quite sure Smythe will have enough intelligence to hire a hansom of his own."

Hatchet frowned slightly. "Excuse me, Mrs. Jeffries. But I don't quite see the point of sending Smythe off."

Of course you don't, Mrs. Jeffries thought, you're a male. She could tell from the smug expressions on Luty and Mrs. Goodge's faces that they knew precisely what she'd been doing. But naturally she kept her thoughts to herself. "The point is we want to know who was on that list of names the inspector got from Henry Alladyce. The inspector may not be home until very late tonight. If Smythe follows him for a few hours today, we might find out the names of some of the suspects."

"Meaning that the inspector will go and interview them." Hatchet nodded knowingly.

"That's correct. I'm sure all of you realize that we don't have much to go on so far. Even a couple more names might be worthwhile."

"But I don't understand," Betsy said. "Aren't we going to concentrate on finding out as much as we can about the victim. That's how we usually do it.''

Betsy had a valid point. That was generally how they'd conducted their previous investigations, and usually the method had been most successful. "Of course we are," the housekeeper replied quickly. "But even with doing that, we frequently have several other suspects to concentrate on as well." That much was actually true. "So far, we've only got the Frommers. If neither of them is the murderer, we'll be at a loss to help the inspector solve this case."

"Oh. I guess then I'd best wait until this afternoon's meeting to tell everyone what I found out early this morning." Betsy sank back against her chair, her expression glum.

Their plan to meet before Lady Cannonberry and her guest arrived had gone awry. No one, save Mrs. Jeffries and Mrs. Goodge, had been available at ten o'clock. Everyone else had been late.

"Well, it wouldn't be fair to Smythe to have a meeting now," the housekeeper offer.

"Fiddlesticks," Luty cried. "I'm bustin' to tell what I found out. I was out at the crack of dawn this mornin'.''

"I don't see why you're so proud of yourself, madam." Hatchet sniffed disapprovingly. "You ought to be ashamed. Waking up a member of the House of Lords at six A.M. is unforgivable."

Luty grinned. "You're just jealous 'cause I got to him first."

"Hmmph." Hatchet pursed his lips.

"Can it wait, Luty?" Mrs. Jeffries asked. "I really don't like the idea of Smythe missing out, especially as I'm quite sure he had something to tell us all too. He acted quite eager when the inspector was here."

Luty made a face. Eager as she was to share her information, she wanted to be fair too. "Oh, all right, then.
I'll wait till this afternoon. But if someone else comes up
with the same thing I found out, I'm goin' to be madder
than a wet hen."

"What time are we meeting this afternoon, then?" Mrs.
Goodge asked bluntly. "I need to know, as I've got a lot
to do. I'm going to have to restock my supplies." She
glared at the inspector's empty plate. "Never seen the
man eat so much at one sitting."

"Why don't we meet at five o'clock?" Mrs. Jeffries
suggested. "Hopefully Smythe will have returned by
then."

"And what do we do in the meantime?" Wiggins
asked. He didn't fancy talking to anymore shopkeepers.
One time Betsy might forgive; she was a good-hearted
girl, after all. But twice, no; she'd box his ears if he
poached on her patch again.

"We do precisely as Betsy has suggested." Mrs. Jeffries smiled kindly at the maid. "We concentrate on learning as much as we can about the victim. Wiggins, I think
you ought to visit the Frommer house and see if you can
make contact with a servant. Perhaps locate the footman
who left before you could speak to him yesterday." She
looked at the maid.

"I know," Betsy said. "I'll go back and have a thorough go at the shopkeepers and"—she gave Wiggins an
impish grin—"anyone else I see hanging about."

"There's still plenty for me to do," Luty announced
gleefully. "I'll drop in on a new friend of mine that's got
a few connections. She knows what's what in this town."

"Who?" Hatchet demanded suspiciously. "Is it someone I know?"

"Now just never you mind." Luty brushed him off

with a wave of her hand. "You just drop me off on Park Lane and send the carriage back at four."

"Hmmph." Hatchet stood up as well. "In that case, madam, I shall endeavor to follow up on my own leads. I take it we're free to find out whatever we can about the entire Frommer household?"

"Of course," Mrs. Jeffries replied.

The cook began stacking plates onto a tray she whipped out from under the table. "I'd best get crackin'. Mrs. Collins from next door has a laundry boy comin' in about ten minutes, and later this afternoon Lady Afton's dressmaker will be in the neighborhood. She always stops in for a cuppa." She frowned at the empty scone plate. "Let's just hope they like Victoria sponge; that's about all I've got left."

Panting heavily, Smythe skidded around the corner just in time to see the inspector's hansom—at least he hoped it was the inspector's—halt at the Uxbridge Road. Thanking his lucky stars for the heavy traffic, he spotted a four-wheeler dropping off a fare just up the road. Keeping his gaze glued to the cab he was almost sure contained the inspector, he ran toward the wheeler and leapt on board. "Follow that hansom," he ordered the surprised driver. "And don't let 'im see ya."

"Now 'ow am I goin' to do that?" the driver asked. "Anyone with eyes in 'is 'ead can turn about and see a bloody great thing like this"—he smacked the seat—"on his tail."

"All right, then, just keep back and try not to get spotted," Smythe snapped, and pulled a fistful of cash out of his pocket. "I've got a guinea here on top of the fare if you can do it."

"You're on, mate," the driver said cheerfully.

As it turned out, the four-wheeler had no trouble keeping up with the hansom. Smythe breathed a little easier as they followed the cab up the Uxbridge Road and approached the neighborhood where the murder took place. That increased the likelihood that he was following the right hansom. Any lingering doubts vanished when the hansom turned onto the Grays Inn Road and few minutes later onto Argyle Street.

Smythe kept his eyes glued to the cab as it pulled up in front of the Frommer house. "Go past them and pull up a bit futher up the road," he ordered the driver.

The four-wheeler moved another fifty yards and then pulled into the pavement. "This far enough?" the driver asked.

Smythe hesitated. It was close enough for him to get a good look at what was going on, but was it far enough away to keep the inspector from getting suspicious? "This'll do," he called softly.

He stuck his head out and watched as Witherspoon and Barnes stood on the pavement talking softly. Finally they turned and started toward the row of houses, but it wasn't the Frommer home at which they stopped; it was the one next door. Taken aback, Smythe watched the inspector and Barnes walk up to the front door and bang the knocker.

"Cor blimey," he muttered. "That's odd." Mrs. Jeffries had already told them that police had taken statements from the neighbors, none of whom had heard or seen a thing. If that were true, what was the inspector up to?

"Wait 'ere," he instructed the driver.

"Not to worry, mate," he said, "I'm not goin' nowhere. Not without my guinea."

Keeping a sharp eye on the doorway through which the

inspector and Barnes had disappeared, Smythe got out. He'd have to be quick about this; he didn't want the inspector coming out and haring off on him. Smythe stood on the pavement and examined the surrounding area, looking for anyone who could give him the information he needed. "Ah." He grinned as he saw a housemaid scrubbing the front steps of a grand house just up near the corner. She'd do. She'd do just fine.

"I'm sorry, Inspector. I don't really know what I can do to help you. I've already made a statement." Charles Burroughs smiled disarmingly. He was a tall, handsome, dark-complected man who appeared to be in his late thirties. His mouth was wide and generous under a sharp blade of a nose, and his eyes were a dark, almost sapphire blue. As the sun spread out across his high cheekbones, it revealed deep lines on his face. "Yesterday two police constables interviewed me and my entire household. We told them everything we knew, but I'm afraid it wasn't very much."

"Yes, sir, we're aware of that," Witherspoon replied. "But we'd like to ask a few more questions if you don't mind."

"Fine, then." Burroughs stepped back from the door and held it open. "Do come in."

As soon as the two policemen stepped inside, Burroughs closed the door behind them and started down the hall. "I'm afraid I can't offer you tea," he said. "It's the staff's day out. I'm here alone."

"That's quite all right, sir," Witherspoon replied as they walked through a set of wide oak double doors into the drawing room. "We're not thirsty." He took a quick look around, carefully noting that the place was exquisitely and expensively furnished. The drapes were heavy red damask, the carpet a richly patterned Wilton and the settee and chairs upholstered in bold, bright reds and blues. A huge, hand-carved rosewood cabinet dominated one end of the room. Through its glass doors, china figurines, gold plates and silver knickknacks could be seen. Tables covered with delicate cream-covered lace were at both ends of the settee, and opposite the door, a fireplace with a carved marble mantel held a triple set of ornately gilded mirrors.

Burroughs gestured at the settee. "Please be seated, gentlemen." The inspector and Barnes settled themselves as Burroughs took a seat on the chair next to them. He clasped his hands together and smiled, waiting patiently.

"Mr. Burroughs, how long have you lived here?" Witherspoon asked.

Burroughs raised his eyebrows slightly. "Three months, Inspector."

"And where did you live before you moved to London?"

Burroughs crossed his legs. "I don't see what my movements have to do with Mr. Ashbury's death," he said.

"I realize it sounds quite an unusual question," the inspector replied, "but we do have a valid reason for asking."

"May I know that reason?"

The inspector hated situations like this. On the one hand, he was such an essentially honest man that it was difficult to look another human being in the eyes and tell a lie. On the other hand, if he let Burroughs know the real reason he was asking, it might harm the investigation.

"We've had a report that you're in the habit of quarreling with your neighbors, sir," Barnes said quickly.

''And that these quarrels led to violence at your last place of residence.''

Burroughs stared at them for a moment and then burst into laughter. ''I don't know who you've been talking to,'' he finally said, ''but I assure you, gentlemen, I do not quarrel with my neighbors. I'm actually considered quite an amiable fellow. However, if you want to confirm my story, you'll have to send someone to Denver, Colorado. That's where I last resided. My next-door neighbors were a lovely family called Robb. I left all of them hale and hearty, and most kindly disposed to me, when I came here.''

Witherspoon shot his constable a grateful look. Barnes had managed to get the needed information out of the witness without revealing everything that Henry Alladyce had told them. The inspector made a mental note to send a cable to the authorities in Denver.

''You're an American, sir?'' he asked. ''Born and bred.'' Burroughs replied.

''Then you never met Roland Ashbury before you came to live next door to him?'' The inspector wanted to be crystal clear on that point.

''Absolutely not, sir.'' Burroughs shrugged. ''Unless, of course, he happened to come to Denver. In which case, I don't recall ever meeting the man.''

''Had you ever met Mrs. MaryAnne Frommer?'' Barnes asked.

''No, not until I came here.'' He uncrossed his legs and leaned toward them. ''But I will tell you, if anyone had a reason to end up with a bullet in his brain, it's that brute of a husband of Mrs. Frommer's. He's the most diabolical man I've ever met. He treats her terribly.''

''In what way?'' Witherspoon didn't want to be side-tracked, but at the same time he wanted to gather as much information as possible. "How did he treat her badly? Did he beat her?"

"He did." Burroughs hesitated. "Well, I never actually saw the man raise his hand to her; if I had, I'd have stopped him. Where I come from we don't take the beating of helpless females lightly."

"Then how do you know he beat his wife?" Witherspoon pressed. Gracious, he was getting a lot of information at one time. He only hoped that Mrs. Jeffries was right and that his "inner mind" was cataloging it all correctly. He wasn't sure he could even remember much of it.

"I've seen the bruises," Burroughs stated flatly. "Her upper arms were black-and-blue. When I asked her about them, she insisted she'd bumped into the side of a tallboy. I didn't believe her."

"So you're friendly enough with the Frommers to ask such a personal question?" Barnes asked.

Burroughs hesitated for a split second before answering. "That's a difficult question. I'm not quite sure how to reply. I'm not really all that friendly with anyone in the Frommer household. As a matter of fact, after seeing what kind of people they really are, I've taken some pains to avoid them."

"Then how did you come to see the bruises?" the constable pressed. "Did she show them to you?" Barnes had seen enough domestic violence to know that most women who'd been beaten were so ashamed they went to great pains to hide the marks of their ill-treatment.

"No," he admitted. "It's a rather awkward situation and I wouldn't like you to get the wrong impression. I saw the bruises out in the garden. As you know, our gardens are joined at the back; they're separated by a stone wall. I was out watching some starlings in the oak tree when I happened to see Mrs. Frommer in her nightdress; she was confronting her father, having some sort of argument with him. They were on the other side of their garden, which is quite wide, so I couldn't hear what they were saying. . . . Also, I believe both of them were deliberately keeping their voices down. Mr. Ashbury started to walk away; she grabbed his arm and pulled the old man back, then she yanked the sleeve of her nightdress up to the shoulder and shoved her arm right under his nose.'' He pursed his lips in disgust. ''Ashbury pushed her aside and walked away. I couldn't believe it. Even from where I stood, I could tell she was terribly distraught, terribly upset.''

''How did you see the bruises if they were so far away you couldn't hear what they were saying?'' Witherspoon asked.

''There's a stone bench on their side of the wall,'' he explained. ''Mrs. Frommer rather stumbled over to the bench and sat down; then she covered her face with her hands and wept. I saw the bruises because her sleeve was still rolled up. I guess I must have walked toward her, wanting to offer comfort or something. I don't know; I simply found myself standing behind her, shocked as I realized what she'd been showing to her father. Without thinking, I asked her about them.'' He shook his head sadly. ''She was quite startled and jumped up. As she ran off back toward her house she called out that she'd banged up her arm by running into a tallboy. It was nonsense, of course. Frommer had beat her.''

''But you don't know that for a fact, sir,'' Witherspoon reminded him.

''Oh, but I do,'' Burroughs declared. ''Later that day, Fiona, my parlor maid told me she'd heard gossip from the servants at the Frommer house. There'd been a terrible row that morning, Andrew Frommer had gotten furious at his wife for something or other, and like most cowards, he'd used his fists on his wife. Apparently her own father had done nothing to help her, but had barricaded himself in his quarters and pretended that nothing was amiss.''

"Did your parlor maid happen to mention what the row was about?'' Witherspoon decided if he was going to listen to gossip, he might as hear all of it.

Burroughs wrinkled his brow in thought. "Let's see . . . ah, yes, now I remember. Mrs. Frommer didn't want to go to the house in Ascot. She wanted to stay in town.''

"You do understand we'll have to confirm this information with your servants?'' Witherspoon said.

"Of course. They'll be back later this afternoon.''

The inspector wasn't at all sure what it would mean even if the servants confirmed the rumor that Frommer beat his wife. That might be useful knowledge if it had been Andrew Frommer who was the victim. But he wasn't. "Mr. Burroughs, are you absolutely certain you've no prior acquaintance with the victim?''

Burroughs shrugged. "As far as I know, I never even saw the man until I moved in next door to him.''

"Do you own a gun?'' Barnes asked.

"Yes, I own a revolver. An Enfield.'' He laughed. "I'm afraid it's a carryover from my living in the American West. Everyone has guns.''

Witherspoon nodded. "May we see it, sir?''

"It's locked in my desk''—he stood up—"in my study. If you'll come with me, I'll show it to you.''

The policemen followed him down a long hall to wood-paneled room. Bookcases lined two of the walls, a huge rolltop desk sat in the corner and several huge, overstuffed chair were planted in front of the fireplace. Burroughs pulled a small brass key out one of the many cubbyholes

on the top of the desk. He unlocked the bottom drawer
and removed a small, flat blue case.

Carefully he put the case on the desk and flipped open
the lid.

Then he gasped. The case was empty.

''Prompt as always.'' The tall, gaunt-faced man smiled
pleasantly at Hatchet and stepped back, pulling the door
wide open. With a dramatic flourish, he waved Hatchet
inside. ''Do come in and make yourself comfortable.''

''Thank you.'' Hatchet stepped inside, took off his top
hat and gloves and sat down in a Queen Anne chair that
had certainly seen better days. But then, virtually everything in Newton Goff's life had seen better days. Hatchet
ought to know: he'd once worked for the man. But he'd
worked for him before Goff became a thief. ''How have
you been keeping yourself?'' he asked.

''I've managed to avoid being arrested''—Goff
grinned—''if that's what you're asking. I'd offer you
something to drink, but I'm afraid all I've got is whiskey
and I know you don't indulge.'' He walked over to a
small cabinet sitting under the window. Opening the door,
he reached inside and took out a bottle. ''You don't mind
if I indulge? I always find it's so much more civilized to
conduct business over a nice drink.''

Hatchet nodded. He didn't care how much Goff drank
as long as the man was still able to ferret out information.
''By all means, drink up.''

Goff set the bottle on the top of the cabinet and reached
inside, pulling out a glass.

''Do you still have reasonable sources of information
available to you?'' Hatchet asked, watching as Goff
poured the whiskey into a shot glass that didn't look altogether clean.

"Of course. That's how I've managed to stay alive all these years. What is it you want to know?"

"I'm not certain," Hatchet admitted. "A man by the name of Roland Ashbury was shot the other day. He ran a shipping agency. It's down near the East India Docks. He lived with his son-in-law, Andrew Frommer."

"The politician?" Goff raised an eyebrow.

Hatchet nodded. "That's right. I want you to find out what you can about either of them."

Goff looked doubtful.

"Is there a problem?" Hatchet pressed. "I thought you said you had numerous resources."

"I do." Goff tossed the drink back. "But getting information on a politician might be expensive. They cover their tracks pretty well—if, I mean, there's anything to be covered. Do you think he did the shooting?"

"I don't know." Hatchet was grasping at straws. He'd no idea what was going on and he had the distinct impression that none of his cohorts did either. He wasn't even sure that coming here had been a wise move. But there was nothing else he could think of to do. They needed more information. "But I want you to find out what you can about him. See if there's any skeletons in his closet. Don't worry about what it costs; I can afford it."

"All right," Goff agreed. "Check back with me tomorrow. I might have something for you then." He tossed back the rest of the drink and studied Hatchet for a long moment. "Why do you care?" he asked.

"Pardon?" Hatchet had gotten to his feet. Goff's question took him by surprise.

"Why do you care who killed this fellow?" Goff pressed. "Did you know him?"

"No, but I care all the same. There is such a thing as justice."

Goff gazed at him and then shook his head, his expression puzzled. "Do you really expect me to believe that? That you're sticking your nose in this murder simply because you're interested in justice? That you're getting nothing out of it for yourself?"

"Yes," Hatchet replied. "I do." He clamped his mouth shut, refusing to say another word on the subject. Goff could think what he would. He wasn't here to convince the man of anything.

"I'm not sure I believe you, Hatchet." Goff shrugged and turned toward the dirty window. "All I know is you sure have changed. Used to be you didn't give two figs about anything except yourself."

"As you said, Goff," Hatchet replied softly, "I've changed."

"He's plum disappeared, 'e 'as." The small, ruddy-faced gardener slapped the stack of straw mats down on the ground next to the black currant bushes.

Wiggins quickly looked around, wanting to make sure that there weren't any policemen still hovering in the garden of the Frommer house, which was right next door. He'd made the acquaintance of the gardener by offering to help him carry these flat straw mats from a wagon out front of the house into the garden. It was a proper kitchen garden too, he noted, similar to the ones Mrs. Goodge was always going on about. Rows of black currant bushes trailed along the back wall. Gooseberry and red currant bushes flanked the side wall and rows of vegetables were planted in straight lines running up toward the house. Several fruit trees were planted in the grassy space between the currant bushes and the vegetables.

"Thanks fer the hand, lad," the gardener said. "I'd like to pay ya, but I've no coin with me."

"That's all right, I don't mind 'elpin' out. Matter of fact, like I told ya, I was 'opin' to see my friend from next door. But when I went round to the back, they told me 'e'd gone."

"That's right; that's what our scullery maid heard. The lad hasn't been seen since the day of the murder." The gardener bent down and picked up a long pole which was lying beside the stack of mats. He stood up and plunged the pole directly into the center of the bush. "He were out in the country, and then, on the day of the murder, he completely disappeared. But Minnie—that's our scullery maid—said she can't believe Boyd had anything to do with the killin'. He'd no reason to want to harm the old man."

"But Boyd was supposed to see me today." Wiggins was making it up as he went along. "I've brought him a message from home."

The gardener laughed and picked up a mat. Taking a ball of thin rope from his pocket, he quickly looped it around and between the straws on the top of the mat and then drew it tight, forming a sort of skirt. "Message from home? For Boyd? You're jokin', lad. Boyd ain't got no 'ome. Afore he got taken in by Mrs. Frommer, 'e was at St. George's Workhouse in Hanover Square."

"I mean I brought him a message from my home, from my auntie Jeffries. She was invitin' 'im to come for Sunday tea." Wiggins watched, fascinated, as the gardener looped the twine through a hole in the top of the pole and then, standing on his tiptoes, hoisted the mat skirt over the top, anchoring the thing to the top of the pole. The entire top part of the bush was now covered with the mat.

"Oh." The gardener picked up a third mat and placed

it carefully around the base of the bush, taking care to make sure the mat was loose enough not to crush the tender shoots on the tips of the branches. "I see. Well, you're goin' to have to disappoint yer auntie. Boyd's gone, and I don't think he's comin' back."

"Why'd he leave like that? I wonder."

The gardener shrugged. "Probably saw something that made him uneasy." He fitted a fourth mat onto the bush, effectively covering it completely. Then he stepped back and surveyed his handiwork. "He were right fond of Mrs. Frommer, he was."

Wiggins didn't wish to push his luck, but he had to find out more. He'd learned that you could get a lot more information if you were a bit sly about how you asked your questions. "What's that for?" he asked, pointing at the matted bush. "It looks like a wigwam. You know, one of them houses that indians live in in America. I saw a drawing of one in the *Illustrated* last month."

The gardener laughed. "It's a covering to keep the currant bushes from ripening all at once. Mind you, these bushes should have been covered a month ago. Bein' as we're in July, it might already be too late. If you can keep the sun off it, it'll delay the fruit ripening. That's the idea." He grabbed another pole and started for the next black currant bush. "I've not tried it before, but my wife's the cook and she's mighty tired of having to put up jams and jellies by the bushelful because all these currants ripen at once. So I'm tryin' this to see if we can push some of the bushes back."

"You're right clever." Wiggins was sincere about the compliment, but he's also found that people tended to keep talking to you if you said nice things to them.

"Thanks, lad. I'm sorry about yer friend."

He sighed dramatically. "I am too. Boyd's a nice lad.

My auntie was lookin' forward to seein' 'im again. She's goin' to be right disappointed.''

"You might try havin' a look over on Hanover Square," the gardener suggested as he plunged the pole into the next bush. "Boyd still went over that way occasionally. I think he was friends with one or two of them poor blighters at the workhouse."

"Thanks," Wiggins said. "I'll do that. I would like to find 'im. 'E's a good friend. At least now I know where to start lookin'. Good thing I run into you." He jerked his head toward the Frommer house. "They'd no idea where 'e'd gone."

The gardener frowned, his eyes growing speculative as he glanced at the house next door. "They'll have plenty of ideas soon enough," he said darkly. "As soon as everyone realizes what Boyd takin' off like that means, they'll be fallin' all over themselves with ideas about where to look for the lad."

"What do ya mean?" But Wiggins knew what the man meant.

"There's been murder done there, son," the man said darkly. "And when murder's been done, they like nothing better than to blame it on the likes of us. Take me word fer it, they'll be runnin' to the coppers soon enough with all kinds of tales about the poor lad. Everyone would rather it be some poor servant than one of their own kind."

"Well . . ." Wiggins hesitated, he didn't want to overplay his hand here, but he did want to hear as much as possible. "It *is* odd, Boyd leavin' like that. I mean, it's not like 'im. Makes you wonder."

The gardener gave him a sharp look. "I thought you said you was his friend."

"I am," Wiggins protested. "But it's odd."

"It's not a bit odd." He yanked a mat off the stack. "He's devoted to Mrs. Frommer, he is. I reckon he took off for one reason and one reason only. Because she told him to."

"I'm thinkin' maybe a guinea's not enough," the cabbie said to Smythe. They were trotting along St. Martin's Lane. Bored with sitting in the four-wheeler, Smythe had come up and taken a spot next to the driver. "I mean, you've tied my rig up all day."

"Bollocks," Smythe retorted. "Who do you think you're kiddin', mate? You'd not make a guinea for one day's work, so don't go tryin' to up the price 'ere." It wasn't the money he objected to, it was the idea of being taken advantage of that set his teeth on edge. He glared at the driver.

The intimidating expression obviously worked, for the poor fellow almost fell off the seat as he tried to pull away from his frowning passenger. "All right, all right," he said quickly. "You can't blame a bloke fer tryin'. It's tough to make ends meet these days. I'm out on this rig for twelve, sometimes even fourteen hours a day. I've got a wife and three kids to feed. I didn't mean no harm."

Smythe sighed and stifled the shaft of guilt that crawled out of his gut. He didn't like being taken advantage of, but he couldn't really blame the man for trying. He knew what it was like to be poor. He'd been poor most of his life. "No offense taken. Just a minute, now; they've stopped. Drive on past and pull on ahead of them."

Smythe turned his body away from the hansom as they trotted past. As soon as the four-wheeler pulled in at the curb, he whipped his head around and saw the inspector and Barnes get out. They had just started up the stairs of a lovely, small white house when the door flew open and one of the most beautiful women Smythe had ever seen stepped out.

Elegantly dressed in a teak-colored afternoon gown, matching hat and gloves, she had exquisite features and a slender figure. She spoke to the two men, and a moment later they disappeared inside the house.

Smythe jumped down off the seat. "Stay here," he ordered the driver in a soft voice. Taking care to avoid being seen, he nipped across the road to a tobacconist's on the corner. He didn't waste time trying to be subtle. What was the use of being rich as sin if he couldn't use his money to serve the cause of justice? Reaching into his pocket, he pulled out a couple of florins and slapped them on the counter. The old woman folding newspapers didn't even look up; she merely put her wrinkled hand on the coins. "What can I get you, sir?"

"Information," he said. She looked up then, her expression curious. He pointed to the house. "Who lives there?"

"There? That house." The old crone laughed. "Why, it's that fancy woman that lives there, sir. Her name is Hartshorn, Eloise Hartshorn."

CHAPTER 5

"Please sit down, gentlemen," Eloise Hartshorn said as she led them into a small, very feminine-looking sitting room and gestured at an ivory-colored settee. The walls were done in pale pink, the curtains were cream-colored lace and a fawn-colored carpet covered the floor.

Barnes and Witherspoon both sat. The inspector tried not to stare, but it was really very difficult. Miss Hartshorn was quite a lovely woman. Small, slender and titian-haired, she had delicate features and lovely blue eyes.

Removing her gloves, she gracefully sat down on the love seat opposite the settee. Tossing the gloves to one side, she folded her hands in her lap and smiled patiently. "How can I help you, sir?"

"Er, uh, we'd like to ask you a few questions about Roland Ashbury," Witherspoon said.

Her smile disappeared and her expression became serious. "I'm surprised it took you this long to get around to me. I haven't been hiding, you know."

"Hiding?" Witherspoon repeated in confusion. "Goodness, Miss Hartshorn, we know that. We simply didn't realize you'd anything to do with Mr. Ashbury until after we'd spoken to Henry Alladyce."

"So you learned about me from Henry, did you?" She shrugged, the gracefulness of her movement making the gesture look eloquent. "I knew we wouldn't be able to keep it quiet much longer. Not that it mattered." She laughed. "Roland was such an idiot. He actually was stupid enough to think I'd care if he went running to Andrew."

"Running to Andrew?" Witherspoon said. "You mean Andrew Frommer?" Alladyce had only said that Miss Hartshorn disliked the victim; he hadn't told them why.

"Who else would I mean, Inspector." She sighed and leaned back against the overstuffed pillow of the settee. "Roland was a despicable man. I loathed him. He tried to blackmail me. But I wasn't having any of it. I told him to go right ahead and tell Andrew everything. I was finished with Andrew anyway. God knows what I ever saw in the man in the first place." She gestured helplessly. "Perhaps he turned my head because he was a member of Parliament. In any case, it doesn't matter. Once I discovered what brute he was, I wasn't interested anymore." She laughed again. "It really took the wind out of Roland's sails when I told him that too, silly fool. I didn't care if he did tell Andrew about Charles and me."

Barnes looked at the inspector. So far, they were getting far more than they'd hoped. "Are you saying you were once . . . er . . . involved with Mr. Frommer and that Mr. Ashbury tried to blackmail you because he'd discovered you were now involved with Mr. Burroughs?"

Witherspoon nodded gratefully at the constable. Fellow knew just the right way to put things.

"That's exactly what happened," she said. "There's no reason for me to lie about it. Far too many people know about me. Most of Andrew's servants knew and MaryAnne suspected we were seeing each other. Not that she cared, mind you. And after having gotten to know Andrew better, I can understand why."

"How long were you involved with Mr. Frommer?" Witherspoon asked.

"About six months," she replied. "Roland Ashbury found out that Andrew and I were seeing each other. I think he followed Andrew here one afternoon. The day before he went to their country house in Ascot, Roland showed up on my doorstep. He demanded money to keep quiet. I laughed in his face. He said if I didn't give him money—quite a bit of money—he'd tell Andrew I was now seeing Charles Burroughs. I told him to go right ahead, that it would save me a great deal of trouble and a very unpleasant scene."

"I see." Witherspoon was flabbergasted. "Did he go to Mr. Frommer?"

"I'm sure he did," she said nonchalantly. "But I don't think that's why Andrew killed him. Andrew would murder for money or power, but he certainly wouldn't kill over losing me."

"You're accusing Mr. Frommer of murdering his father-in-law?" Barnes exclaimed. "What reason could he have for wanting Mr. Ashbury dead?"

That was precisely what the inspector wanted to know.

Eloise Hartshorn hesitated for the briefest of moments. "I'm not sure," she began. "All I know is that Roland Ashbury didn't seem unduly surprised when I told him I wasn't paying him a penny. He simply sneered at me and said if I wouldn't pay, there was someone else who would. I can only guess that he meant Andrew.''

"But I thought he was in awe of his son-in-law?'' Witherspoon said. "Our information has made it very clear that Mr. Ashbury wanted nothing more than to stay in Mr. Frommer's good graces. Are you sure he wasn't referring to Mr. Burroughs?''

"Don't be absurd. Charles was no more likely to pay that pompous fool than I was,'' she snapped. "Why should he?''

"Perhaps to protect both his and your reputation,'' Witherspoon suggested. He was only guessing, of course. But sometimes even the wildest conjecture might turn out to hit the mark.

"You are joking, Inspector, aren't you?'' She looked very amused. "Women like me don't have reputations. I should have thought someone in your profession would have realized that. Besides, Andrew Frommer wanted Roland dead. Furthermore, he was there the afternoon the man was shot. I know; I saw him coming out of the house.''

"You *saw* him?'' Barnes prompted. "Where were you?''

She smiled triumphantly. "Right next door. You can see the back of the Frommer house from Charles's bedroom window. At four o'clock, Andrew Frommer came running out the back door like the devil himself was on his heels.''

Everyone was on time for the afternoon meeting. Mrs. Jeffries, who'd gone on an errand of her own and then spent the remainder of the day going over what little information they'd acquired, was eager to hear from the others. "Who would like to start?'' she asked.

Wiggins bobbed his head. "Let me. I've 'eard plenty and I'm afraid I'll forget it if I don't get it out." When no one objected, he plunged straight in. "I've got two things to tell. The first one I 'eard this mornin'. I 'ad a chat with a shopkeeper." He tossed Betsy an apologetic glance, even though he'd apologized special-like before their botched-up morning meeting. "And 'e give me an earful." He gave them all the details he'd learned from his encounter with Nat Hopkins. His voice rose in excitement as he told them of Andrew Frommer's "fancy woman" and the fact that young Emma had actually seen her.

"Did you get her name?" Betsy interrupted eagerly.

Wiggins's face fell. "No, I was goin' to, but ya see, I think I might 'ave made a muck-up of the whole situation."

"Muck-up?" Mrs. Jeffries repeated. "In what way, Wiggins?"

He swallowed nervously. "I told Nat Hopkins who I worked for; I told 'im I worked for the inspector. Well, I 'ad to say somethin', I'd been asking the feller questions and 'e was gettin' a mite suspicious, so when he was moanin' that the coppers weren't goin' to come around and question 'is niece, I thought 'ere's my chance to learn even more. So I told 'im who I worked for, thinkin' 'e'd keep on talkin'." Wiggins sagged in his chair. "But it didn't work out, ya see. Right after I said that, is wife come along and shouted for 'im to come 'elp 'er. I was thinkin' I'd find a way to tell the inspector 'e ought to go along and interview this Emma. I was goin' to do that at tea this mornin' when the inspector showed up so unexpectedly, but there weren't a good way to bring it up, not with Lady Cannonberry bringin' that Mr. Pilchard with 'er and the inspector actin' so funny."

No one said a word. It was a given that while in the midst of the investigation none of them were supposed to mention they worked for Inspector Witherspoon. Better to be discreet than take the chance of their inspector finding out members of his own household were questioning witnesses. But as they'd all found reason in the past to violate this rule, no one wanted to criticize Wiggins.

Mrs. Jeffries's expression was thoughtful. "Don't worry, Wiggins, we'll find a way to get the information to him. What's this girl's full name?"

"All I 'eard was 'Emma,' " he replied, "but she lives with Nat Hopkins and 'e owns the shop down on Badgett Street around the corner from the Frommer house."

"Too bad you didn't get the name of Frommer's fancy woman," Mrs. Goodge mused. "That would have been right useful. At least it gives a reason why Andrew Frommer might want to murder his father-in-law. Maybe he got tired of putting up with the old bloke and did him in to make sure he couldn't tell anyone anything."

"I'm sorry." Wiggins shook his head, his expression glum. "I didn't 'ave time to get 'er name."

"Not to worry, lad," Smythe said cheerfully. "I think I know who she is. Eloise Hartshorn. She's one of the people the inspector interviewed today. She's a right beautiful woman, that's for certain. I can see why Frommer . . ." He trailed off as he caught sight of the fierce glare Betsy was directing at him.

"You said there were two things you needed to tell us, Wiggins," Mrs. Jeffries said briskly. "What was the other one?"

Wiggins took a deep breath. He wanted to get this part right. "I learned a bit more about that missin' footman from the Frommer household," he said. He told them what he'd learned from the gardener. He took great pains to make sure he got every detail right and made doubly sure he repeated the gardener's assertion that the lad had disappeared to protect MaryAnne Frommer. "Anyway," he finished, "I was thinkin' I'd 'ave a nip over to St. George's and see if anyone there knows anythin' about this lad. It's important we find 'im."

"Do you really think this boy knows anything?" Hatchet asked.

" 'Course 'e does," Wiggins declared. " 'E scarpered, didn't 'e?"

"But 'e scarpered the morning before the murder took place. So 'ow could 'e know anythin'? Smythe asked thoughtfully. "Unless, of course, 'e 'eard somethin' or saw somethin' earlier that scared 'im."

"You should pursue locating the lad," Mrs. Jeffries said. "But do please be careful."

When Wiggins nodded, she looked at the others. "Who would like to go next? Betsy?"

"I didn't learn anything." Betsy wrinkled her nose at the footman. "None of the shopkeepers I spoke to had anything interesting to say. Mr. Frommer pays his bills promptly and most of the household shopping is done by the housekeeper, not Mrs. Frommer. No one knew anything about Mr. Ashbury."

"Don't be discouraged, Betsy," Mrs. Jeffries said stoutly. "You'll do better tomorrow."

"I might as well go next," Smythe said. "I've not got much, but I did follow the inspector to a couple a places. The first one was right next door to the Frommer 'ouse. Bachelor lives there and 'is name is Burroughs, Charles Burroughs. I couldn't find out anythin' else about 'im, though. There wasn't time before the inspector come out. Then 'e went to talk to this Eloise Hartshorn."

"The pretty one?" Betsy asked archly. She smiled sweetly at the coachman.

"Right." He grinned. "She were pretty. The inspector was in there a fair amount of time. When he come out he went back to the station. As it were gettin' late, I decided to nip on back 'ere." Smythe didn't tell them that he'd also nipped into his bank and taken out a wad of cash. He had an appointment tonight and he was going to need it.

"Mrs. Goodge, have you anything to report?" Mrs. Jeffries's own news wasn't so important that she was in any rush to impart it.

"Not really. I only had a couple of people stop in today." She shook her head in disgust. "Good thing, too, as I'd not much to feed them. But I've got the word out, and tomorrow, there'll be an army of people trooping through here. Now that I've got them names from Smythe"—she shot the coachman a grateful smile—"that'll give me a lot to work with." Her broad face suddenly creased in a thoughtful frown. "But there's something I'd like to know. Where'd that cake that Ashbury served for tea come from?"

"The kitchen?" Wiggins suggested.

"Of course it come from a kitchen," Mrs. Goodge said impatiently. "But what kitchen? The Frommer household had been on holiday for two weeks. You don't leave a cake sittin' in the larder for weeks on end."

"But you bake our Christmas cake in August," Wiggins argued.

"This wasn't a bloomin' Christmas cake," the cook snapped.

"It was walnut," the housekeeper murmured.

"Thank you," Mrs. Goodge said promptly.

"And you're right to wonder where it came from," the

housekeeper continued. She looked at the maid. "As a matter of fact, that's something you ought to do straightaway. Tomorrow. Check with all the bakers in the area. Find out who bought that cake."

"Are you thinkin' it might 'ave been the killer?" Smythe asked. "Surely no one is that stupid."

"You'd be surprised how stupid some criminals are," Mrs. Jeffries replied. "But you're probably right. I doubt the killer walked into a local baker's shop and bought it. But someone must have. I do think that we ought to know who."

"Maybe Ashbury brought it from the country," Luty suggested. "From what I hear, he's about as cheap as they come."

"Is that all you found out, madam?" Hatchet grinned broadly. "That the victim was a cheapskate?"

Luty frowned at her butler. "It's early days yet in this investigation. Don't ya worry yourself about me, Hatchet. I'll find out plenty."

"In other words, madam"—the butler smiled gleefully—"that is all you found out."

"But I thought you was eager to tell us something earlier today?" Mrs. Goodge said. "Something you heard from your friend in the House of Lords."

"I was," Luty replied. "But seein' as how Wiggins and Smythe has already mentioned Eloise Hartshorn, they've kinda stole my thunder. That's really all he had to tell me. He was just repeatin' some gossip. The only other thing he mentioned was the scandal involvin' Ashbury's son, Jonathan, but that was years ago."

"He disinherted the boy, didn't he?" Mrs. Goodge nodded. "That's what my sources said. The lad married a servant girl, a Russian immigrant, and they left the country."

Luty nodded. "The boy and his family died when the wagon they was in got washed away. Just goes to show what kind of man Ashbury was. He wouldn't even help his own flesh and blood."

"You saw Dr. Bosworth today?" Betsy asked Mrs. Jeffries. She rather liked the good doctor, and better yet, she knew it niggled Smythe that she would bring the man's name up. She shot the coachman a quick glance out of the corner of her eyes. He looked annoyed.

"Yes, I went around to the hospital right after tea." She pursed her lips thoughtfully. "He'd not done the postmortem, but he'd managed to have a look at Dr. Potter's report. It's as we thought. Ashbury was killed by a bullet, probably from a revolver."

Smythe pushed his way through the crowded, noisy pub, one hand over his pants pocket to protect against pickpockets as he scanned the small room. He spotted a familiar figure leaning up against the bar.

"Hello, Blimpey." Smythe wedged himself in next to the short, rotund fellow. "Glad to see yer on time."

"Am I ever late when there's money involved?" Blimpey asked with a wide grin. He wore a brown-and-white-checked coat that had seen better days, a dark, porkpie hat covered with so much grime its original color was anyone's guess and a wilted gray shirt that had once been white. A bright red scarf was tossed jauntily around his squat neck. Blimpey nodded at his empty glass. "Wouldn't say no to another."

Smythe caught the publican's eye. "Another one 'ere," he called, pointing to Blimpey, "and I'll 'ave a pint of yer best bitter."

"Ta," Blimpey said amiably. "Well, me lad, how ya been keepin'?"

"I'm doin' all right," Smythe replied, pulling out a handful of coins and slapping them on the counter as the barman put their drinks in front of them. "Same as always."

"How's that sweet girl of yours?" Blimpey said chattily. "My, but she's a lovely one. When the two of you tyin' the knot? I could tell by the way ya hovered over her so carefully that she's right special to ya."

"You saw me and Betsy? Where?"

"At the Crystal Palace." Blimpey smiled slyly. "A few months ago. It was at the Photographic Exhibition. Grand, wasn't it?"

Surprised, Smythe retorted, "You was at the exhibition?"

"Don't sound so shocked," Blimpey countered. "You're not the only one who can get out and about. I like lookin' at interestin' things too."

"More like ya was pickin' pockets." Smythe reached for his beer. He wasn't sure how he felt about someone like Blimpey knowing too much about his courtship of Betsy. It made him feel vulnerable. He didn't mind Mrs. Jeffries and the others knowing he was crazy about the girl; that was different, that was family.

Blimpey's face fell; he actually looked hurt. "I'll have you know, I don't do that anymore," he said with dignity. "I don't have to. My current occupation is far too lucrative. Now, why don't you tell me what it is you're wantin' from me tonight?"

Blimpey's current occupation was the reason that Smythe had arranged to meet him. After years of petty thieving and picking pockets, the man had realized his phenomenal memory could be put to much better use than dodging coppers.

So now he bought and sold information. His clients

ranged from people like Smythe to politicians and, on occasion, even Scotland Yard itself.

"No offense was meant," Smythe said apologetically. Not that he was overly concerned with hurting Blimpey Groggnis's tender feelings; he just didn't want him so annoyed he didn't do a good, quick job. Smythe felt a bit funny about his current mission. Somehow, it didn't seem fair. Especially as it was becoming a bit of a habit. He'd hired the man on several of the inspector's cases now. But in his own defense, he thought quickly, he did plenty of investigating himself. It just seemed silly to run all over London trying to find out things when for a few bob he could pay Blimpey and be sure of getting it fast and quick. And it wasn't like he couldn't afford it, either.

He had plenty of money. More than he knew what to do with, and that was causing him no end of bother as well. It was one of the reasons he couldn't "tie the knot" with Betsy.

"None taken." Blimpey's good humor was restored as quickly as it had disappeared. "Now, who am I onto this time?"

"Did you hear about that murder at the MP's house?"

"All of London's 'eard of that one." Blimpey chugged his drink. "Andrew Frommer. It was his wife's father who was killed, wasn't it?"

"Right," Smythe agreed. "And I want to know everything there is to know about both of them. The husband and the wife."

"You think she might have done her old man in?" Blimpey asked conversationally. Nothing surprised him.

"It's possible." Smythe shrugged. "I've got a few more names fer you as well. Find out what ya can about Charles Burroughs; 'e lives right next door to the Frommers."

Blimpey didn't bother to write anything down. "Who else?"

"Eloise Hartshorn. She lives at number four Tacner Place in Chelsea. I think she might be Frommer's mistress. Then there's a bloke named Henry Alladyce. 'E was the victim's partner. They ran a shipping agency over on Russell Street. That's right off the East India Docks."

"I know where it is." Blimpey finished off his pint. "Is that it, then?"

Smythe nodded. "Yeah, for right now. How long do ya think it'll take to find out anythin'?"

"Meet me here at noon tomorrow," Blimpey replied. "I ought to have something by then."

The inspector arrived home for dinner only an hour past his usual time. "I do hope dinner is ready," he commented as he handed his hat to Mrs. Jeffries. "I'm quite famished. By the way, do you happen to know how long Lady Cannonberry's houseguest is staying?"

"Dinner is on the table, sir." Mrs. Jeffries led him down the hall and into the dining room. "Mrs. Goodge has made a lovely meal for you, sir." She gestured at the table. "She thought you might enjoy a cold supper, sir, as it's so hot today." Actually, the cook had been too busy using her ovens to bake for her sources to bother making much of a meal for the inspector. Betsy and Mrs. Jeffries had been the ones to put together his dinner from what fixings they'd found in the dry larder.

"Excellent." He pulled out his chair, whipped his serviette off the plate and reached for the platter of sliced ham. He speared a double portion and dumped it onto the china. "This does look good."

"I've no idea how long Mr. Pilchard is staying with Lady Cannonberry," she continued. She reached for a bowl of fresh mixed greens and handed it to him. "How was your day, sir? Are you making any progress on the case?"

"Well"—he made a face as he popped two hard-boiled eggs next to the greens—"I think so. I interviewed two other people who might have had a reason to kill the victim. But honestly it's all such a muddle, I can't make heads nor tails of it."

"Really, sir? And who were they? If, of course, you don't mind my asking."

"One of them is a neighbor. Charles Burroughs. Nice enough chap." Witherspoon shook salt onto his eggs. "Very cooperative. He told us something most interesting." As he ate he told her about the interview, taking care to get all the details correct. Talking the case out with Mrs. Jeffries was always so helpful. "So you see," he said, "I had quite a good impression of the fellow, thought he was being honest and everything until I spoke to Eloise Hartshorn. That's when it all got terribly, terribly confusing. As a matter of fact, I think Miss Hartshorn might be lying. Could you pass me those greens?"

She complied with his request, noting that not only was he demolishing the last of the greens, but he'd also eaten all the ham. "Why do you think she might be lying, sir?"

"Because"—he scraped some more greens onto his plate—"I think she's in love with Charles Burroughs and she's trying to protect him. She claimed she saw Andrew Frommer leaving his own house by the back door at a quarter to four on the afternoon of the murder. She said she witnessed this from the window of Charles Burroughs's bedroom." He broke off as a bright, red blush swept his cheeks, and then forced himself to go on. "But that's not true. We interviewed Mr. Burroughs's servants on the way home this evening, and all of them testify that

Miss Hartshorn wasn't in the Burroughs house the afternoon of the murder. So she couldn't have been in his bedroom and couldn't have seen what she claimed she saw.'' He shook his head and popped another bite into his mouth. As he demolished his dinner he told Mrs. Jeffries about his interview with Eloise Hartshorn.

As always, she listened carefully, storing every little bit of information in her mind. Finally, when it appeared he'd told her everything, she said, ''But I don't understand why Henry Alladyce wanted you to interview Charles Burroughs in the first place. I can see why he'd give you Eloise Hartshorn's name. But why Burroughs?''

''Oh.'' Witherspoon looked surprised. ''Didn't I tell you?''

''No, sir, you didn't. From what you've told me, Burroughs's only connection to the family is that he lives next door. The fact that he knows Andrew Frommer beats his wife couldn't be the reason that Alladyce sent you to him in the first place. Not unless Burroughs told Alladyce what he'd seen.''

The inspector swallowed a huge bite of egg. ''He hadn't. Alladyce thought I ought to see him because he knew that Burroughs had a gun.''

Incredulous, she stared at him. ''That's it? He was suspicious of the neighbor because of a gun? But, sir, half of London owns weapons of some sort.''

''True.'' Witherspoon scanned the empty serving bowls. ''But most of them aren't revolvers. Burroughs has a revolver. The same kind of weapon used in the murder.''

''How did Alladyce know what kind of gun had been used?''

''From the newspaper.'' He frowned. ''Stupid of us, really, letting that information get out to the public.''

Mrs. Jeffries knew it was common practice for the police to keep some details out of the press. "How did Alladyce know that Burroughs had the gun? Are they well acquainted?"

"Not really. Alladyce only met him once, in front of the Frommer house. He knew about the gun because he happened to see Burroughs cleaning it a few weeks back. He'd taken the weapon in the garden to clean and Alladyce saw it over the fence. He said Burroughs wasn't trying to hide what he was doing, he was simply sitting at the lawn table in his shirtsleeves cleaning his gun. Burroughs confirmed this. He admitted he'd been doing just that. Even knew when it must have happened. It was the day before the Frommer household went to Ascot."

"I still don't think that's enough of a reason to consider the man a suspect," she said, shaking her head.

"Normally I'd agree with you." Witherspoon licked his lips. "But in this case, considering what I learned from Eloise Hartshorn, I'm glad I went to see Charles Burroughs. You see, the revolver he owns is missing. It's completely disappeared."

They only had time for a brief meeting the next morning. Mrs. Jeffries brought them all up-to-date on what she'd heard from the inspector. She also assured Wiggins that she'd managed to plant the idea in the inspector's mind that he ought to interview any servants who'd recently left the Frommer household. Therefore, he could stop worrying about Emma not being able to tell her tale. By the time everyone had left to do all their own snooping, she'd still not decided what she ought to do. She sat at the table, gazing blankly ahead, trying to sift all the bits and pieces of information into some sort of coherent pattern. But nothing, absolutely nothing came to mind.

Mrs. Goodge ushered in a young man wearing a footman's livery. "Oh," she said, when she spotted the housekeeper sitting at the table, "you're still here? I thought you'd gone off with the others."

The words weren't rude or even unfriendly, but Mrs. Jeffries had the distinct impression the cook wanted to pump her source in private. She finally decided what she ought to do. "I was just leaving," she said, smiling at the skinny lad as she rose to her feet and hurried over to the coat tree. Reaching for her hat, she said, "I ought to be back by tea."

She left by the back door, hurried up to Addison Road and from there onto the Uxbridge Road. She found a hansom in front of Holland Park Gardens. "Take me to Chelsea," she ordered, getting inside.

"None of the alibis are right, sir," Barnes said as he and the inspector waited on Ladbrook Road for a passing hansom cab. The police station, where they'd just come from, was directly behind them. "I don't know why people bother lyin' to us. Do they think we don't check up on them?"

"I'm afraid that's precisely what most of them think." Witherspoon raised his arm as a cab clip-clopped toward them. "Argyle Street," the inspector instructed the driver when the hansom pulled over. As soon as he and the constable were safely inside, he allowed a sigh to escape him. Not only was this case becoming a bit of a muddle—don't they all, he thought—but he was rather distressed about Lady Cannonberry. He'd popped over early this morning hoping to have a word with her before breakfast, only to discover that she and Mr. Pilchard were al-

ready out and about. They'd taken the early train to
Brighton. Drat. He'd so wanted to ask her to dine with
him later in the week.

"Well, sir?" Barnes asked.

Witherspoon came out of his daze to find the constable
staring at him expectantly. "I'm sorry," he said, "I'm
afraid I didn't quite hear you."

Barnes nodded sympathetically. He'd arrived at Upper
Edmonton Gardens this morning just in time to see the
inspector leaving Ruth Cannonberry's front porch. The
glum expression on Witherspoon's face and a discreet
question or two had elicited enough information for the
constable to guess at the cause of the inspector's preoc-
cupation. Ah, first love, he thought, it didn't matter
whether one was fifteen or fifty. It hit with the force of a
gale, spun the unlucky man to and fro a few times and
then knocked him on his backside. Poor fella. "I asked
who we wanted to question first?"

The inspector forced himself to keep his mind on the
case. "Why don't we see who's available?" he finally
said. "It could well be that Mr. Frommer is at his office."

But Mr. Frommer wasn't at his office; he was at home.
When the butler led the two policemen into the study,
Frommer looked up from his desk with a puzzled, ab-
stracted expression. It took him a moment before he recognized his visitors. "Back again? Have you caught the
killer yet?"

"No, sir, we haven't," Witherspoon replied.

"Why not?" Frommer put down his pen and leaned
back in the chair. "What's taking so long? It's most
awkward for me, being part of a household where an un-
solved murder has been committed. My constituents
don't like it. The party doesn't like it. I don't like it.

Now, why can't you fellows catch the lunatic that did this thing?''

Witherspoon hadn't much cared for Mr. Frommer the first time he met him. Since hearing Burroughs's contention that the man was a wife beater, he cared even less for him. He'd no doubt Burroughs had been telling the truth, though as to why he felt that way he couldn't say. But the inspector had long ago learned to listen to his inner voice, and right now that voice was telling him this man was a blackguard and a cad. However, that didn't mean he was a killer. "I expect it would be easier to catch the murderer," he said carefully, "if we didn't have to waste so much time sorting out the lies people tell us.''

Frommer's self-satisfied expression vanished. His eyes grew wary. "I don't know what you mean.''

"Don't you, sir?" Witherspoon walked closer to the desk. "You told us you came to London on the four o'clock train, sir. But that's not true. We've a witness who placed you on the two forty-five.''

Frommer shot to his feet. "Your witness is lying. You were already here when I arrived, and that was well into the evening. It had gone half-past six.''

"Our witness isn't lying, sir," Barnes said firmly. "He's a policeman. He stood right next to you on the platform at Ascot and then watched you get into a first-class compartment. When the train arrived at London, he saw you get off.''

"He's mistaken," Frommer sputtered. "It wasn't me.''

"It's no mistake, sir," Witherspoon said. "He knew quite well who you were. You're the MP for his district. Now, sir, why don't you tell us where you were on the afternoon of the murder?''

Speechless, Frommer gaped at the two men and then

flopped back into his chair. "All right," he muttered, "I'll tell you. But it's to go no further than this room. You must give me your word on that."

"I'm afraid I can't do that," Witherspoon said gently. "I may have to give evidence in court and I can't promise to keep any information secret."

"Now, see here," Frommer snapped. "It's a matter vital to the national interest—"

"No, sir, I'm afraid it isn't." Witherspoon sighed inwardly. Honestly, people sometimes thought the police were such fools. "The chief inspector has already been in contact with the home secretary and Whitehall. You were doing nothing official or even unofficial in your capacity as a member of Parliament that afternoon. As a matter of fact, according to your chief whip, you missed an important meeting of your own party that day. Now, could you please tell us where you were?"

"Yes, Andrew, do tell us."

The inspector and Barnes swiveled around to see MaryAnne Frommer standing in the open doorway. Though she was covered from head to toe in mourning black, the bonnet on her head and the black parasol she carried signaled the fact that she was getting ready to go out. She didn't take her eyes off her husband. "Well, where were you?" she goaded. "You weren't at Ascot. You weren't at your office and you certainly weren't helping any of your constituents."

"I don't have to answer to you," he finally sputtered.

"True, you don't." She smiled sweetly, a smile that took fifteen years off her middle-aged face. "But I do believe the inspector is waiting for a reply."

"Your wife is correct, sir," Witherspoon interjected hastily. He wasn't sure what he was trying to do; he only knew he didn't wish to give Mr. Frommer further reason to get angry with his wife. "We do need an answer." He looked at Barnes. "Could you please escort Mrs. Frommer into the drawing room and take her statement?"

"That won't be necessary," Mrs. Frommer said. "I know why you're here and I'm quite prepared to tell you the truth."

The inspector was very, very confused. "Er, if you'd like to go with the constable . . . I'm sure he'll be pleased to take your statement."

"There's no reason to go anywhere," she said flatly. "You're here to find out why I lied about the day my father was killed, aren't you?"

Frommer shot to his feet again. "What are you talking about, MaryAnne?"

"Don't look so shocked, Andrew." She pushed past the policemen and flopped down on the chair opposite her husband's desk. "I was on the two forty-five train that day. With you."

"Now, lad, why don't you drink up?" Mrs. Goodge handed the footman a third cup of tea. "Would you like more sponge?"

"Umm. yes." Matthew Piker nodded vigorously as he stuffed the last bite of scone into his mouth. He completely ignored the crumbs that fell from his lips and dotted the chest of his dark blue footman's uniform. "This is good. Mrs. Hampton's a good mistress, but she's a bit stingy with food. I'm always hungry."

"So many of them are like that." Mrs. Goodge clucked her tongue sympathetically and silently sent up a prayer of thanks that her aunt Elberta had finally come in useful. She'd accidentally dropped the box containing Elberta's rambling letters when she'd been rummaging

about in her bureau drawer for one of her ''special'' recipes. When she'd picked the letter up, it had opened onto
a page that mentioned Elberta's late husband's two neph-
ews worked for Eugenia Hampton, a dreadful shrew of
a woman to be sure. But she lived just up the road from
the Frommer house. Mrs. Goodge hadn't wasted a moment. She'd sent off a note to young Matthew Pike in-
viting him to come around for tea on his afternoon off.
He'd arrived wary, but curious. It wasn't often the likes
of him got invited to tea in a fine kitchen. ''We're very
lucky,'' she went on. ''The inspector's quite the generous man.''

''Must be funny, workin' for a copper?'' Matthew
gasped quietly as he saw the slab of sponge cake the cook
loaded onto his plate.

''It's not so bad,'' she said, handing him the cake. ''We
get to hear all about his cases. They're interesting.''

''Well, we had us a murder,'' he boasted. ''Bet you've
'eard of it; it were in all the newspapers. Old man up the
road got himself shot while he was havin' tea.''

''Oh yes.'' She nodded. ''I know all about that one.
His name was Roland Ashbury.''

''Is your inspector on that one, then?'' Matthew asked,
somewhat disappointed because he'd been looking forward to having all the details coaxed out of him with more
cake and tea.

''He is indeed,'' Mrs. Goodge replied. ''And he likes
to discuss his cases, he does. For instance, I'll bet you
didn't know that the man was murdered with a revolver.''

''The whole neighborhood knows that,'' Matthew shot
back, ''and just about everyone knows whose gun it were
too.''

''Charles Burroughs's.''

His mouth dropped in surprise. ''Blimey, I guess you

do know all about the case.'' He pursed his lips and stared at his plate. Then he brightened. ''But I'll bet you didn't know something else. Something that no one except me knows.''

CHAPTER 6

Mrs. Jeffries eyed the small but elegant house warily, wondering if she was about to do something very foolish. She hesitated by the letter box, in her hand an old envelope she'd found in her skirt pocket. Using the envelope as a prop, she pretended to double-check the address, all the while keeping her gaze on the white-painted door of the house across the street. What if the woman refused to answer her questions? Refused to cooperate at all? What if she told the inspector? Mrs. Jeffries pursed her lips as she weighed the odds. To go in or not to go in, that was the question. She smiled at a maid who was vigorously sweeping the door stoop of the house behind her. The maid simply stared back, no doubt beginning to wonder why someone was lingering so long in front of a letter box.

Mrs. Jeffries was just about to start across the road when the front door opened and a tall handsome man emerged. A woman, small, elegantly dressed and quite beautiful, came out right behind him. He gave the woman his arm and the two of them descended the stairs and began walking up the street.

Mrs. Jeffries didn't hesitate. She turned and walked in the same direction the couple had taken, but she stayed on her side of the road. Traffic was brisk. Hansoms, four-wheelers, drays and loaded wagons kept up a moving screen between her and the two on the other side. When she reached the corner, she saw them turn onto Guildford Street. She hurried after them, taking care to keep them in sight yet staying far enough behind not to be noticed.

They went past the Statue of Coram, the Foundling Hospital and from there onto Lansdown Place and into Brunswick Square. Mrs. Jeffries was breathing heavily by the time the couple in front of her circled the square and headed into the burial grounds. From the way they kept their heads close together in conversation without so much as a glance behind them, she was fairly sure they'd no idea they were being followed.

The man suddenly led the woman off the path and into the cemetery itself. Mrs. Jeffries was close enough now to see the expresssion on his face. He was worried, very worried.

They finally stopped in front of a large marble statue of a winged angel surrounded by a grouping of cherubs. Mrs. Jeffries halted as well. She desperately wanted to know what her prey were discussing, but she needed to stay out of sight. She surveyed the scene carefully and, after the briefest of hesitations, decided the headstone might be large enough to conceal her. Moving cautiously, she darted off the path and crept up on other side.

"But why must I leave?" she heard the woman ask. "I've already spoken to the police. They know about us."

"You shouldn't have told them anything," the man insisted. "They're not fools. Now they know you had a motive. The old bastard tried to blackmail you."

She gave a cynical laugh. "He tried, but he didn't succeed. I told him to go ahead and tell. I was going to break it off anyway. But it's not me I'm worried about, Charles, it's you. Why did you admit to having a gun?"

"Because I had to," he said harshly. "Too many people have seen it."

Mrs. Jeffries could hear the shuffle of feet as the man's agitation increased. She huddled closer to the headstone.

"It doesn't matter, darling. The police will realize the gun must have been stolen," the woman cried. "You didn't have any reason to kill him."

There was a long silence, so long that Mrs. Jeffries was beginning to think they might have discovered her presence and were in the process of tiptoeing away. But finally the man spoke. "That's where you're wrong, my dear. I had the best reason of all to want him dead."

"But you didn't even know him till you came here?" The woman sounded as though she couldn't believe what he was saying. "You couldn't have hated him enough to murder him. You just couldn't."

"You don't really believe that, dearest," he said softly. "If you did, you wouldn't have made up that lie about seeing Andrew Frommer."

"It wasn't a lie," she hissed. "I did see him."

"Darling, I'm touched by your devotion, but you weren't even at my house that afternoon. The police will find that out soon enough. My servants won't lie." There was the thump of feet and the rustle of clothing as they began to move. "Come on," Mrs. Jeffries heard him say, "let's walk."

Mrs. Jeffries waited a few seconds, giving them time

to move farther away. The moment she judged they were far enough down the path not to hear her, she hurried out from her hiding place.

Her face fell in disappointment. Coming directly toward her was a huge black coffin, in front of which walked a sad-faced cleric. Somehow a funeral procession had gotten between her and her quarry. She stepped to one side so they could pass. By the time she could politely make her way past the mourners, her prey were gone.

The inspector and Barnes followed Mrs. Frommer into the drawing room. Witherspoon waited until she'd sat down on the sofa before quietly closing the door. He didn't think Mr. Frommer would dare interrupt them, especially as he'd left a fresh-faced police constable on duty outside the study. But he was taking no chances. The man had been furious at his wife. Witherspoon, despite not knowing what to make of MaryAnne Frommer, didn't wish to conduct the interview in her husband's presence. He was afraid her answers might enrage Frommer to the point that he'd do violence to his wife the minute the house was empty of police. The inspector wasn't having any of that.

MaryAnne Frommer cocked her head to one side and gazed at him quizzically. "You're wondering why I lied earlier, aren't you?"

"Yes, madam, I am." He crossed the room and, without being invited, sat down on the other end of the sofa. "You originally told us you'd come back to London on a late train because you'd gone to the vicarage."

"I knew you'd find out the truth." She laughed. "I suppose expecting a vicar to lie for one is expecting a bit much, don't you agree? Of course, when I arrived home and found out that Papa was dead, lying no longer mattered."

Witherspoon didn't think he could be any more confused. "Could you explain yourself, please."

"I told everyone I was going to the vicarage so I wouldn't have to come home on the same train as Andrew." She broke off with a short, harsh laugh. "I thought he'd be going on the four o'clock train. Imagine my surprise when I came hurtling onto the platform and saw him. I jumped back so fast I almost tripped."

"I take it your husband didn't see you?" Witherspoon asked.

"Andrew isn't particularly observant." She shrugged. "Once the train pulled in, I waited till he got into a first-class carriage and then got on myself. When we arrived at Waterloo, I kept well back, making sure that he didn't see me. When I saw him leave the station, I hurried out and hailed a hansom. Then I went to Mortimer Street, to the offices of Henley and Farr."

"Who is that, ma'am?" Witherspoon asked.

"They're a firm of solicitors." She smiled wanly.

The inspector nodded encouragingly. "What time was your appointment?"

"I didn't have one. I went to them because they were the only solicitors in town who I thought might represent me. They aren't frightened of Andrew, you see."

Witherspoon didn't see, but before he could formulate a question that didn't sound too terribly odd, she continued.

"What I needed from them was rather delicate. The sort of thing most solicitors wouldn't want to handle in any case." She sighed. "Especially when the husband in question is an MP. Andrew isn't averse to using his position to make someone's life miserable. He's done it before. Frequently. That's why I had to go to Henley and Farr. They've gone up against Andrew several times and won."

"What did you want them to do for you, ma'am?" Barnes asked softly.

"I wanted to find out if I could obtain a divorce." She smiled sadly. "You see, I had grounds now. Andrew's got a mistress. I have witnesses. Several of them."

"I see." Witherspoon knew that obtaining a divorce was very difficult. From what he'd learned of Frommer's character, he didn't much blame Mrs. Frommer for wanting to leave this marriage, but something was bothering him. Something she'd said. He frowned, trying to remember precisely what it was.

The constable, after waiting a moment of two for the inspector to speak, finally asked, "Who did you see at Henley and Farr?"

She made a disgusted face. "No one. The whole trip was absolutely wasted. The office was closed; there weren't even any clerks there. There was a notice on the door saying that they were closed until Monday next. Can you believe it? The whole office gone on holiday at the same time."

Barnes glanced at Witherspoon. The inspector's face still wore an expression of fierce concentration. The constable carried on. "What did you do then?" he asked.

"What did I do?" she repeated, with a cynical laugh. "What could I do? Nothing. I was very disappointed, of course. Who wouldn't be? I didn't want to face going home, so I went for a long walk."

Again the constable glanced at his superior. He didn't want Witherspoon thinking he was getting above himself by asking so many questions. But the inspector still looked preoccupied, so the constable pressed on. "Did you see anyone you know?"

She shook her head. "Not that I recall."

Barnes scribbled her answers in his notebook, more to

give the inspector time to finish his thinking than anything else. The constable had quite a good memory. But he'd learned that putting something in writing didn't hurt. Especially when one had to give evidence in court. He glanced up. Witherspoon was now stroking his chin, his expression still preoccupied. There was nothing for it but for him to keep on. "Where were you between three-thirty and four o'clock?" he asked.

She looked puzzled by the question. "I just told you." Her expression cleared as she realized the implications of what was being asked. "Gracious, that must have been when Father was killed."

"Yes, ma'am." Barnes wondered if the inspector was ever going to ask another question. "As far as we can tell, that would be the time of death."

"And I've no alibi now." Again she laughed. "I assure you, Constable. Much as I disliked my father, I certainly didn't kill him. I was nowhere near the house at that time."

Witherspoon started slightly, as though her answer had pulled him back into the conversation. As a matter of fact, her statement had reminded him of what was bothering him. "You admit you didn't like your father."

"I admit that," she replied. "I told you that before. I didn't like my father at all. He was never a real father to me. He always put his own interests first, but much as I disliked him, I didn't murder him."

Witherspoon nodded slowly. He wanted to ask this next question very carefully. "Could you tell me why you said that once you'd found out your father was dead, lying wouldn't matter." He was rather annoyed at himself for taking so long to recall that particularly interesting comment she'd made. Especially as she'd made it only a few moments ago. He admonished himself for being so distracted. He really must keep his mind on the interview at hand. But gracious, it was so very easy to get muddled.

She stared down at her hands and a long, heartfelt sigh escaped her. "I meant that if I'd known Papa was dead, I wouldn't even have bothered going to the solicitors. I'd have left. I've some money of my own. With my father dead, Andrew couldn't have forced me to come back. That's what he did, you know. One other time when I left him, he made me come back by threatening me."

"How did he threaten you?" Witherspoon asked quickly. "If you've money of your own, how could he have made you come back?"

She looked away for a moment, and when she turned back to the Inspector, her expression was grim. "He told me he'd toss Father out into the streets if I didn't come home. At the time I was sure he meant it. But after I found out what my father did, after the way he'd behaved recently, I wouldn't have cared about what Andrew could do to him. I wouldn't have let anything stop me. I was quite prepared for the worst."

Witherspoon thought back to his conversation with Henry Alladyce. He'd gotten the impression that Roland Ashbury was cheap, but certainly not destitute. "Your father, then, couldn't afford his own home?"

"That's not the point, Inspector." MaryAnne Frommer smiled bitterly. "My father has plenty of money. But he claimed he couldn't live on his own because he had a weak heart. It was rubbish, of course. He was as healthy as a horse. He only made the assertion because he wanted to stay on here."

"What did your father do to you?" Witherspoon asked. "You said a few moments ago that once you found out what he'd done . . ."

"He told Andrew where I was living," she cried angrily. "I'd written to him to give him the address of the rooming house where I was staying. I hadn't wanted him to worry. But instead of taking my part, instead of helping me get away from that monster I was married to, my own father led him right to me. I never forgave him for that. Never."

Witherspoon looked at the constable, making sure that Barnes was getting all of this down. Whether Mrs. Frommer realized it or not, she'd just given them a motive for murder. "So you hated your father," he prodded gently.

"Of course I did. My father couldn't have cared less about me," she countered flatly.

"You realize you've just given us a motive, don't you?" Witherspoon warned. He wasn't quite at the point of cautioning her officially, but she was definitely climbing to the top of the suspect list.

MaryAnne Frommer didn't look in the least alarmed. "Why would I kill him? I'd devised the perfect revenge against the man. I was going to leave. Andrew would have tossed him into the street. That would have hurt my father ten times more than getting a bullet in his skull. He wouldn't have been able to stand the humiliation of being a nobody."

"Living here meant that much to him?" Barnes queried.

"It meant everything to him," she said passionately. "He stayed because despite Andrew treating him like a half-witted servant, he loved basking in Andrew's limelight. He loved living in a big house with an important man, an MP. Don't you understand, as long as he was a member of this household, people treated him with respect. He got invited to the best gentlemen's clubs, he was asked out to dine, his opinion was solicited. If he was tossed out on his ear, all that would end. My father was terrified that if he lived on his own, he'd just be another stingy businessman with no entrée into the circles of his betters.''

"Stingy businessman," Witherspoon repeated. "But your father's business partner says the business is doing well." He really didn't know what to make of all this; it was most odd. Most odd indeed. Tonight, when he got home, he'd have to have a good long think about the whole situation.

MaryAnne Frommer's brows came together. "Business partner? You mean Henry?"

"He said he was your father's partner," Witherspoon replied. "Isn't that correct?"

She looked doubtful. "Well, I suppose he *would* say that. But actually Papa and Josiah Alladyce had quite a different arrangement worked out. Papa set it up when my brother Jonathan went to live in the United States."

"I'm sorry," the inspector said, "but I don't quite understand." He didn't know if this matter would turn out to be pertinent to the case, but he'd learned that the most seemingly unconnected events could end up being important.

"It's an old story, Inspector"—she sighed again—"and one that does none of us any credit. For when it happened, I was just as unreasonable as Father. Pride, I suppose. Anyway, it doesn't matter now. My brother and his wife and son have been dead for over fifteen years. They died in California. They were killed when the wagon they were sleeping in was washed away in a flood. But the point is, when my father disinherited Jonathan and had no son to leave his half of the business to, he forced Josiah Alladyce—that's Henry's father—to draw up an agreement about the disposal of the company's assets when they either died or retired. The agreement is very specific in its terms. Whoever died first would leave his half of the business to the other one until both partners were dead or retired. Then the business would be sold and the assets split between my father's heirs and the Alladyce heirs. That's why I'm surprised that Henry calls himself a partner. He's not. Well, I suppose he is now that Father's dead. But he wasn't before.''

Barnes asked, ''How much is the business worth?''

''I'm not certain,'' she replied. ''Quite a lot, I think. I know Father hadn't spent a penny of the profits that he didn't have to after Josiah Alladyce died. I do believe that annoyed Henry. Mind you, Henry does pull his living out of the firm.''

Again Barnes glanced at Witherspoon. The inspector nodded slightly in acknowledgment. It was obvious now that they had one more suspect on their hands.

There was an air of suppressed excitement around the table as they all took their places for their afternoon meeting. For once, Mrs. Jeffries thought, everyone is on time. She could tell by their expressions that most of them had found out something useful. She couldn't wait to tell them what she'd learned.

''Can I go first?'' Luty asked eagerly as she scanned the faces of the others, daring someone to deny her request. ''I'm gonna bust if I don't git it out.''

''Go ahead, Luty,'' Mrs. Jeffries replied. Her own information, important as it was, could wait.

''Well, as you all know, I've got plenty of ways of findin' out things.'' She shot her butler a glare as a faint snort of derision issued from his direction. ''And I found out something real interestin' about Andrew Frommer. He's broke. He spent a bundle campaignin' in the last election. So much so that he's up to his nose in debt and that fancy house of his is mortgaged to the hilt. That means he's got a motive for murderin' his father-in-law.''

"I don't see how his financial condition could be that affected by Roland Ashbury's death,'' Hatchet said thoughtfully. "Even if Mrs. Frommer inherits from her father, it would be her money, not his.''

"So?'' Luty demanded.

"So''—Hatchet gave her a sly smile—"we know that Mrs. Frommer loathes her husband. If she inherits from her father, I don't think she'll be sharing it with her spouse. Furthermore, how much could the victim actually have to leave to anyone? He didn't even own his own home and his business certainly doesn't appear to be all that prosperous. I know. I went along and had a look at the place.''

"He's got plenty to leave,'' Mrs. Goodge said darkly. "He hasn't spent a penny of the profits off that business since his partner died five years ago. MaryAnne Frommer's the heir, you see. That business may not look like much, but I found out that Ashbury and his partner bought the building some years back, and the warehouse next to it. The whole lot's worth a fortune now.''

"Seems to me that just about everyone 'ad a reason for wantin' Mr. Ashbury dead,'' Wiggins said. "Even 'is own kin.''

"Especially his own kin,'' Mrs. Goodge declared stoutly. "Ashbury was a horrible man. He disinherited his own son because the boy married a servant, and forced Mrs. Frommer to stay with that brute of a husband of hers. But now that he's dead, she can leave him. She'd left him before, you see. But her own father told Frommer where she was stayin' and he went and drug her home.''

"Whaddaya mean, 'he drug her home'?'' Luty asked, her eyes narrowed dangerously.

"Just what I said," Mrs. Goodge replied. "Frommer went to the flat where his wife was living and made her come home with him. He's a wife beater."

"And she went with him?" Luty exclaimed, her expression incredulous.

"What else could she do?" Mrs. Goodge said. "He was her husband. I'm sure her landlord didn't want that kind of trouble, especially as Frommer was an MP."

"MP or not," Luty snapped, "they'd be havin' snowball fights in hell before I'd let some wife-beatin', no-good cowardly varmmit come draggin' me home."

"My sentiments precisely," Mrs. Jeffries agreed. Gracious, the information was coming along so fast she could barely absorb it all. They must be a tad more orderly or she, along with the rest of them, would get confused. "But let's let Luty finish talking and then we'll move along to Mrs. Goodge. Both of you seem to have found out an awful lot."

"I'm done," Luty announced. "All I learned was that Frommer was broke and iffen Mrs. Frommer ain't gonna share with him, I guess that leaves him out as a suspect."

"Not necessarily," Mrs. Jeffries murmured. She made a mental note to ask Lady Cannonberry about the Married Woman's Property Act. One of the delightful things about being friends with a radical is that they were usually well up on all the most recent legislation. "We'd better check on what Mrs. Frommer's position would be. Legally she might not have been able to stop her husband from using her money or selling her property. Especially if it was left to her in trust and that trust is administered by her husband."

"But even Ashbury wouldn't have done that," Betsy cried. "It wouldn't be right. Surely he knew Frommer was a brute."

"He'd do it all right," Mrs. Goodge interjected. "Any man that would let his own son and his wife lose their home and almost starve to death wouldn't care tuppence for his daughter's happiness."

"Ashbury let his son's family starve?" Smythe asked.

"Almost." The cook shook her head in disgust. "He disinherited the boy when he married. The girl was a servant, a Russian immigrant. They, along with the wife's family, moved to the United States and bought a small farm somewhere out west. There was a drought or something horrid like that; you know how things like that are always happening in America. The family lost the farm. Jonathan Ashbury wrote his father for help, begging him to lend him some money. Ashbury never even answered. A few months later, when the family had been forced out of their home, the wagon they were sleeping in was washed away in a flood. All of them were killed except for the daughter-in-law's brother."

"Cor blimey," Wiggins muttered. "Ashbury really was a monster."

"That's right," Mrs. Goodge agreed. "So it's no wonder his own daughter stopped speakin' to him. I only hope the stupid old fool didn't tie up the girl's inheritance and give Frommer control of it."

"We don't know what Frommer can or can't do," Mrs. Jeffries said. "I think it may well depend on how Ashbury wrote his will. Apparently he spent more time trying to please his son-in-law than he did worrying about his daughter's well-being."

"And as Frommer's an MP," Smythe muttered, "there's no tellin' what he could do even if the money was left free and clear to his wife." He caught Betsy's eyes and gave her a wary smile. He didn't want her thinking he approved of any man hitting a woman. He'd noticed that when women heard about another female being knocked about, they tended to tar all men with the same brush.

"Does this mean that Mr. Frommer is still a suspect?" Wiggins asked.

"Of course," Mrs. Jeffries replied.

"But 'e's got an alibi," the footman pointed out, "and so does Mrs. Frommer."

"What difference does that make?" Luty exclaimed. "We've had half a dozen cases where the one with the best alibi ended up bein' the killer."

"I don't think it's Mr. Frommer," Wiggins stated, shaking his head. "I think it's her, Mrs. Frommer. She really hated her father, especially after he come and drug 'er 'ome."

"How do you know that?" Mrs. Goodge demanded.

"Because I talked to Bobby Vickers," he said casually. " 'E's a good friend of that footman that's taken off from the Frommer household. He told me that Boyd—that's the lad's name—'ad said that 'e was worried that Mrs. Frommer was goin' to do somethin' awful. She were desperate to get away from 'er 'usband."

"Oh bother, Wiggins." Mrs. Goodge crossed her arms over her chest. "That's silly. If Mrs. Frommer was goin' to commit murder because her situation was so awful, why would she murder her father? Seems to me she'd have killed her husband."

"You have a point, Mrs. Goodge," Hatchet agreed. "My sources of information all agreed that Mrs. Frommer despised her husband and would have done anything to get away from him."

"Why'd she marry him in the first place?" Betsy murmured.

"She married him because her father made her,"

Hatchet replied. Goff had come through with a bit of information. Not much, but at least he could contribute something. "Andrew Frommer is from an old and well-respected family. But like many such families, they've no money. The estate was lost years ago and there was only a small yearly income for Andrew. Not enough to support his political ambitions and certainly not enough to finance a campaign. Then he met Roland Ashbury at a party political dinner. Ashbury was in trade, of course, but he'd money and a daughter. Frommer, to his credit, at first resisted Ashbury's attempts to buy a husband for his daughter. But he eventually gave way and asked MaryAnne to marry him." He toyed with the handle of his teacup. "But the marriage went sour from the start and Andrew Frommer made no secret of the fact that he considered it his father-in-law's fault. He blamed him for getting him stuck in a loveless marriage."

"He wants an heir too," Mrs. Goodge added. "I've got that on good authority. He dreams of startin' a political dynasty. 'Course, he can't do that without a son." She smiled, thinking of the way the poor lad had blushed earlier today when he'd told her about overhearing Frommer bragging to one of his associates that as his wife was barren, he'd have to "take matters into his own hands" to procure a son. It had taken her ten minutes to pump that bit of information out of Matthew Piker. "But Frommer's been talkin' about the neighborhood that he's got that problem well in hand," she finished.

Mrs. Jeffries knew she had to take control of this situation. There was far too much information being bandied about. So much so that she wasn't sure she'd even remember it all.

"Please, everyone, can we do this one at a time? I'm getting very confused." She looked at Luty. "Now let me see if I understand you. You found out that Frommer finances are in a mess.''

Luty nodded vigorously. ''That's right.''

''And I found out that he's a wife beater and that Mrs. Frommer had run off from him and that he and her father had drug her home,'' Mrs Goodge announced proudly. She'd also found out another bit or two, but she was saving this for their next meeting. Sometimes she'd found her sources could be most unreliable and she could have dozens of people through the kitchen without learning a ruddy thing. Well, it wasn't so much that she'd found out anything as it was that she'd thought of something and she considered it might be important.

''I see.'' Mrs. Jeffries nodded encouragingly and then looked at Hatchet. He repeated what he'd learned and she turned her attention to Smythe and Betsy, both of whom had been somewhat quiet. ''Betsy?''

The maid smiled and shrugged. ''No luck yet, Mrs. Jeffries, but I'll keep at it. I'm going back out before supper to have a word or two with one of the housemaids who works for Charles Burroughs. I'm meeting her at the Lyons Tea Shop on Oxford Street.'' She glanced at the clock and then got to her feet. ''I'd best be off. I told her I'd be there at five o'clock.''

Smythe hated for Betsy to be out late in the afternoon; he was always worried that she'd get caught up in her investigation and end up on the streets after dark. ''Now, why would you want to talk to Burroughs's 'ousemaid?''

''She might know something.'' Betsy shrugged. ''After all, it might have been Burroughs's gun that killed Ashbury.'' She was desperate to find out something and at this point she was willing to talk to anyone.

''But 'e'd no reason to murder the old man,'' Smythe persisted.

"We don't know that," Betsy said. "We don't know that at all."

"Betsy's right," Mrs. Jeffries interjected. "Burroughs did have a good reason to murder Ashbury. Unfortunately I don't know what that reason is."

Andrew Frommer seemed to have aged ten years in the past half hour. He sat slumped behind his desk, his expression morose, all arrogance gone. "What did she tell you?" he asked.

"Quite a bit," Witherspoon replied. Without being invited, he took a seat on a cane-backed chair opposite Frommer's opulent desk. He nodded for the constable to take the empty one next to him. "Your wife states that both of you came back on the early train. That, along with the PC who saw you on the earlier train, is more than enough evidence to warrant further questioning."

"Where was she when the old man was killed?" he asked.

The inspector certainly wasn't going to answer that question. Eventually there wouldn't be any police constable on the premises, and who knew what kind of vengeance Frommer would take on his wife if the man knew she'd gone to a solicitor. "More to the point, sir, where were you?"

He jerked his head up. "I went for a walk," he mumbled. "I had a lot on my mind."

"Did anyone see you, sir?" Barnes asked.

"Lots of people saw me," he replied.

"Anyone who actually knew you?" the constable persisted. "Anyone who could confirm your whereabouts between the hours of three and four o'clock?"

Frommer shook his head. "No. Not that I recall."

"Where did you walk, sir?"

He swallowed heavily. "Look, Inspector, if I tell you the truth, can you promise to keep it confidential?" He held up his hand as he saw the inspector start to protest. "I swear, this has nothing to do with Roland's murder. But it isn't the sort of information I want made known. It could ruin my career."

Witherspoon mentally debated his options. He didn't like Andrew Frommer; the man was a brute and a bully, but that didn't necessarily mean he was Ashbury's murderer. Also, there was the small matter of Eloise Hartshorn's statement that she'd seen him leaving here on the afternoon of the murder. Not that Witherspoon was accepting her statement at face value. Not yet. "I'll try to keep what you tell me confidential if, indeed, it has no bearing on this case."

Frommer heaved a sigh of relief. "Good, good. It doesn't, believe me. Well, let's see, where to begin?" He gave a weak laugh and put his elbows on the desk. "I did come back to London on the early train. There was someone I wanted to see. I got to the station and I took a hansom to Tacner Place; that's over near the Foundling Hospital in Chelsea."

"Who were you going to see, sir?" The inspector already knew the answer to that question, but he wanted to see how genuinely honest Frommer would be.

"A woman by the name of Eloise Hartshorn," he replied, his expression was now speculative. "But I expect you already knew that."

Witherspoon nodded but kept quiet.

"Eloise wasn't home. I was disappointed, but as I hadn't told her I was coming, I couldn't really get angry."

"What time was it that you were at Miss Hartshorn's?" the inspector asked.

"I believe it was close to three-fifteen or so. After that

I went for a walk. I had a lot of thinking to do.''

Witherspoon said nothing for a moment. ''What were you thinking about, sir?''

''I don't think that's any of your concern,'' Frommer snapped.

''I'm afraid it is, sir. You see, I think you were thinking about the awful row you'd had with your father-in-law before you both left Ascot.''

Frommer's face darkened with anger. ''Are you back to that? I've told you, Roland and I didn't *have* an argument. My wife imagines things. She's a dreadfully stupid woman . . . just because she couldn't abide her father she thinks that everyone hated him. I'd no reason to quarrel with Roland. No reason at all.''

''But you did, sir,'' Witherspoon said calmly. He hoped the information he'd received from Ascot was reliable. ''You were furious with him because he wouldn't loan you any more money.''

''Who told you that ridiculous story?'' Frommer leapt to his feet. ''It's a lie. A damned lic.''

''Are you denying that you asked your father-in-law for a loan?'' Barnes queried.

Frommer hesitated and the inspector pressed his advantage. ''We know all about your financial situation, sir. We know that you're completely without funds. Roland Ashbury has made the last two payments on your bank loan, hasn't he, sir?''

''All right, I'm a bit short at the moment, I'll admit that. Roland was glad to help me. He was always glad to help,'' Frommer insisted.

''Not this time, though,'' Witherspoon said. ''This time he told you he wouldn't do it and you were angry. Very angry. I believe you actually threatened him, didn't you?

Told him if he knew what was good for him he'd pay up.''

Frommer paled. "I didn't mean I'd kill him," he said, his voice a hoarse whisper. "I only meant that I'd ask him to leave this house. It's still my house, you know."

"But it wouldn't be for much longer, would it, sir? Not if you stopped paying your bank loan." Witherspoon watched Frommer carefully.

"You can't possibly believe I killed him," Frommer insisted. "Why, I was at Chelsea at three-fifteen. Eloise's maid will testify to that."

"But you could easily have made it here by three thirty-five," Barnes pointed out. "And as the body wasn't discovered until almost four, you'd have had ample time to murder the man."

CHAPTER 7

"What do you think, sir?" Barnes asked as they walked toward the hansom station at the corner.

"I'm not sure," Witherspoon replied. "Frommer could have murdered him, but we've no real evidence. That's the mucky bit about this case, Constable. There are so many who could have killed him, so many who apparently wanted him dead, but we've no proof that any of them actually did it. Mrs. Frommer could just as easily have done it, as could Henry Alladyce or the servants . . . or—I don't know; we'll just have to keep digging. Any word on that missing footman yet?"

"No, sir, nothing. We've sent the lads around the workhouse, but no one there admits to seein' the boy. Mind you, that lot isn't all that happy to be cooperating with us in any case, so who knows if he's been there or not. Do you think he's important?" Barnes ran his hand over his forehead, wiping off a line of perspiration trickling out from under his helmet onto his cheek. The day was waning, but the summer air was heavy and humid.

"I'm not sure. According to Miss Donovan and the other servants, the boy hasn't been seen since the morning of the murder. Which would mean he'd disappeared hours before the murder and probably has nothing to do with it. But I don't like it, Barnes. I don't like it at all. But there's not much about this case that I do like. It certainly is turning into a muddle, isn't it?"

They'd come to the curving junction of Manchester Street and Grays Inn Road. This late in the afternoon, traffic was heavy. On the pavement, a boardman advertising this evening's performance of a pantomine spotted Constable Barnes in his policeman's uniform and made a mad dash in the other direction. As did a young shoe-black. A mush-faker pushing a ginger-beer cart yelled a catcall at the retreating boy and boardman and then grinned broadly as the policemen came steadily on, seemingly oblivious to the consternation their appearance on the street had caused.

A row of hansoms formed a line across the road, some of them disgorging passengers in front of the Throat and Ear Hospital. Barnes didn't know what to think; he was as confused as his inspector. "It *is* a muddle, sir. But about the missing footman, well, coincidences do happen," he ventured. "Should I get us a cab, sir?"

"Let's walk." Witherspoon pointed to his left. "There's a grocer's up a ways."

"You're going to do the shopping?"

"Oh no, no." The inspector laughed. "There's a witness we need to interview. It may come to nothing, but I want to stop in and have a word with the grocer's niece. She used to work for the Frommers."

Witherspoon started briskly up the street. He was glad

he'd remembered this bit of information; why, goodness, poor Wiggins had mentioned the girl almost two days ago. "She might be able to help us. Oh, I say, look, there's a fruit vendor. Yoo-hoo, boy." He waved his hands at a boy pushing a large coster's cart just up ahead. "Hang on, lad," he called. He quickened his steps and Barnes had to run to catch up with him.

The coster stopped and waited for the policemen to catch up to him. He bobbed his head respectfully as Witherspoon and Barnes trotted up. "What can I get ya, guv?" he asked. "The fruit's good and ripe."

"My, my, these do look good." The inspector licked his lips as he eyed a basket of ripe peaches. "How much?"

"Fourpence each, sir," the lad replied. "But I'll let you 'ave two at that price seein' as 'ow it's gettin' late and they'll not keep overnight."

"I'll take them." Witherspoon reached in his pocket and pulled out some coins. Dropping them into the boy's hand, he deftly scooped up two of the ripest-looking fruits and tossed one to Barnes.

"Thank you, sir." The constable watched as the inspector stuffed the peach in his mouth and took an enormous bite. This was twice now that Witherspoon had stopped to buy something to eat. Earlier, on their way to the Frommer house, he'd bought a lemon halfpenny ice from an Italian iceman. Barnes had been horrified; everyone knew those ices weren't fit to eat. But before the constable had been able to protest, Witherspoon had gulped the thing down. What on earth was wrong with the man?

"Aren't you going to eat yours?" the inspector asked. "They're awfully good."

"I'm sure they are, sir, but I'm not really hungry now.

If you don't mind, I'll save mine till after supper.''

"As you like, Constable. Ah, here we are. Hopkins Grocers.'' He stopped beneath the green-stripped awning and polished off the rest of the peach. He pulled out a pristine white hankerchief and delicately wiped his fingers, taking care not to get the fabric near the dripping pit he held between his left thumb and forefinger. "Hmm . . . what can I do with this?'' he asked, frowning as he glanced at the tables of assorted goods out on the pavement. "There doesn't seem to be a dustbin out here.''

"Can I help you gentlemen?'' The grocer stepped out of the front door.

"Have you a dustbin?'' Witherspoon held the pit out.

The grocer, to his credit, made only the slightest of faces. "Give it to me, sir. There's one inside. Is that all you needed?''

"Actually we've come to speak to a Miss Emma.'' Witherspoon smiled at the grocer. "I believe she used to work for Andrew Frommer.''

"That she did, sir.'' He broke into a huge, satisfied grin. "That she did. You're the police, then, come about that murder at the Frommer house?''

"I'm Inspector Gerald Witherspoon and this is Constable Barnes.''

"Come inside, gentlemen, and I'll get the lass. I'm Nat Hopkins, the proprietor.'' He bustled back through the door with the two policemen right behind him. They stopped in front of the counter and waited. Hopkins walked to the back of the store, opened a door and stuck his head inside. "Emma,'' he shouted. "Come down here, lass. There's some coppers want to have a word with you.''

"All right,'' a muffled female voice replied.

Nat hurried back to them, his expression bright with

anticipation. "Nice of that lad of yours to pass on my message," he said, bobbing his head at the inspector. "Smart lad. Come in to buy some boiled sweets and we got to talking. When he found out that our Emma used to work for that rotter, he was right excited. Said you wasn't like other coppers, said you'd take the trouble to listen to the girl. She's heard plenty, she has."

"You wanted to see me, sir?"

Witherspoon and Barnes whirled about to see a young girl of about sixteen standing behind them. Small and slender, she was a beauty. Her hair, so dark a brown it was almost black, was pulled back off her face and lay in a thick braid down her back. Her features were perfect, her eyes a dark luminous green. Witherspoon knew that if Wiggins had seen the girl, he'd have fallen in love on the spot. "Yes, miss, we understand you used to work for the Frommer family. Is that correct?"

"Yes, sir," she replied calmly. "But Mr. Frommer sacked me a few weeks back. He wouldn't even give me a reference, sir, so I've been unable to find another position."

The door opened and two customers, both women, stepped inside. They'd been chatting to each other, but their conversation died when they caught sight of Barnes in his uniform.

"Would you like to step back to the parlor?" Hopkins offered quickly. "Emma'll show you the way."

They followed the girl and a few moments later were standing in a small, neat room comfortably but not opulently furnished.

"Would you like to sit down?" Emma offered, gesturing at the sturdy horsehair settee.

"Now, Miss Emma," Witherspoon said as soon as the three of them were settled. "Can you think of anyone who might have had a reason to dislike Mr. Ashbury?'' He started with that question because he'd realized the girl wouldn't know anything about the murder itself and he thought he might as well take the bull by the horns.

''Oh, sir, I expect there's lots of people that didn't like Mr. Ashbury; he weren't a very likable person, if you take my meanin' sir.'' She smiled timidly. ''I don't like speakin' ill of the dead, sir. But he wasn't a good man.''

Witherspoon nodded encouragingly. As he couldn't think of the kinds of questions he ought to be asking, he'd decided that perhaps just keeping the girl talking might be the best way to proceed. ''Would you elaborate on that a bit, please?''

Emma's perfect brows drew together in a confused frown. ''Pardon?''

''He means would you tell us exactly in what way Mr. Ashbury wasn't very nice?'' Barnes interjected.

''Oh.'' She gave him a bright smile. ''That'll be easy. He was awful particular, he was. Worse even than Mr. Frommer. He was the one got me sacked.'' She broke off and looked at them, her expression earnest. ''It's true, it is. I swear. I'm a good girl and I worked right hard. It weren't fair of them to sack me because of an accident. It could have happened to anyone.''

''I'm sure you're a very hard worker.'' Witherspoon offered her an encouraging smile. ''Why don't you tell us what happened.''

''Well, it was a few days before the family was set to be goin' to the house at Ascot,'' she began. ''The whole staff was to go. My aunt and uncle weren't happy about me goin' off. The reason they liked me workin' for the Frommers was because it was close to home, but there was naught they could do about it. Anyway, I'd gone up in the attic to fetch Mr. Ashbury's boxes so he could pack.

As I said, he's a right particular sort, and as there was three of them up there, I weren't sure which one he wanted, so I had Boyd haul down all three of them."

"You took them to Mr. Ashbury's quarters?" Witherspoon added, hoping to hurry her narrative along a bit.

"Oh no," she replied. "We took them out to the garden to be aired. Well, I'd forgotten that Mr. Burroughs was comin' round for tea that afternoon, so I left the boxes out next to the table so they could get the afternoon sun."

"Open or closed?" Barnes asked.

"Closed." She frowned. "They was locked, so I couldn't open them. I remember I was goin' to ask Mr. Ashbury for the keys so I could give them a proper airing. Anyway, then I went about my business. I was upstairs polishing the railings when Boyd come runnin' up sayin' that I'd best help him get them cases moved, as Mr. Ashbury and the others were outside and that Mr. Burroughs had arrived for tea." She made a face. "I flew down the stairs, I did. But it was too late. They was already outside. Mr. Ashbury started to give me the back of his tongue for leavin' them out where everyone could see them, but that nice Mr. Burroughs made a jest of the whole thing. I still think that Mr. Ashbury would have sacked me right then, he were so angry. He hated looking like he was lower class, sir. Hated it worse than anything, and those cases of his were a right tatty-looking bunch. But he was too cheap and mean to buy new ones, even though Mrs. Frommer had been after him about it the week before."

Barnes asked, "Why didn't he sack you then?"

"Mr. Alladyce arrived to give Mr. Ashbury some papers."

"Henry Alladyce?" the constable clarified.

"Yes, sir. I was ever so pleased to see Mr. Alladyce. He took Mr. Ashbury's mind right off me." Emma grinned. "He started giving poor Mr. Alladyce a tongue-lashing for leaving the office in the middle of the day."

"So Mr. Ashbury was distracted? That's why you didn't get the sack?" Witherspoon was finding her story just a bit difficult to follow. Plus, he wondered why Charles Burroughs was having tea at the Frommer house. He'd made it perfectly clear he didn't think much of his neighbors.

She nodded eagerly. "That's right. Anyway, Mr. Alladyce took no notice of Mr. Ashbury. He was too busy staring at Mr. Burroughs. He was downright rude. He kept on and on, asking Mr. Burroughs if they'd ever met. Mr. Burroughs laughed and said not unless Mr. Alladyce had been to Colorado, but Mr. Alladyce wouldn't leave it alone. He kept sayin' he never forgot a face and he was sure he'd met Mr. Burroughs before. Well, by that time Boyd and I had finished moving the cases, so I thought I'd best ask Mr. Ashbury for the keys so they could be aired out before we brung 'em upstairs. Mr. Ashbury didn't like bein' interrupted, but he didn't want to make any more of a fuss. I think Mr. Burroughs had shamed him, sir; I think he'd made some kind of comments about how it were only lower-class people that were mean to servants in front of guests. But Mr. Ashbury were still angry with me, I know that."

"How do you know?" Barnes asked. His weathered face was creased in a frown, as though he too were having trouble seeing the point of her story. But like the inspector, he'd learned to be patient. Especially with the very young.

"Because he was givin' me that funny smile of his, the one he used when he was feelin' like he'd pulled one over on you."

"I'm sorry." Witherspoon's eyes narrowed behind his spectacles. "I don't quite understand."

"It's the truth, sir," she said earnestly. "He did have a mean smile. Ask anyone. Every time he'd gotten one of us in trouble or told some big tale or just done something horrid to someone, he had this nasty, smary smile that just made you wish you could smack him in the face. Beggin' your pardon for bein' so bold, sir. But that's how it made all of us feel, sir."

"All right." Witherspoon decided to accept her statement at face value. "Go on, what happened then?"

"Well, I asked him for the keys, sir," she repeated. "He kept them in his pocket, on a small brass ring. He pulled off the three little keys and said that only two of the cases was to be aired. The other one was nothing but old letters and daguerreotypes and stuff like that. It was to be taken back upstairs. The first case I unlocked was the one with the papers, so I sat it next to the back door so Boyd could haul it back up to the attic. Then I opened the other two and took them to the other end of the terrace so they could get the best of the sunshine. I could hear Mr. Ashbury goin' on and on on the other side of the garden. Anyway, I got up and turned around, thinking I'd slip back in through the door off the terrace so I wouldn't have to face Mr. Ashbury again. Well, blow me, if I didn't run smack into a big terra-cotta pot. Someone had moved the ruddy thing till it were almost directly behind me and I'd slammed straight into it. It toppled over against the stone tiles and smashed into dozens of pieces." She sighed. "I knew I was in for it then. Breakin' their things would get you sacked right fast, and this was an expensive pot. Everyone come runnin' to see what had happened. I tried to explain that someone had moved the pot, but it were no good; Mr. Ashbury kept on and on until Mr.

Frommer sacked me. I left that very day. It didn't even help when Boyd went to Mr. Frommer and told him that I were tellin' the truth: someone had moved that pot, someone who wanted to get me sacked. I thought it had to be Mr. Ashbury. He never liked me. It was the kind of mean thing he'd do.''

Witherspoon didn't know what to say. The story was quite sad and unfair; the girl shouldn't have lost her position merely because of an accident, regardless of the circumstances. "I'm sorry, my dear," he said. "You were treated very badly."

"They treated everyone like dirt, they did."

"Even Mrs. Frommer?" Barnes asked.

Emma smiled cynically. "She was all right, but no one took any notice of her. Not her husband and certainly not her father."

Barnes smiled kindly at the girl. "Do you really think it was Ashbury who moved the pot?"

Witherspoon couldn't tell if he was humoring her or not. But to Emma, the question was deadly serious.

"That's just it," she said. "The only person who I think would be mean enough to do it was Mr. Ashbury. But when I asked Lottie the kitchen maid if she saw him come around to where I was, she claimed that Mr. Ashbury hadn't moved from his chair, so it couldn't have been him. Lottie's got no reason to lie to me, and as she was the one whose job it was to keep an eye on the tea party to see if they needed anything else, then she'd know. Besides, I could hear him talking while I was opening the cases. He couldn't have nipped around and moved that pot and then nipped back."

"So no one left the table while you were opening the cases?" Witherspoon asked. He too was now curious as to how the pot got moved.

"No one, sir." She shrugged. "It's a right mystery. That pot was in its proper place by the back door when I went around to the terrace, that's for certain. I'd have noticed if it wasn't."

"Wouldn't you have heard it being moved?" the inspector asked curiously. "Terra-cotta pots are quite heavy."

"This one wasn't, sir," she answered. "It were one of them thin ones. Come from Italy it did. They'd only bought it a few days earlier. Besides, it was empty, so it wouldn't have weighed much. And I wouldn't have heard it in any case, not with Mr. Ashbury brayin' loud enough to wake the dead on the other side of the terrace wall."

"I see." Witherspoon frowned thoughtfully. Deep inside his mind, something slid into place and then just as quickly slipped away. Before he could grasp the elusive thought, it was gone. His frown intensified. He chewed on his lip as he tried to will the idea back, but it was no use.

"Sir?" Barnes voice was concerned. "Are you all right?"

"Yes, yes, I'm fine. Right as rain, as it were." He forced himself to smile. Apparently, his inner voice didn't wish to speak to him anymore today. But he'd learned one thing. Everything the girl had told him was important. Most important. Either that, or her statement had triggered him into thinking about something else, something connected. Too bad he couldn't recall what it was. Oh well, he'd think of it sooner or later. As Mrs. Jeffries always said, he had to learn to trust his instincts. "Are you absolutely certain that no one left the table? They were all still there taking tea, both the Frommers, Ashbury, Mr. Alladyce and Mr. Burroughs?"

"Mr. Alladyce had gone, sir. He'd left while Mr. Ashbury was giving me the keys.'' She laughed harshly. ''Just like the old tartar not to invite the poor man to stay to tea. He was like that, he was. Unless you were big and important, he couldn't be bothered with you. Not like that nice Mr. Burroughs. He was nice to everyone. Even poor Boyd.''

''Boyd?'' Witherspoon queried. ''What was wrong with Boyd?''

''He's not right, now, is he?''

The inspector had no idea what she was talking about. ''What's not right about the lad? I know he's gone missing, but I didn't know there was anything wrong with him.''

She frowned angrily. ''He's gone missing? When?''

''The morning of the murder,'' Barnes replied. ''But what's wrong with him?''

''He's a bit slow,'' she replied, with a shake of her head. ''You know, he's not too smart. Not so stupid that he couldn't work, but not very bright either. I can't believe he'd run off. He's devoted to Mrs. Frommer. He'd do anything for her.''

''Well . . .'' Witherspoon sighed. This case was even more complicated than he'd thought. ''He's gone now.''

Emma studied the two policemen. ''You don't believe that poor Boyd had anything to do with it, do ya?''

''We've no evidence that he did,'' Barnes replied. ''But as he's disappeared, he is a suspect. Especially as we know that Mr. Ashbury wasn't very kind to him.'' The constable had tacked that part on; in truth, they didn't know anything at all about the way Ashbury had treated the footman. But given what they'd learned of the victim, Barnes was fairly certain the man hadn't been good to the lad.

''Boyd wouldn't hurt anyone,'' she insisted. ''He's not

smart, but he's the sweetest lad you'd ever meet. And he wouldn't know how to shoot a gun. He's scared of them, he is.''

"Most people are frightened of weapons," Witherspoon said kindly. "But we've found that being afraid doesn't stop people from using them."

The inspector tried to keep his spirits up as he turned the corner onto Upper Edmonton Gardens. He was terribly confused about this case, but he refused to be downhearted about it. As Mrs. Jeffries always said, he'd figure it out in the end.

Just then a four-wheeler pulled up, and the inspector, thinking it might be an urgent message from the station or the Yard, stopped. He smiled as Lady Cannonberry emerged. His smile faltered as Morris Pilchard got out right behind her.

She spotted him immediately. "Oh Gerald, this is lovely. I had so hoped to see you."

"I was just on my way home." He swept his bowler off and bobbed his head. "I'm happy to see you too."

"Good evening, Witherspoon." Morris Pilchard elbowed his way between them. "How is your case going? Caught the killer yet? Of course, one doesn't expect you to work miracles, does one? Actually I'm amazed that you chappies manage to catch anyone at all. No offense meant, but the police don't seem to be very good at it. They never caught that Ripper fellow, did they?"

"Well, no—" Witherspoon began.

"Don't be ridiculous, Morris," Ruth interrupted. "The police do a fine job and I'll have you know that Gerald is a brilliant detective. Do you have any idea how many murderers he's caught?"

"Now, now, dearest." Pilchard patted her arm. "Don't

upset yourself. I wasn't casting aspersions on your neighbor's good character. I'm sure he does the best he can."

Dearest? Witherspoon's heart sank as the meaning of Pilchard's familiarity toward Ruth sank in. Her defense of him was nice, but she was the sort of person who would defend anyone who was being berated unfairly. "Thank you, Ruth. But you're much too kind. I don't catch murderers all on my own. It's a team effort. I could do nothing without the rest if the force."

"You're much too modest, Gerald. You're the best detective they have at the Yard," she said earnestly. "I know you're probably terribly busy, but can you dine with us tonight?"

"Dinner?" The inspector's spirits soared. "At your house? Gracious, I should love to."

"Good, then it's settled." She smiled and patted his arm.

"Are you sure it won't put your cook to any trouble?" Witherspoon asked.

"Not at all, Cook always prepares far more than we eat," she assured him. She smiled at her houseguest. "Gerald can tell you about some of his more interesting cases," she told the sour-faced man. "You'll be fascinated."

Pilchard's mouth curved in disapproval. "I hardly think murder is a proper topic for dinner conversation."

"I think it's a better topic than dung beetles," she said sweetly, "and that's what you talked about last night."

"I must go home and tell the staff," Witherspoon said eagerly. "Then I'll pop right over, shall I?"

"That'd be lovely, Gerald." She took Pilchard's arm and, ignoring his frown, led him toward her front gate. "We'll expect you in fifteen minutes. That will give us time for a glass of sherry before dinner."

"I shall be there," he called happily. Turning, he dashed up the road toward his own front door. Taking the steps two at a time, he fairly flew inside, almost crashing into Mrs. Jeffries. "Oh gracious," he exclaimed. "I *am* sorry. But I'm in a frightful hurry."

"Oh dear, sir," Mrs. Jeffries said sympathetically. "Has something happened on the case? Are you going to make an arrest?" She certainly hoped that wasn't true. She couldn't make heads or tails of what was going on with this murder, and unless the inspector had had a confession or an eyewitness turn up, she didn't see how he could have solved the crime.

"No, no, no, Mrs. Jeffries," he said happily. "I'm going to Lady Cannonberry's. She's invited me for an impromptu supper. Do tell Mrs. Goodge that I'm ever so sorry," he called over his shoulder as vaulted up the staircase to his room. "I hope she didn't go to a lot of trouble with tonight's dinner."

"She didn't, sir," Mrs. Jeffries replied. "It was only a cold supper. It'll keep." This also meant that she wouldn't have a chance to find out what the inspector had learned until late tonight when he came home. She hoped he wouldn't be so tired that he'd go right to bed. She didn't want to wait until breakfast tomorrow.

Upstairs, the inspector washed his hands, combed his hair and changed into a fresh shirt. He'd just called down the backstairs that he was leaving when there was a knock on the front door. Mrs. Jeffries, coming in from the drawing room, reached it first.

As it was after dark, the inspector frowned as he saw her turn the doorknob. "I say, Mrs. Jeffries, do let me get it." He hurried up the hall, but his words were too late. She'd already pulled the door wide open.

Witherspoon's frown intensified. A police constable, a

rather familiar-looking one, stood on the door stoop.
"Beggin' your pardon, sir," the lad said, talking over the
housekeeper's shoulder directly to the inspector, "but I've
been sent to fetch you to the hospital."

"Hospital? I'm sorry, Constable . . ."

"Martin, sir. Theodore Martin. We met a few months
back on that murder at old man Grant's house."

"Oh, yes, yes, I thought you looked familiar. What's
happened? Why do I have to go to the hospital?"

"There's been a shooting, sir," Martin explained.
"Constable Barnes was just goin' off duty when the word
come in and he thought you'd want to know right away.
It's a Mrs. Frommer, sir. She's been shot."

As soon as the front door closed behind the inspector, the
household sprang into action. Betsy was dispatched to
Lady Cannonberry's to express the inspector's regrets
about dinner, Smythe was sent off to Howard's, the livery
where the inspector's carriage and horses were stabled and
Wiggins was put in a hansom to deliver the news to Luty
and Hatchet. Mrs. Goodge and Mrs. Jeffries settled in the
kitchen to discuss this new turn of events. Their main
concern was how they could learn all the details of this
latest development without having to wait for the inspector to return home and tell them.

In less than an hour all of them, except Smythe, were
back and gathered about the kitchen table.

"This is sure puttin' the fox amongst the chickens,"
Luty declared. "Just when I was fixin' to figure this one
out too. Do we know who did the shootin'?"

"Not yet," Mrs. Jeffries replied. "Smythe has taken
the horse and carriage to the hospital. He's using the pre-
text that the inspector may need it this evening. Naturally
he'll find out what he can."

"Which hospital is it?" Hachet asked.

"The one on Grays Inn Road," she answered. "The Royal Free."

"Smythe might not be able to get away," Betsy said. "He'll probably be stuck there as long as the inspector is."

Mrs. Jeffries nodded. "I know, dear. But knowing Smythe, even if he's stuck, he'll find out what he can."

"Why do they git to go?" Luty asked, glaring at her butler. "I can go just as easily."

"It wouldn't be right, madam," Hatchet said quickly. "A lady such as yourself doesn't go about the streets at this time of the evening."

"Oh, pull the other one, Hatchet," she snorted in disgust. "I've been out more times at night than you've had hot dinners. Why don't you just admit it, you like hoggin' all the fun."

"Really, madam, I hardly think that's fair."

"Fiddlesticks," Luty snapped. "I'd be in the carriage, and besides, I'd have Dickson with me."

"Dickson, madam, wouldn't say boo to a goose in barnyard," Hatchet shot back. "He is an excellent driver, but he certainly couldn't defend you against any street ruffians."

"I don't need defendin'," Luty countered. She was getting tired of always being the one waiting for news. "I'm pretty danged good at takin' care of myself. You just don't want me to go because you're afraid I'll git the jump on you."

Since this was absolutely true, Hatchet would have died before admitting it. But as he'd not found out much of anything, even after paying Goff to snoop about, he was getting quite desperate for clues. "Don't be ridiculous, madam. Our investigations are a cooperative effort."

"Indeed they are," Mrs. Jeffries said quickly. "And as there is quite a bit I haven't had a chance to share, we women will have a brief meeting of our own while the two of you"—she smiled at Wiggins and Hatchet—"go over to the hospital and find out what Smythe has learned. You ought to be back in a couple of hours or so. We can compare notes then."

MaryAnne Frommer lay upon the narrow bed at the end of the ward. Her eyes were closed and she was deathly pale. A coarse but clean white sheet was drawn up under her chin. A gray-haired doctor stood opposite her. "I don't mind admitting I don't know all that much about gunshot wounds," he said. "But we'll do the very best we can."

"Is she going to live?" Witherspoon asked.

"I don't know. She's lost a lot of blood." The doctor shook his head. "The surgeon got the bullet out. It's a clean wound; it entered her side and doesn't appear to have damaged any of her internal organs. If she dies, it'll be because of blood loss or infection."

"Can I speak with her?" Witherspoon asked. "It's important. We have to know who did this to her, especially if there's a chance she's"—he hesitated, torn between his duty as a policeman and his compassion as a human being—"not going to recover. It's imperative we try and find out if she knows who did this to her."

"You can try"—the doctor looked doubtful—"but I don't think she'll be able to tell you very much. I doubt she'll respond at all."

"Who brought her in?" Barnes asked.

"A young man," the doctor replied. "He brought her in a hansom. He and the driver carried her inside to the casualty ward. As soon as we realized she'd a bullet in her, we sent her directly into surgery.''

Witherspoon looked around the ward. Except for two nursing sisters and another doctor, all of them tending to patients, no one else was about. ''Where did this young man go?''

''I can't help you there. I didn't see him. I'm Dr. Hall,'' he said. ''I've got to finish my rounds. Have one of the sisters come find me if you need me. We'll keep a close eye on her.'' He nodded toward Mrs. Frommer. ''You can depend on that.''

''Thank you, Doctor,'' the inspector replied. ''We won't be long. We've only a few questions to ask.''

''If she does respond, try not to upset her. She's in pretty bad shape.'' Dr. Hall smiled briefly and moved on to the patient in the bed across the aisle.

Witherspoon looked at Barnes. ''What do you think? Should I try to ask her what happened?''

Barnes hesitated, his expression uncertain. He'd been a copper for a long time. Sometimes, no amount of experience prepared you to make the best decision. ''I don't think we've any choice, Inspector,'' he whispered. ''She might die. At least if we can find out who did this to her, they'll not get clean away with it.''

Witherspoon took a deep breath and leaned over the bed, placing his lips as close to her ear as he dared. ''Mrs. Frommer,'' he whispered.

She moaned softly.

''Mrs. Frommer''—he tried again—''can you hear me?'' His instincts were to go away and let her rest, but he couldn't do that. The constable was right: if she died, he wanted to make sure he arrested her murderer.

She moaned again, but this time it sounded a bit like a ''yes.''

"Do you know who did this to you?" Witherspoon pressed. "Did you see who shot you?"

"Tashaa . . ." she muttered. "Tash . . . bro . . ."

"Can you understand her, sir?" Barnes asked anxiously.

The inspector shook his head and cocked his ear only inches from her lips. "I'm sorry," he said, "but you'll have to try again. Do you know who shot you?"

"I'm afraid she's probably not going to make any sense at all," Dr. Hall interrupted. He'd come back when he heard Mrs. Frommer moan. "We gave her quite a bit of laudanum after the surgery."

Witherspoon straightened up. "Are you saying that even if she says something, it might not be true?"

"I ought to have mentioned it before, but frankly I didn't think you'd get any reaction at all from the poor woman. I wouldn't put too much stock in anything she tells you," he said. "Her system is full of opium. She probably doesn't even hear you. I'd suggest you wait until tomorrow to question her."

"We can't," Witherspoon said simply. "By your own admission, she might not live through the night."

She spoke suddenly.

This time they heard her quite clearly. She said one word.

"Andrew."

CHAPTER 8

Hatchet and Wiggins, with Smythe in tow, were back within the hour. "The inspector is spendin' the night at the 'ospital," Smythe explained as he dropped into the chair next to Betsy, "so he sent me along home. I ran into these two 'ere and we 'otfooted it back as soon as we could."

"Unfortunately, we left so quickly we hadn't a chance to ask very many questions," Hatchet said disapprovingly. "Smythe, for some reason of his own, seemed to feel it was imperative we get back right away."

"Yeah, 'e 'ustled us out of there right fast," Wiggins agreed as he shot the coachman a quick frown. "I didn't 'ave time for much of anythin' except a quick word or two."

"If you'll just give me a chance to tell you," Smythe charged, "you'll see it were right important we got back here as quick as we could. We may be going out again."

Wiggins's frown vanished. "Goin' out?" he said eagerly. "Where?"

"Oh, that sounds most interesting," Hatchet added. "Where are we going? Back to the hospital? Over to the Frommer house?"

"That's not fair," Mrs. Goodge protested. "We've been stuck here for an hour waitin' to find out what's what, and you're thinkin' of dashin' off again?"

"How come you git to go out?" Luty demanded.

"Please, everyone." Mrs. Jeffries held up a hand to silence them. This was becoming ridiculous. Now they couldn't even start a meeting without things getting completely out of hand. Men, she thought in exasperation, sometimes they were all little boys. The merest hint of adventure could get them completely offtrack. "Let's hear what Smythe has to say before we start deciding who does or doesn't need to go out tonight." She turned to the coachman. "Tell us what happened?"

"MaryAnne Frommer was shot." Smythe reached for the teapot and poured the hot brew into his mug. "She's still alive, but the doctor don't know if she'll make it through the night. 'Er 'usband's nowhere to be found, neither. I overhead one of the police constables tellin' Constable Barnes that they couldn't find the fellow. The Frommer servants said 'e weren't 'ome and they didn't know when 'e was expected."

"Poor lady was shot right in 'er own back garden," Wiggins said in disgust. "She'da died if it 'adn't been for Boyd turnin' up like 'e did. 'E's the one that sounded the alarm."

"How did you find that out?" Hatchet demanded.

"I 'ad a quick word with the lad after 'e finished talkin' to Smythe," Wiggins admitted. "You were busy listening to them constables natterin' on down at the end of the ward.''

"The missing footman's turned up?" Mrs. Goodge said. "When?"

"This evening," Hatchet interjected smoothly. He gave Wiggins a quick grin. "Eavesdropping is sometimes most rewarding. According to the statement the butler gave to the police, they knew the footman was back when he started pounding on the kitchen door and screaming for help. The butler raced outside and found Mrs. Frommer lying on the ground unconscious. The footman had gone to fetch a hansom. It was Boyd and the hansom driver who got the woman to the hospital."

"Why didn't he fetch a policeman?" Mrs. Jeffries asked. "There should have been constables nearby. The Frommer house had a murder in it only a few days ago."

"Apparently the only constables left in the area were doing rounds on foot," Hatchet explained. "Frommer had enough influence with the Home Office to get rid of the policeman who'd been watching the house."

"Seems to me she owes 'er life to Boyd," Wiggins declared. "If 'e'd not come to meet 'er, Mrs. Frommer woulda laid there bleedin' to death."

"Didn't anyone hear the gunshot?" Luty demanded. "They ain't exactly quiet, you know."

All three men answered at once.

"Someone may have," Hatchet said. "The constable I overheard said they'd been instructed to do a house-to-house for witnesses who may have seen or heard something."

"Boyd said 'e been about the neighborhood for a good few minutes waitin' for Mrs. Frommer to come out, and 'e never 'eard nothin'," Smythe offered.

"No one 'eard the shot when Ashbury were killed either,'' Wiggins added firmly. ''Maybe the killer's got a special way—''

''*Please,*'' Mrs. Jeffries shouted. She was almost out of patience. ''We really must hear from you one at a time.'' Her expression was stern as she looked at the three men. ''I don't know about any of you, but the more I learn about this case, the more confused I get. So far, we've a lost footman who now turns up at a very suspicious time, an attempt on Mrs. Frommer's life and a missing husband. None of it makes any sense. Now, the only way I'm going to be able to make heads or tails out of anything is if all of us share our information in a calm, logical fashion. Is that absolutely clear?''

''You tell them, Mrs. Jeffries,'' Betsy exclaimed. ''I'm so confused I don't know what I should even be asking when I'm out and about.''

''Me too,'' Mrs. Goodge muttered. ''I've had half a dozen sources through this kitchen today and I'm so addled, I couldn't think of a ruddy thing that made any sense.''

Mrs. Jeffries softened her expression as she gazed at the now shamefaced men. ''I realize you weren't deliberately trying to confuse us. I'm sure you're all doing your best, but it would be so much easier for the rest of us if you would speak one at a time.''

Everyone was silent for a moment, then Smythe grinned. ''Looks like you've finally found a way to shut the three of us up.'' He laughed. ''Sorry, everyone. It'll not 'appen again. And I know what you mean about this case. It's right confusin'. So much as 'appened tonight, I'm not sure 'ow to begin.''

''Why don't you just tell us what happened this evening?'' the housekeeper suggested. ''Start from when *you* arrived at the hospital.''

Smythe nodded in agreement and took a quick sip of tea. "By the time I got there, the inspector had already gone into the ward. I was right surprised, though, because I'd expected to see Mr. Frommer or someone from the household awaitin'. But there weren't no one but a scared-lookin' lad. It turned out that was the missin' Boyd."

"Was he wearing his uniform?" Mrs. Jeffries asked. She didn't know why, but for some reason, that seemed a pertinent question.

"No, but as 'e were the only one sittin' on the bench outside the ward, I figured 'e might 'ave something to do with Mrs. Frommer. I asked 'im who 'e was, and the lad were so surprised to be spoken to, he answered me without thinkin'. The boy were right torn up about Mrs. Frommer, that was for certain," Smythe said sympathetically. "Anyway, as soon as I 'eard 'is name, I asked 'im where 'e'd been. 'E were a bit skittish at first, but after we'd chatted a few moments, I got 'im to talkin'."

He'd had gotten the lad to speak by being honest. He'd told Boyd whom he worked for and assured him that Inspector Witherspoon wouldn't rest until he'd found MaryAnne Frommer's assailant. " 'E told me 'e'd been in 'idin' since the day of the murder."

"Hiding?" Luty said. "Why? Did he shoot Ashbury?"

"No, but he were in the house when the killer did."

"He was a witness?" Mrs. Jeffries asked. "He saw who did it?"

Smythe shook his head. "No, 'e only heard it. 'E was up in the attic when the killin' was done."

"The attic," Betsy said. "What was he doing there?"

"He'd gone up to get somethin' for Mrs. Frommer. That's why 'e'd slipped off early that mornin' from the 'ouse at Ascot. Boyd 'adn't run off," Smythe explained. "Mrs. Frommer 'ad sent 'im on an errand."

"What kind of errand?" Mrs. Goodge asked. She felt calmer now that Mrs. Jeffries had laid down the law.

"Money," Smythe replied. "Seems that Mrs. Frommer 'ad some money 'idden up there. She sent Boyd into town fer it and told 'im to meet 'er in front of 'er solicitors' office. She were so desperate to get away from Frommer, she were willin' to pay out all she could get 'er 'ands on to the solicitors so they'd take 'er case. But Boyd never showed up. 'E claims that while 'e was up in the attic, 'e 'eard Ashbury come into 'is rooms below. Scared the boy to death; 'e'd been told the 'ouse was empty. He laid low for a few minutes and then 'e 'eard someone else come in, but 'e couldn't tell who it was."

"Not even if it were a man or a woman?" Luty asked incredulously.

"Not even that," Smythe replied, his expression somber. "The walls in them old 'ouses is thick. Boyd says for a good 'alf 'our 'e couldn't 'ear anything, so 'e made up 'is mind to get the cash and slip down the stairs and out the back way. Then all of a sudden, a muffled poppin' sound."

"The gunshot," Mrs. Goodge muttered. "Probably done through that pillow that's gone missin'. Sorry." She waved her hand. "I'm doing it again, aren't I? Jumping in without waiting for my turn. Go on, Smythe, finish up."

"Well, as I said, Boyd 'eard this poppin' sound and 'e really got scared. 'E started down the stairs, but 'e stopped when 'e 'eard footsteps runnin' out of Ashbury's rooms. Poor lad flattened 'imself against the wall, but 'e needn't 'ave worried. The killer were in such a 'urry to get away, 'e wouldn't 'ave stopped to look behind him up to the attic."

"What did Boyd do then?" Mrs. Jeffries asked.

" 'E was real confused, 'e didn't know what to do,'' Smythe explained. "At that point 'e didn't know that Ashbury was dead. All 'e'd 'eard was a funny noise; 'e didn't know it was a gun. He knew 'e had to get out of there, so 'e started down as quiet as 'e could. 'E'd got to the other side of Ashbury's door when he accidentally dropped the carpetbag containing Mrs. Frommer's money.''

"Cor blimey, she must 'ave 'ad a lot of it,'' Wiggins exclaimed, "if it took a carpetbag to carry it!''

"It wasn't all filled with money.'' Smythe motioned impatiently with his hand. "There was some old papers and letters in there too. Mrs. Frommer had told Boyd to get them from one of her bureau drawers. Anyway, 'e dropped the ruddy thing on the floor and it make a bloomin' racket. Boyd said 'e were sure that Mr. Ashbury'd come barrelin' out and box 'is ears. But 'e didn't.''

"Why didn't he leave then?'' Mrs. Goodge asked curiously. "That's what I'da done. That's what most people would have done.''

"He were too scared,'' Smythe replied. "Boyd's not too bright, but 'e's not dumb as a lamppost, neither. 'E knew something were wrong. Bad wrong. So 'e stuck 'is 'ead in the room and didn't see anything. But 'e 'ad a feelin', as it were, so even though 'e was so scared 'is knees were shakin', he went inside. He told me peekin' over the back of the old man's chair was the 'ardest thing 'e ever did. But 'e did it and 'e saw Ashbury sittin' there all wide-eyed and starin', so 'e gently moved the bloke's 'ead. That's when 'e saw Ashbury'd been shot.''

"Why didn't he raise the alarm right then?'' Mrs. Jeffries asked.

" 'E was scared the police'd think 'e did it. 'E'd moved the body, 'e'd got blood on his 'ands and 'e'd got the blood on 'is clothes too. 'E took off and went into 'idin'.''

"What about Mrs. Frommer?" Luty demanded. "If he's so devoted to her, why didn't he meet her in front of the solicitors' office and tell her what had happened. I know Ashbury weren't much of a father to the woman, but Nell's bells, Boyd knew the man was dead."

"The lad weren't thinkin' clearly," Smythe said defensively. "Besides, 'e'd been stuck up in the attic so long, 'e'd already missed his meetin' with her. Remember, there was blood all over 'im. All 'e could think to do was run and hide. That's what 'e did. 'E took off and hid out down on the docks by the river."

Mrs. Jeffries tapped her finger against the rim of her empty teacup. "What made him go to the Frommer house today?" she asked curiously.

Smythe smiled sadly. "Boyd couldn't stand bein' separated from 'er, from Mrs. Frommer. 'E'd decided to tell her the truth about what 'appened, about what 'e'd 'eard."

"Did he bring the money with him?" Betsy asked.

Smythe grinned broadly. "No, but 'e told me where 'e'd put it. Gave me real good directions too. It's over near the Greenland Dock. That's why I wanted to get right back 'ere tonight. I thought you might want the three of us"—he indicated the other two men with a nod in their direction—"to go out and see if we can find this 'ere carpetbag."

Mrs. Jeffries eyed the coachman speculatively. Smythe was doing his best to appear calm and collected, as were the other two, but it was quite clear from the sudden sparkle in his eyes that he wanted nothing more than to go. On the other hand, the woman were getting a bit tired of sitting and waiting for the menfolk.

"That's a very rough area this time of night," she said thoughtfully. She had no choice except to let the three of them go and collect the bag. But, really, there was no point in making it easy for them.

"But I think it might be important, Mrs. Jeffries," Smythe argued. "Not the money so much as the papers. I mean, Mrs. Frommer was goin' to take 'em to her solicitors. She told Boyd they was as important as the money."

Mrs. Jeffries pretended that she had to think about it. If she gave in too quickly, Betsy and Luty might have a fit. "Do you think you could find Boyd's hideout in the dark?"

" 'Course I could." Smythe looked slightly offended.

"I wasn't doubting your abilities," the housekeeper said quickly. Really, men were so easily affronted. "All I meant is that it's quite dark and the docks are rather notorious for having poor lighting."

"I'll take a lamp," he offered. "I don't know why, Mrs. J, but I got a feelin' this is important. The carriage is right out back. We could get over there and back in a couple of 'ours."

"I'll be most happy to accompany you," Hatchet offered.

"Now just hold yer horses here," Luty put in. "I kin go just as well as you. As a matter of fact, I've got my Peacemaker right outside in our carriage. . . ."

"Really, madam," Hatchet rebuked. "You promised me you'd leave that wretched thing at home."

"I did no such thing," she shot back. "I promised I wouldn't carry it in my muff. I didn't say a thing about not hidin' it under the seat in the carriage."

"Luty," Mrs. Jeffries said quietly. This was precisely what she'd feared would happen. She considered it only luck that Betsy wasn't demanding to go as well. "I really would like you to stay here."

"Why?"

"If the inspector should unexpectedly return while
Smythe is gone, at least with Hatchet gone as well we'd
have a reasonable answer as to why you were here so late
at night. We could always say that Hatchet had taken your
carriage to go rescue Smythe because he'd thrown a
wheel." It was a very weak excuse, but it was the very
best Mrs. Jeffries could come up with at the moment. She
didn't want their elderly friend out on the docks at this
time of night. Even with a Colt .45 for protection.

"Oh cowpatties, Hepzibah, you never want me to have
any fun." Luty tossed her butler a quick glare and then
turned back to the housekeeper. "But seein' as how you
put it like that, I guess I'll have to stay. But I'm tellin'
ya, I'm gittin' tired of the men havin' all the fun."

"Not to worry, Luty," Mrs. Goodge said. "Our turn's
coming. I can feel it in my bones."

"You really ought to go on home, Constable," Witherspoon whispered to Barnes. They'd gone out to the hallway and sat down on a bench. The ward sister had
promised to call them if there was any change in Mrs.
Frommer's condition. "There's no point in both of us
missing a night's sleep."

Watching for changes in the wounded woman's condition wasn't the only reason the inspector was staying.
Whoever had shot Mrs. Frommer hadn't killed her. He
was afraid the murderer might try again. To that end, he'd
stationed police constables on the front door and the door
leading to this ward. They were to report anyone acting
suspiciously.

At the end of the hallway, the double doors suddenly
flew open and a woman swathed in a bold, emerald-green
evening cloak charged though.

"My goodness," Witherspoon murmured. "It's Miss Hartshorn. What on earth could she be doing here?"

Eloise Hartshorn, an anxious expression on her lovely face, hurried up to the inspector. "Is it true?" she asked without preamble. "Has MaryAnne Frommer been shot?"

"Yes, I'm afraid she has," the inspector replied. He was very confused now. But he was also rather curious as to how the woman had learned the name so quickly. "How did you find out about it?"

"One of the Frommer servants came to my house. They were looking for Andrew," she replied. "He wasn't there, of course."

"I see," Witherspoon said. He was very puzzled. Why would Andrew Frommer's former mistress be so concerned about the man's wife that she rushed to the hospital upon hearing the wife had been shot? He wasn't quite sure how to phrase the question, though. "Er, uh, why have you come here, Miss Hartshorn? Do you know anything about this?"

Eloise ignored his question. "Is she dead?"

He hesitated, not certain of how much information he ought to provide. "No, but she's lost a lot of blood," he finally admitted. "The doctor doesn't know if she'll live. Have you any idea where Mr. Frommer might be? We'd like to inform him of his wife's condition." He watched her face carefully, hoping that he could see something in her expression that might help with this baffling case.

"Oh, I shouldn't worry about telling Andrew." She sneered. "I'll wager he already knows all about it. As a matter of fact, Inspector, that's why I came. I think Andrew Frommer murdered Roland Ashbury and then shot his wife." She clutched Witherspoon's arm. "You've got to help me. I think he's going to come after me next. Andrew's desperate for money."

• • •

Smythe was as good as his word. It was almost two hours to the minute when he, Hatchet and Wiggins returned to the warm, cozy kitchen of Upper Edmonton Gardens.

He grinned as he put the worn carpetbag in the center of the table. "Would you like to do the 'onors, Mrs. J?"

"I think the three of you have earned that right," the housekeeper replied. She ignored the disgruntled expressions on the faces of the female contingent around the table. They, of course, had had the advantage of discussing all the details of the case in the warmth of the cozy kitchen. Mrs. Goodge had proposed an interesting theory. "Go on," she ordered with a smile, "open it."

"I'll do it." Hatchet reached for the top of the bag and unclasped the heavy, brass prongs in the center. Opening it wide, he eased back, nodding at Smythe and Wiggins to have the first look inside. The others crowded closer as well, their gazes on the open bag.

"Cor blimey," Wiggins cried. "Looks like she 'ad a bundle stashed in that attic."

Smythe whistled and then reached inside. He pulled out a stack of pound notes tied with blue ribbon. The stack was a good two inches thick.

"Wonder 'ow much that is," Wiggins whispered in awe.

"What else is in the bag?" Mrs. Jeffries said. She was quite sure that the money had nothing to do with Ashbury's murder. They already knew that the footman had been dispatched on his errand hours before the killing. Which, of course, should imply that the money had been in the attic for a good while. Now she wanted to make sure that whatever else was in the carpetbag was equally innocent.

Smythe reached inside again. The sound of rustling paper filled the quiet room as he pulled out a small stack of letters tied with string. "Just this," he said, handing them to the housekeeper.

"Are they letters?" Mrs. Goodge demanded to know. She wanted to get on with this bit so she could think further about her theory.

"Just a moment." Mrs. Jeffries slipped off the string, which was quite loose, and laid the stack on the table. She picked up the first envelope and gazed at the address. "It's a letter to Roland Ashbury," she murmured.

"Roland Ashbury," Betsy repeated. "Why would Mrs. Frommer want her father's old letters?"

"I don't know. Let's have a look." She slipped the top one out of the envelope, taking care not to damage the fragile page. "It's dated October tenth, 1875."

"Read it," Betsy said. "I'll bet it's important. I'll bet it's something to do with the murder."

" 'My dearest father,' " Mrs. Jeffries began to read:

"I am writing to you because I am in desperate need. I had hoped that time would soften you somewhat and make you want to heal the breach between us. But as you did not respond to my earlier missive wherein I informed you of the birth of your first grandchild, I can only conclude that you are still angry at me for disobeying you and marrying Natasha. I'm sorry that such is the case. But she has made me a good wife and I love her dearly.

"I will get right to the point. We are in dire need of money. There has been a series of calamities recently. I will not bother you with the details; suffice to say, if you do not send me my share of my dear late mother's estate, I will be ruined. The bank will foreclose on our farm and we will lose everything.

Surely you must see the rightness of my request. If you do not wish to communicate with me, kindly have your bank send the particulars of the transfer of funds directly to the First Bank of Boulder.
Your loving son,
Jonathan Ashbury''

Mrs. Jeffries, not understanding how this could have any bearing on the case, yet feeling instinctively that it did, frowned as she put the letter to one side. "This is very peculiar."

"It couldn't have anything to do with the murder," Hatchet murmured. "That letter is fifteen years old."

"Maybe it does," Betsy countered. She bobbed her head at the other letters. "What's in those?"

Mrs. Jeffries picked up the next one and scanned it quickly. "It's another one from Jonathan. He appears to be getting more desperate. Listen to this: 'The bank has already started foreclosure proceedings. They've already taken my plow to be sold at auction. We are desperate. Natasha's brother lost his job at the mine, so the last of our income has disappeared. If you ever had any vestige of feeling for your own flesh and blood, you'll send the money without delay.' "

She shook her head in disgust and picked up the next envelope off the stack. After she'd studied it for a few moments, she said, "More of the same. Jonathan's family is virtually starving." She grabbed the next one, read it quickly and sighed. "Poor Jonathan just gets more and more desperate in each letter."

"How many are there?" Luty asked.

"This is the last one." Mrs. Jeffries picked up the buff-colored envelope. As she extracted the letter something dark fell out and landed onto the table. "It's a photograph,'' she exclaimed, laying the letter to one side and picking it up.

She studied it for a moment and then smiled sadly. ''I think it's a picture of Jonathan and his family.'' She held it up and they all leaned closer.

The picture showed a tall, dark-haired man dressed in a morning suit standing next to a woman with a baby in her arms. Next to the woman stood a young man who couldn't have been more than twenty.

''It's sad, isn't it?'' Betsy murmured. ''Seeing them like that, all done up in their nice clothes, and knowing what's going to happen to them.''

''What does the letter say?'' Mrs. Goodge asked eagerly, trying to push things along a bit.

Mrs. Jeffries opened it up. ''There isn't a salutation,'' she said, ''it simply begins, 'I hope you are happy now. We are ruined. The bank has taken the farm and anything else they could get their hands on. Natasha's brother is so sick with the fever that he'll probably be dead by the time you get this. I want you to know you have my undying hatred. How anyone could let their own flesh and blood be turned out is beyond me. You are a mean and miserable man and a thief. You stole my inheritance. One of these days you'll stand before the Almighty and have to accept judgment for what you've done.' ''

''Cor blimey, Ashbury was a mean-'earted bloke, wasn't 'e?'' Smythe pursed his lips in disgust. '' 'Ow could 'e do it? 'Ow could 'e let his own family suffer like that?''

Betsy sighed. ''They must have died right after.'' She picked up the picture, her gaze on the baby held in Natasha Ashbury's arms. ''How awful, turned out and hungry and then washed away in a flood.''

''Yes it *is* awful,'' Mrs. Jeffries agreed. She, like the

others, was saddened by the fate of that poor family. But she couldn't see what connection it could possibly have with Ashbury's murder. "I wonder if the photograph came with the letter."

"Probably," Luty stated. "I imagine Jonathan wanted to rub old Ashbury's nose in it—by sending that there photograph, he'd make him see who he was hurting. Then when the family died, I expect the old feller really felt bad."

"I wonder why it was mixed in the stuff that Mrs. Frommer wanted?" Betsy asked. She continued to hold the picture. "What could she want with these letters and this picture?"

"I don't know," Mrs. Jeffries replied, and reached for the picture. As her gaze scanned the somber faces in the photograph, something nudged her in the back of her mind and then just as quickly disappeared. "Like you, I can't think of one reason why she'd want to show them to a solicitor. Perhaps she only wanted to put them in a safe place."

"What shall we do now?" Hatchet asked, nodding at the open carpetbag on the table. "How are we going to get this to the inspector? We can hardly admit we went haring off down to the docks and pinched evidence that by rights should have gone directly to the police."

"Don't worry about that," Mrs. Goodge said resolutely. "We'll think of something. We always do. Now, I've got this idea—"

"And it's quite an interesting idea," Mrs. Jeffries interrupted. She rose to her feet. "But we're all so tired tonight, none of us can think straight. Smythe, I'd like you to take charge of the bag. We'll meet again tomorrow morning at nine. Is that all right with everyone?"

"But what about my idea?" the cook protested. She

was sure she was right. "It's a foolproof way to catch the killer. I need an answer if it's to work. Getting the ingredients this time of the year won't be easy. I'll have to send over to Covent Garden directly tomorrow morning so I can do the bakin'."

"That'll be fine," the housekeeper replied. "Now, I suggest we all get some rest. We're going to have long day tomorrow."

Mrs. Jeffries didn't bother to light the lamp as she stepped into her small sitting room. From outside in the hall, she could hear the creak of the floorboards as Smythe and Wiggins marched up the stairs to the own quarters. She made her way across the darkened room to the chair by the window. Sitting down, she stared out into the night.

A long, heavy sigh escaped her. This case was perplexing. Perhaps one of the most confusing ones they'd ever had. She wasn't one to admit defeat, but for once, her usual optimism was at a very low ebb. She leaned her head back against the chair and took long deep breaths, trying to force her body to relax. She'd discovered her mind worked better when she was calm. Soon she felt a lightness of spirit as her breathing became slow, rhythmic and even. She let her mind drift aimlessly, deliberately keeping herself from worrying about what had gone wrong on this case.

Thoughts and ideas floated in and out of their own accord. To begin with, the victim was a monster. Virtually anyone who was close to him might have a motive to murder him. Any of them could have done it too, she thought. None of the alibis were worth much.

She took another long deep breath as the details of the case seemed to sort themselves into a semblance of order of their own accord. The victim had been murdered by someone he knew very well. Someone he planned to meet that afternoon. It could be any of the suspects. Andrew Frommer could have followed him into town and murdered him. With his father-in-law dead, he might have access to his wife's estate.

Henry Alladyce could have done it as well. He certainly benefited from Ashbury's death. As could Eloise Hartshorn. They had only her word for it that she was going to end her relationship with Frommer. She might have decided that she didn't want Ashbury telling Frommer about her affair with Charles Burroughs . . . Mrs. Jeffries caught her breath as the face from the photograph flashed into her mind. She thought back to the day she'd followed Eloise Hartshorn and Charles Burroughs into the burial grounds. She remembered his face. His handsome, worried features. She remembered his words.

Suddenly she sat bolt upright in her chair. Now she knew why something had bothered her about that photograph. Charles Burroughs was Natasha Ashbury's brother.

Of course he had a reason to murder Roland Ashbury. He wanted revenge.

CHAPTER 9

Mrs. Jeffries's immediate problem was the inspector. How could she communicate what she'd learned to him? The carpetbag was useful evidence, of course. But how to get it to him without admitting their part in the investigation?

She got up and began pacing her sitting room. She knew the room well enough that even in the dark, she easily managed to avoid crashing into furniture.

For several hours she paced and thought, considering all the angles of the problem. Finally, long after midnight, she hit upon a solution, and thus allowed herself a few hours rest before getting up and setting her plan in motion.

In the interests of fairness, she ought to tell the others what she was up to, but there really wasn't time, she thought as she climbed the stairs to the attic box room.

Knocking softly, she roused Wiggins from a sound sleep. "What is it, Mrs. Jeffries?" he asked, sticking his head out. "Is somethin' wrong?"

"No, Wiggins," she whispered softly. "But I do need you to help me. Do you remember how to find Boyd's hiding place?"

" 'Course I do," he said, yawning.

"And you can find it again?" she clarified.

" 'Course I can." He rubbed the sleep out of his eyes. "Why?"

"Because I've thought of a way of our getting the carpetbag to the inspector without his knowing of our involvement," she answered. "However, I do need you to take the bag and get over to that hiding place."

"You want me to find Boyd?"

"For this plan to work, we need him."

"But what if 'e's not there," Wiggins hissed softly. "What if 'e's scarpered off again?"

"I've thought of that," she replied. From inside the room, she heard Smythe snoring. "And I don't think he'll have gone off anywhere. He's no place else to go. I think he'll go right back to his hiding place. He was safe there."

"If you say so, Mrs. Jeffries," Wiggins said halfheartedly. "I'll give it a look."

"Excellent, Wiggins," she replied quietly. "I knew I could count on you. I wouldn't be sending you out at this time of the morning, except that I think it's important."

"Do you know who did it, then?" he asked excitedly.

Mrs. Jeffries allowed herself a small, smug smile. "I think so," she replied. "And if all goes well, the rest of you will understand everything by tonight."

"I'll nip out, then," he said. "Just give us a minute to get ready. Where's the bag?"

"It's in my quarters," she said. "Come along as soon as you're dressed and get it. I'll give you the money for a hansom as well."

She hummed as she went down the stairs a little while

later. As she neared the kitchen she stopped in the doorway, surprised to find Mrs. Goodge already up and about. The cook generally didn't stir herself until seven-thirty.

Mrs. Goodge glanced up and saw her standing there. "Good morning," she said cheerfully. "Lovely day, isn't it? I do hope it's not goin' to be too hot. I want these to bake properly." She was standing in front of the worktable by the sink, kneading a mound of white dough on a marble slab.

"Good morning," the housekeeper replied. Her heart sank as she saw what the cook was preparing. Mrs. Goodge apparently hadn't given up on her idea. Well, Mrs. Jeffries thought magnanimously, there was no reason why the cook's theory couldn't be correct as well. The two ideas weren't mutually exclusive. "Goodness, you are up and busy early today. Are you baking something delicious for your sources, then?" she asked hopefully.

"Oh no, this isn't for them," Mrs. Goodge said. "It's for the inspector. I know I'm right. All he's got to do is take these round when he interviews the suspects. Once I explain to him what to look for, we'll have our killer by the end of the day."

"Now, Mrs. Goodge, your idea was only a theory," Mrs. Jeffries warned.

"Most ideas are only theories until they're proved right." The cook picked up her rolling pin and gave the dough one very light roll across. The cream-colored substance was spotted with dark brown dots. "These'll be ready in twenty minutes or so. We should know by then what the inspector'll be up to today. If I need to, I'll take these along to him wherever he is."

Mrs. Jeffries didn't have the heart to continue this conversation. There was no point in telling the cook that even though her theory might be right, the killer would be caught because his motive was now exposed and not because of his eating habits. "I don't expect you'll have to take them anywhere," she replied. "I think he's here."

Through the small window at the other end of the kitchen, she saw the wheels of a carriage pulling up in front of the house. Mrs. Jeffries hurried over and had a good look. "He's just now getting out of a hansom."

"I'm ready for him." Mrs. Goodge pointed at the table, where the teapot, creamer, sugar bowl and several cups and saucers were stacked on a brown wooden tray. "Just give us a minute and I'll get the kettle onto the boil so he can have some tea."

A few minutes later Mrs. Jeffries found the inspector in the drawing room. His face was drawn and tired, his eyes red-rimmed from lack of sleep and his hair stood straight up as though he'd just run his hands through it.

"Good morning, Mrs. Jeffries." He greeted her with a wan smile. "I trust all is well with the household."

"We're fine, sir," she replied. "You're the one we're concerned about. Smythe told us what happened. You must be exhausted. Mrs. Goodge has made up a nice tray for you, sir. There's some toast and tea. We weren't sure if you wanted a full breakfast."

"That's most kind of her," he replied. "Most kind, indeed. Actually I'm not very hungry. Constable Barnes and I ate a quick meal in the wee hours of the morning. The nursing sisters at the hospital took pity on us and got us some breakfast from the hospital kitchen. The food wasn't very good, but one doesn't like to complain. I should love a cup of tea, though."

Mrs. Jeffries put the tray down on the table next to his chair and poured him a cup of the steaming brew. "Is Mrs. Frommer still alive?" she asked, handing him his cup.

"Yes." He smiled happily. "Her breathing improved enormously this morning. The doctor thinks she might be past the worst. She was well enough to be moved into a private room. It'll be easy to keep a watch on her if she's not on the ward. There's simply too many people coming and going on the wards. Until this killer is caught, I won't risk her. He's tried once. I expect when he realizes he's failed, he might try again. That's why I left a police constable outside her room when I decided to come home and freshen up."

"Aren't you going to have a rest, sir?" she asked in alarm. "You've been up all night."

"I'll be fine," he assured her, taking a huge gulp from his cup. "I've too much to do today to sleep."

"Really, sir?" She set a plate of toast on the table next to him. "The investigation is going well, then?" She needed to keep him here until Wiggins returned.

He made a slight face. "I wouldn't exactly say that; it's still all a bit of a muddle. But after last night we've a number of new leads to follow up. For starters, we'll have to open an investigation into who tried to kill MaryAnne Frommer."

"You think it's the same person who shot her father, don't you?" Mrs. Jeffries asked. Her own theory would fall apart if it wasn't. But she was fairly confident that wasn't going to happen.

"Oh yes, the two are definitely connected." He gulped more tea. "And with that in mind, the first thing on my agenda today is to locate Andrew Frommer."

"Didn't he come to the hospital at all last night?"

"He hadn't been there by the time I left this morning, nor has he returned home. I don't mind telling you, Mrs. Jeffries, this looks quite bad for the man. I didn't take

Eloise Hartshorn's accusations all that seriously last night.''

"Eloise Hartshorn," Mrs. Jeffries interrupted. "Was she there?''

"Oh yes." Witherspoon nodded vigorously. "She's convinced that it was Andrew Frommer who shot his wife. She's equally convinced she's going to be next. Though her reasons for thinking so don't really make all that much sense.''

"What are those reasons?''

"Miss Hartshorn seems to feel Frommer has gone insane. As I said, it's all a bit of a muddle. No one heard the shot or has any information about the attempted murder of Mrs. Frommer.''

"What about the servants?" Mrs. Jeffries asked. "Weren't they able to help?''

He frowned slightly. "Not really. All any of them could tell us was that she'd gone up to the attic late in the afternoon, come back downstairs, washed her hands and then had tea. That was the last anyone saw of the poor woman until they found out she was lying in the back garden with a bullet in her side." He sighed. "It's most annoying. We can't locate Mr. Frommer, the footman who helped get the poor woman to the hospital has disappeared—''

"No 'e 'asn't sir," Wiggins said. " 'E's right 'ere.''

Witherspoon turned sharply. Wiggins and a young lad of fifteen or so, stood in the open doorway of the drawing room. The boy was holding a worn carpetbag in his hand. His hair was dark blond and cut close to his scalp. His face was thin, his complexion a pasty pale color and his expression anxious. He wore a dirty white shirt, a brown short-waisted jacket with the two top buttons missing and a pair of badly wrinkled and stained russet trousers. Under the inspector's scrutiny, he shifted his slight weight from one foot to the other and then eased behind Wiggins.

"It's all right," Wiggins assured the boy, patting his arm. "No one 'ere'll 'urt you. The inspector's a nice man, 'e is. Like I told ya, you just tell 'im the truth and everythin' will be all right."

Witherspoon smiled gently. He wasn't precisely sure what was going on, but he realized this poor lad was scared out of his wits. "Wiggins is right," he said softly. "No one here will hurt you. Please, do come closer and sit down."

The boy hesitated and looked at Wiggins, who nodded encouragingly. "Go on. You can 'ave some tea."

Mrs. Jeffries had already poured the boy a cup. She held it out as he slowly made his way across the drawing room and, still staring at the inspector out of wide, frightened eyes, sat down on the end of the settee. He dropped the carpetbag by his feet. She handed him the tea and then moved quietly to the other end and sat down herself. Wiggins, who'd followed the lad, propped himself against the side of the settee next to the housekeeper.

"Did you bring that bag for me to have a look at?" Witherspoon asked the boy.

"Yeah." He gulped some tea. "It's Mrs. Frommer's. She wanted it."

"She told you to bring it to her?" he asked.

"Yeah."

"When?" Witherspoon prompted.

"I don't know." The lad sniffed and rubbed his nose. "Before it were done."

"Before what were done?" the inspector pressed.

"The murder. Mr. Ashbury's murder. She sent me before."

"I see."

"Was it on the day you were all to come back from Ascot?"

Boyd bit his lip in confusion. "I don't know. I don't remember so good."

"Why don't you tell me what you do remember?" Witherspoon suggested.

"I hid," the lad replied. "I was scared."

"I see." He nodded, trying to encourage the boy to keep on talking. But Boyd shut up and stared down at the carpet.

"You got the bag from the Frommer house on the day of the murder, right?" the inspector said.

"I guess." Boyd didn't sound so certain. "I think, I'm confused."

Mrs. Jeffries realized that at this rate of questioning, they'd be here all day. "Excuse me, Inspector. I don't mean to interrupt, but, well, sir—" She broke off and jerked her head toward the hall.

"Is something wrong, Mrs. Jeffries?" he asked. "You seem to have devloped a twitch . . . oh . . . yes." He leapt to his feet as he realized she was trying to tell him something.

"If you'll excuse us, boys," Mrs. Jeffries said, "we'll be right back."

As soon as they were in the hall, she said, "I'm not trying to tell you your business, sir, but I've had some experience in dealing with people like Boyd." When he continued to stare at her blankly, she went on: "I mean, sir, he's scared of you, and probably of me as well. I think if we let Wiggins get him talking, you'll find out that you can get all of your questions answered far more quickly."

The inspector thought about it for a moment. "You know, I think you're right," he agreed. "Wiggins," he called, sticking his head into the drawing room, "Could you come here, please?"

The plan worked like a charm. Within half an hour Boyd had told his tale and departed with Wiggins downstairs for a hearty breakfast.

Meanwhile Witherspoon, with a very helpful Mrs. Jeffries making comments as they went along, was giving the contents of the carpetbag a very thorough going-over.

"How on earth did she manage to get all this money?" he asked as he put the stack of notes to one side.

"She'd money of her own," Mrs. Jeffries said, and then clamped her mouth shut as she realized that she'd not got that bit of information from the inspector. "I mean, perhaps she'd money of her own," she continued as the inspector shot her a puzzled look, "or perhaps she'd managed to save it out of the household accounts over the years. Some women are quite clever money managers."

"I expect it's the former," Witherspoon replied as he pulled out the stack of letters. "From what the constable and I learned, she did inherit some money from her mother. Which, of course, explains Miss Hartshorn's hysterics last night. Though why she thought she'd be next is beyond me."

"So that's why Miss Hartshorn felt that Frommer had attempted to kill her?" Mrs. Jeffries queried. She wanted to cover her mistake as thoroughly as possible, seeing as how she might have to do some very fancy juggling to lead the inspector down the path she wanted him to go. "I'm afraid I don't understand."

"That was one of the reasons." Witherspoon peered at the faded ink on the front of the top letter. "She claimed that Frommer is desperate for money. According to her rather convoluted reasoning, Frommer murdered his father-in-law so Mrs. Frommer would inherit Ashbury's half of the business. Then he tried to murder Mrs. Frommer so he'd inherit her money. Supposedly he was going to kill Miss Hartshorn because she was the only one capable of putting all the pieces together and ruining Frommer's plan.''

''You don't believe her, do you?'' Mrs. Jeffries task would be much more difficult if the inspector thought that Andrew Frommer was the killer. Much more difficult indeed.

Witherspoon sighed and put the letters down on the tea tray. ''I don't know what to believe.'' He picked the first one up and tapped it absently against the side of the tray. ''At first I dismissed her ravings as hysteria, but as I said, it doesn't look good that we can't locate Frommer. Where could he be? We've checked his office, his club, even with his party's chief whip, but no one's seen hide nor hair of the fellow. But be that as it may, I don't believe he's our killer.''

''You don't?'' Mrs. Jeffries held her breath.

''No, to begin with, if Mrs. Frommer had died, her husband would lose all rights to Roland Ashbury's half of the shipping agency,'' he explained. ''The constable and I had a word with Ashbury's solicitors yesterday.'' He stopped tapping the envelope and slipped the letter out. ''Remember when I told you he'd changed the will when he disinherited his son?''

''Yes, sir, I remember,'' she said patiently.

''Apparently in an effort to ensure that Jonathan Ashbury had no claim on the estate whatsoever, Ashbury and Josiah Alladyce did their wills up so that only one chosen heir would inherit. For Ashbury, that heir was MaryAnne Frommer.'' He settled back in the chair and flipped open the letter. ''So the last thing Frommer would want is his wife dead. If she dies, the estate all goes to Josiah Alla-dyce's heir.''

"You mean it's a bit like a tontine," she remarked. "Whoever is left gets it all? Isn't that illegal?"

"It does sound a bit like that," he murmured. "But apparently it's not illegal if it's worded correctly in the will."

"Did Frommer know about Ashbury's will?" she asked.

"Oh yes, Ashbury made it quite clear to Frommer sometime back," Witherspoon replied as he turned his attention to the paper in his hand.

Mrs. Jeffries sagged in relief. She knew Andrew Frommer wasn't the killer. He was a monstrous human being, but he wasn't a murderer.

Witherspoon's brows drew together as he read the first letter. Absently he handed it to Mrs. Jeffries to read and then picked up the next one.

His expression changed to disgust as he read the others. By the time he finished the last one, his mouth flattened into a grim, hard line. "It's unbelievable, isn't it, Mrs. Jeffries? How could the man have treated his family so abominably."

She pretended to read the letter before she looked up and met his gaze. "Yes, sir, it is awful." She scanned the area quickly, looking for the photograph. With dismay, she realized it hadn't fallen out of the envelope as it had last night. "Is there anything else in the envelope?"

The inspector picked it up and peered inside. "No, why did you ask? Do you think the letter sounds as if it were missing a page."

Blast, she thought. Now what? "Oh no, sir, I simply wanted to make sure." She forced herself to laugh. "I'll be honest, sir. I know what a thorough policeman you are.

I was just trying to impress you with my own, rather feeble attempt at efficiency.''

"Dear Mrs. Jeffries," he scoffed. "You've no need to impress me at all. Why, you know how much I've come to rely upon you to be my sounding board, as it were. But, as you say"—he reached for the bag, just as she'd hoped he would—"I am thorough. Let's see if there's anything else in here." He pulled it closer and held it wide open. "Goodness, there is something else."

Mrs. Jeffries sent up a silent prayer of thanks. They were heading back in the right direction. This was becoming increasingly difficult and now she had a new fear. What if Constable Barnes arrived before she could use the photograph to get the inspector moving toward the real killer. "What is it, sir?" she asked.

"It looks like a photograph," he murmured. He held it up and stared at it, a look of curiosity on his face. "Oh how sad. I think it's Jonathan Ashbury and his family."

"May I see, sir?" she asked. She kept her ears cocked toward the front of the house. Were those footsteps coming up the front stairs?

"Of course." He handed it to her and then put the carpetbag on the floor. "Have a good look. I think it's quite a good photograph. Amazing what they can do these days."

She didn't answer for a minute. She was trying to determine what was the fastest course of action here. From down the hall, she heard the pounding of the door knocker.

"You know, sir," she said loudly, hoping to distract him, "there's something very familiar about this face."

"That's probably Constable Barnes at the front door." He started to get up. "And yes, there is a resemblance. I think Jonathan Ashbury looks very much like his sister."

"Do sit down and finish your tea, sir," she ordered. "Betsy'll get the door. I expect the constable could do with a cup of tea as well." Panic set in as she realized that she wasn't supposed to have ever seen any of the principals in this case. Blast.

He eased back into his chair as footsteps echoed in the front hall. "He's probably in a hurry, Mrs. Jeffries. As I said, we've much to do today."

"What I meant, sir"—Mrs. Jeffries tried again—"was that I wouldn't know about the resemblance of Jonathan Ashbury to his sister; I've never seen her." She took a deep breath and hoped she could manage to pull this off without arousing his suspicion. "But I have seen one other principal in the case."

Witherspoon raised his eyebrows. "Really? Who?"

She heard Betsy's voice and then Constable Barnes. This was no time for to be subtle. "Charles Burroughs," she announced bluntly. "I accidentally saw him, sir."

"Really?" Witherspoon repeated.

Betsy and Barnes's footsteps came toward the drawing room. Mrs. Jeffries only had few more seconds to make her point. "Really, sir. It was quite accidental, I assure you. I'll tell you the circumstances later, but what is important"—she held up the photograph and pointed to the young man standing next to Natasha Ashbury—"is this. Don't you see it, sir?"

Witherspoon squinted at the picture. "I'm afraid I don't see what you're getting . . . good gracious, you're right."

"Good morning, sir," Barnes said easily as he slipped in behind the maid.

"Barnes, do come have a look at this." Witherspoon pointed at the photograph.

The constable, to his credit, didn't bat an eye; he simply crossed the room and did as he was instructed. "All right, sir,'' he finally said. "It's a nice enough picture, but I don't . . . yes, sir, I see what you mean. This young fellow''—he placed his finger on the figure next to Natasha—"is very familiar. Now, where have I seen that face?''

"It's Burroughs, man. Charles Burroughs.'' Witherspoon leapt to his feet. "And that means we'd best get over there right away. We've found our killer, Barnes, and it isn't Andrew Frommer.'' He charged out into the hall with the constable on his heels. A moment later the front door slammed.

A satisfied smile on her face, Mrs. Jeffries relaxed back against the settee. It had been touch and go for a moment or two there. Thank goodness the inspector had put two and two together and realized that the motive on this murder wasn't money but revenge. As to all the other bits and pieces, well, she was sure that once Burroughs was in custody and had told his tale, they'd sort out the puzzling things that didn't add up as yet.

"I take it from the expression on your face that you know what that was all about,'' Betsy said.

Mrs. Jeffries started. She'd quite forgotten the girl was in the room. "Oh, I'm sorry, Betsy. I was thinking.'' She got up. "But yes, I do know what it was about. If you'll come downstairs, I'll tell you at the same time as I tell the others. Is Boyd still here?''

"Wiggins took him upstairs so he could have a rest,'' she replied. "The boy hasn't slept well since Ashbury's murder.''

The two women made their way downstairs. Mrs. Goodge, who was taking a tray of scones out of the oven, turned as they came into the kitchen. "What's happened?'' she asked.

"We really should wait till the others are all here before

I say anything," Mrs. Jeffries said. "I do so want to be fair."

Mrs. Goodge slammed the tray of scones down hard on the worktable. "Wiggins'll be back as soon as he gets Boyd settled, and Smythe has gone to fetch Luty and Hatchet."

Mrs. Jeffries realized the cook was most put out. "Mrs. Goodge," she asked, "is something wrong?"

"Wrong? What could be wrong?" She put her hands on her hips and glared at the other two women. "Wiggins seems to feel you've solved the case all on your own."

"Now, Mrs. Goodge," Mrs. Jeffries said gently, "that's not true. I'll admit I had to act quickly today. But only because it was the only way I could think of to get the carpetbag back here and into the inspector's possession without him realizing what we'd done."

"Then you haven't solved it?" the cook asked hopefully.

"I wouldn't precisely say that," Mrs. Jeffries hedged. She wanted to let the cook down easily and tried to think of a way to go about it.

"Then you have solved it," she charged.

"Well, more or less." The housekeeper winced as Mrs. Goodge's expression turned thunderous. For the first time she realized the others might consider that she'd been just a tad hoggish on this case. But what could she have done differently?

"You could have at least given me a chance to test me theory," the cook cried. "Was that too much to ask? I've gone to a lot of trouble here. I've been up since before dawn, sendin' street lads to Covent Gardens and over to other places sussin' out information, and for what? So you can come along and solve the case without so much as a by-your-leave. Well, I tell you, I'm annoyed. Right annoyed. I know I was right and all it woulda took was a few minutes with each of the suspects.''

''You're not bein' fair,'' Betsy said. ''Mrs. Jeffries had to act fast. We had to get that carpetbag to the inspector and she figured out a way to do it.''

''It couldn't have waited a day or two?'' Mrs. Goodge asked archly.

It could have, Mrs. Jeffries thought. Charles Burroughs wasn't going anywhere and the police were watching over Mrs. Frommer, so he couldn't make an attempt on her life again. ''Yes, Mrs. Goodge,'' she admitted, ''it could have waited a day or two. I'm terribly sorry. I should have let you test your theory. Or at least told the others about it.''

''Test what theory?'' Smythe asked easily as he came in from the back hall. Luty and Hatchet were right on his heels.

''My theory,'' Mrs. Goodge declared. ''But it's too late now; Mrs. Jeffries has already solved the ruddy case.'' With that, she dusted off her hands and went to the sink to fill the kettle.

No one said anything for a moment. Luty and Hatchet quietly slipped into their chairs. Smythe, with an inquiring look at Betsy, sat down, and Mrs. Jeffries, her conscience troubling her greatly, took her place at the head of the table.

''I'll just go get Wiggins,'' Betsy said softly.

''Please do,'' Mrs. Jeffries said, ''and when you both come down, we'll have our meeting.''

''Will you arrest him, sir?'' the constable asked as they got out of the cab. The inspector had briefed him on the drive over.

''I'm not sure,'' the Inspector admitted. ''But I will ask him a number of questions.''

"Do you think he really is Natasha Ashbury's brother?" Barnes persisted. He gave a quick, worried glance at the front door of the Burroughs house. "Seems to me it could just be a coincidence; the way he looks, I mean. Lots of people resemble each other. Let's face it, sir, your whole case would fall apart if it turns out he's nothing to do with the Ashburys."

"What about both of them being from Colorado?" Witherspoon argued. "Burroughs has already told us he was from Boulder. Jonathan Ashbury's letters prove that they were in Colorado as well. I don't think that's a co-incidence." He sincerely hoped it wasn't. "It's at least worth asking a few questions over."

Barnes banged the door knocker. "I suppose so, sir. But for my money, I'd like to get my hands on Andrew Frommer. We still haven't found the man, and in all my years as a policeman, I've seen that it's generally the guilty that disappears."

The door opened and Eloise Hartshorn stuck her head out. "Hello, Inspector, Constable. Have you located Andrew yet?"

"No, ma'am," Witherspoon replied. "Not yet. But we're still looking. May we come inside, please. We need to ask Mr. Burroughs a few questions."

"He's not here," she said quickly.

"When is he expected back?" Witherspoon asked. He wasn't sure that Miss Hartshorn was being entirely truthful.

She slipped out of the front door and closed it behind her. "He didn't say," she said. "I'll have him get in touch with you when he comes back, all right?"

The door suddenly flew open behind her, revealing a grim-faced butler and an even grimmer-faced Charles Burroughs. "Oh, for God's sake, Eloise, don't be so ridiculous. Did you think the butler wouldn't come and fetch me when you ordered him away from the front door?''

''I didn't want you disturbed,'' she countered, lifting her chin defiantly. ''You need your rest. You were up most of the night.''

''Please stop trying to protect me, Eloise.'' He sighed in exasperation. ''Inspector, Constable.'' He nodded at the two policemen and opened the door wide. ''I've been expecting you. Do come in.''

Mrs. Jeffries told her story quickly and efficiently. ''So you see, as soon as I realized that the boy in the photograph was Charles Burroughs, I realized that he had to be the killer. He came back for vengeance.''

''But why try and kill Mrs. Frommer?'' Luty asked. ''She didn't have anything to do with what Ashbury did to his son.''

''But she had money of her own,'' Mrs. Jeffries countered, ''and it doesn't appear she had been willing to help her brother either.''

She turned to Mrs. Goodge. ''I'm really sorry if you felt I acted untoward here, but honestly I didn't realize that your theory was so very important to you. I'm quite sure you're right.''

''Do you think so?'' the cook asked. She appeared to be somewhat mollified by Mrs. Jeffries's apology.

''Absolutely.''

Mrs. Goodge smiled happily. ''Then that's all right.''

They discussed the case for a while, asking questions and speculating on what the real answers would be when the inspector came home and gave them all the details. No one had any doubts that Mrs. Jeffries was right about Charles Burroughs being the killer.

No one that is, except Mrs. Goodge.

To her credit, she waited till the others had left the kitchen. Then she got up, packed the freshly baked scones into a wicker basket, covered it with a clean cloth and took off her apron. She put on her hat, took one last look around the kitchen to make sure everything was in order, picked up the basket of scones and then slipped out the back door.

CHAPTER 10

Burroughs took them into his drawing room and bade them to sit down and be comfortable. He smiled tenderly at Eloise, his irritation of a few moments ago clearly forgotten. "My dear, I think it would be best if you left us alone."

"I'm staying," she said flatly. She crossed the room and stood next to him. "I'm not leaving your side."

He stared at her for a few seconds and then took her hand and kissed it. "All right, my love. But let's sit down." The two of them went to the love seat across from the settee and sank down on the cushions. Burroughs turned his attention to the policemen. "Gentlemen, I believe you wanted to ask me some questions. But before you do, I've a question I need answered. How is Mrs. Frommer? Eloise told me she'd been shot."

"She's alive," the inspector replied.

"Will she live?"

"Perhaps," he said cautiously. He wasn't sure how much information he wanted to give just at this moment. "You know that she was probably shot in her own back garden?"

"Yes, my servants told me you'd questioned them, but none of them heard the shot."

"That's correct. I understand you weren't home yesterday evening."

"I was at Eloise's house," he replied. "Her servants will verify that."

Witherspoon was in a quandary. He was sure that whoever had shot Mrs. Frommer was also the same person who'd murdered her father. But how could Burroughs be the killer if he wasn't here last night? Eloise Hartshorn's servants might be well paid, but they weren't paid enough to perjure themselves in a murder inquiry, and both the maid and the cook had sworn that Charles Burroughs was at the Hartshorn house all afternoon and evening. Oh well, there was nothing for it but to press on. Eventually the truth would out; it always did.

"Yes, sir." Witherspoon cleared his throat and stifled a yawn. "We know." Perhaps he ought to have had a nap, because all of a sudden he was feeling a bit muddled. "Is Charles Burroughs your real name?"

"Charles Burroughs is my legal name."

Witherspoon was taken aback. "You realize we will check everything you say with the authorities in America," he warned.

"I would expect nothing less," Burroughs replied easily.

"Is Charles Burroughs the name you were born with," Barnes asked.

Burroughs grinned. "Very good, Constable, you're obviously aware of the fact that many people change their

name when they go to America. Quite rightly too. For
many of us it is a new life. Too bad it didn't turn out that
way for my sister and her family. But as to your
query . . ." He looked at the inspector as he spoke. "I
was born Mikhail Ilyich Buriyakin. That's a bit of mouth-
ful for most Americans, so I had it legally changed to
Charles Burroughs."

"What was your sister's name?" Witherspoon asked.

"Natasha Buriyakin Ashbury," he said. "Her husband
was Jonathan Ashbury. They, along with my ten-month-
old nephew, were killed when the wagon they were sleeping in was washed away in a flash flood. They'd lost their
home, you see, and Roland Ashbury, Jonathan's own father, hadn't lifted one damned finger to help them."

Witherspoon was suddenly overwhelmed with sadness.
There was something most likable about Burroughs, most
likable indeed. Now he was going to have to arrest the
fellow. Maybe. "Why weren't you killed?"

"I wasn't in the wagon," Burroughs said. "I'd recently
been very ill; I'd almost died. One of our neighbors had
taken me in to nurse. They'd offered to let Jonathan and
Natasha sleep in their barn that night too, but Jonathan
was too proud. He'd pulled the wagon onto a dried-up
riverbed. Jonathan wasn't from the west, he didn't know
about storms in the mountain and floods roaring down so
fast that you couldn't do anything to save yourself. That's
what happened to them. They were swept away. It took
us two days to find the bodies."

"You blamed Roland Ashbury," Witherspoon stated.

"Who else?" Burroughs shrugged. "It wasn't as if
Jonathan asked for what wasn't his. Jonathan's mother
had left him money; quite a bit of it. All Jonathan wanted
was what was his by right. But the old bastard never sent
it. He never even answered Jonathan's letters. The day we

buried them, I swore I'd get even with him. I swore I'd make him pay."

"So you came to London for the express purpose of exacting vengeance against Roland Ashbury?" The inspector needed to be very clear about the man's actions, since he would, eventually, have to give evidence in court. This murder, apparently, wasn't a heat-of-the-moment sort of crime. That would make a difference to the court.

"It took me fifteen years of hard work," Burroughs admitted, "but I did it. I ended up with a fortune from silver mining. Right before Christmas, I sold up and came here."

"When exactly did you arrive in London?" Barnes asked.

"February fourteenth. I used a private inquiry agent to locate Ashbury," he said. "Luckily, the house next door to my prey was for sale. I bought it and moved in."

"Why didn't you kill Roland right away?" Witherspoon asked.

Burroughs looked at Eloise Hartshorn before he replied. "I found out, Inspector," he said firmly, "that much as I loathed Ashbury, I couldn't kill him in cold blood."

"Are you saying you didn't murder him?" Witherspoon pressed. "Are you saying you didn't shoot him?"

"I did not," Burroughs said flatly. "How could I? I'd spent years dreaming of the day I would put a bullet into that man's skull, but after seeing the suffering of his daughter, after living next door to him, I couldn't find it within myself to actually do it. I kept putting it off and putting it off, and then I met Eloise and everything changed. Vengeance didn't seem important to me anymore."

"Remember, sir," the inspector warned, "it was your gun that was found at the scene of the murder. You've admitted you had a motive and you could easily have manufactured the opportunity, yet you expect us to believe that you suddenly had a change of heart because you felt sorry for Ashbury's daughter and you fell in love.''

"It's true," Eloise cried. "Everything did change when we met each other. Besides, that gun was stolen."

"Now, Eloise, we don't know that," Burroughs cautioned. "We only think it might have been taken."

"When was this, sir?" Barnes asked.

"A few weeks back. We came home from the theater and found a window wide open but nothing missing."

"That's what we thought at the time," Eloise added, "but Charles never checked to see if the gun was still here."

Witherspoon eyed them speculatively. The tale had the ring of truth to it. "Did you fetch the police?"

"We sent for the constable up on the corner," Burroughs replied. "But by the time he came round, we realized nothing appeared to be missing and told him to go. But you can check with him."

"Rest assured we will, sir," Witherspoon said.

"I tell you, Charles didn't do it," Eloise insisted. "He couldn't. He's too decent a man to kill someone, even an odious pig like Roland Ashbury."

"Ashbury tried to blackmail you, didn't he?" Barnes reminded her. "So you had reason to hate him as well."

"Now, see here." Burroughs got to his feet. "Eloise had nothing to do with Ashbury's death or with the attack on Mrs. Frommer. Why would she? She told me herself about her past. Ashbury couldn't blackmail her."

"And it didn't bother you, sir," Barnes said easily. "It didn't bother you that the woman you loved was the mistress of the son-in-law of a man you hated. Seems to me, sir, that it adds a bit more fuel to the fire."

The inspector wondered what his constable was up to, but he wasn't going to interfere. The man did have a point.

"Of course I hated it, Constable," Burroughs snapped. "But I never hated enough to kill in cold blood."

"We were going back to America," Eloise cried shrilly. "I'd already gone and booked the tickets. I'd made arrangements to get both our household things shipped to San Francisco. Show them, darling, show them the tickets. We bought them days before the murder."

"I should like to see them, if you please," the inspector said.

Burroughs nodded, crossed the room and rang the bellpull. A moment later the butler appeared. "You rang, sir."

"Yes, could you please go to my study and bring me the envelope you'll find in the top left-hand drawer."

"Yes, sir." The butler withdrew to do his master's bidding.

While they waited the inspector tried to think of something else to ask. He'd been so very certain of Burroughs's guilt before he spoke to the man; now he wasn't quite so sure. "Er, which shipping company did you arrange to have your things shipped with?" he finally asked.

Eloise laughed harshly. "The only one I could think of was Ashbury and Alladyce. Ironic, isn't it? I hated Roland Ashbury, yet without even thinking about it, I gave him my business. I suppose I didn't realize he was still a part of it. I thought Roland had retired and was completely out of it."

"Will Mr. Alladyce verify that you came to see him and made arrangements through his company?" Witherspoon asked.

"I don't see why he shouldn't," she replied.

"How long before the murder did you go and see Mr. Alladyce?"

She thought for a moment. "Let me see, now. It must have been two, possibly two and a half weeks before Roland's murder. I told him what ship we were leaving on and left a deposit for the packing and shipping charges."

The butler returned and handed a large, buff-colored envelope to Charles Burroughs. "Thank you," he said, dismissing the servant. He opened it, pulled out the contents and nodded in satisfaction.

"Have a look at these, Inspector; the invoice is right on top. You'll see the purchase date is three days before Roland Ashbury's murder, but the sailing date of the ship is two weeks from now. If I'd killed Ashbury, I'd have left town immediately. I certainly wouldn't have hung around packing up two houses."

The inspector took the proffered documents and studied them carefully. There were two first-class tickets for a mid-month sailing of American Lines flagship vessel the *Elizabeth Kristina* to New York. The invoice for the purchase of those tickets was indeed dated three days before Ashbury's murder.

The inspector wasn't sure what to do. The tickets didn't really prove anything, but their very existence argued against arresting Charles Burroughs. Furthermore, Witherspoon thought, the man had made some powerful points in his own defense. If he had committed the murder, why hang about waiting to be caught? Surely he must have expected that there was a risk the police would find out his true identity. Once that had happened, it would be only a matter of time before his motive became apparent. Then, of course, there was the attempt on Mrs. Frommer's life. Burroughs couldn't have done that. He had an alibi. But he could have paid to have had it done. Witherspoon had seen that happen a time or two. Paid assassins were, unfortunately, all too common.

"Excuse me, sir." The butler had quietly come back into the drawing room. "But there's a rather . . . unusual woman who insists on seeing the inspector."

"Do send her in," Burroughs said. He smiled at Eloise and patted her arm. "Don't worry, darling, everything will be all right."

"This way, ma'am." The butler ushered in a plump, gray-haired woman carrying a wicker basket over her arm.

"Gracious," Witherspoon yelped. "Mrs. Goodge, what are you doing here?"

"I didn't mean to disturb you, sir." She shot the butler a malevolent glare. "I asked him to fetch you out to the hall, not march me inside."

"Yes, yes," the inspector murmured, somewhat surprised at the appearance of his cook. "I'm sure you . . . ah . . . ah—what are you doing here?" he finally repeated. "Is everything all right at home."

"Everything's fine." She nodded politely to Barnes and the others. "It was you that we was worried about. Mrs. Jeffries mentioned how you'd been up all night at the hospital with Mrs. Frommer. Well, sir, seein' as how you didn't even take the time for a proper breakfast—"

"I ate at the hospital," he interjected quickly; he had a horrible feeling he knew what was coming next. Barnes was already trying to hide a smile and even the two suspects looked amused.

"That's not decent food," she charged. "But anyway, my point is, sir, you'll be needin' your strength. I've made up a batch of my special scones, sir. They'll keep you going all day. As I said, I didn't wish to disturb you, but I felt it necessary to bring them round." She opened the wrapping cloth, walked over to the inspector and shoved the basket under his nose. "Here, sir. Have one."

Witherspoon had no choice but to take a scone. Before he realized it, she'd darted to Barnes, forced a scone on him and then dashed across the room to the love seat. "Here, sir." She offered the basket to Charles Burroughs. "They're excellent scones, sir. They've got walnuts in them. Do have one."

Burroughs, looking as thought he were having a hard time keeping a straight face, took a scone and bit into it with gusto. "You're right, these are good. Do try one, Eloise."

Eloise Hartshorn gaped at the cook. "I'm not really very hungry," she began. Burroughs reached in the basket, snatched a scone and handed it to her. "Eat it," he ordered. "You've not had a thing in your stomach since you heard about Mrs. Frommer."

Eloise shrugged and took a bite. "They *are* nice," she agreed, a few moments later. "Very nice indeed. These are quite different than your usual scone. They're excellent, Charles; do please remind me to get this recipe from the inspector's cook before we leave for America."

"Of course, dear," Charles replied. "I must say, Inspector. You're quite lucky to have such a devoted cook. I do hope she doesn't mind sharing her recipes."

"We're all devoted to our inspector," Mrs. Goodge said cheerfully. She watched the two of them as they demolished her scones. "And I don't mind sharin' my recipes at all. At least not with the two of you."

"Thank you, Mrs. Goodge." The inspector gulped down the rest of his scone and got to his feet. The pastry was jolly good. How very clever of Mrs. Goodge to think to add walnuts to the recipe. They added quite a crunchy flavor.

"Mr. Burroughs," Barnes said, "I trust you and Miss

Hartshorn won't be leaving London until your ship sails."
He too had wolfed down his scone. He'd not eaten anything since that pathetic meal at the hospital.

"No," Charles replied as he stuffed the last bite in his
mouth, "we'll be right here."

The policemen, followed by Mrs. Goodge, made their
way outside. The cook gave the butler a smug smile as
she went past.

As soon as they were outside, she seized the initiative.
"Inspector," she said, "please forgive me, but I had to
bring you these." She poked at the basket hanging off her
arm. "I remembered what you said the day after the murder. You are brilliant, sir. Absolutely brilliant."

When Mrs. Goodge walked back into her kitchen, the
place was in an uproar. Smythe was just getting ready to
go for the carriage, Mrs. Jeffries was pacing the floor,
Betsy was ringing her hands and Wiggins had just suggested they drag the river.

Smythe spotted her first. "Where 'ave you been?" he
demanded. "I was getting ready to go to 'oward for the
carriage. Then I were goin' to find the inspector and tell
'im you was missin'."

"We've been worried sick," Betsy added.

"Cor blimey, Mrs. Goodge, you shouldn't give us a
scare like that. Me and Fred was just fixin' to go out and
search the riverbank for your 'at."

"Mrs. Goodge?" Mrs. Jeffries queried gently. "I do
believe I apologized for my earlier actions. Surely you're
not so angry at me that you would scare everyone so
badly."

"I'm not at all angry at you," Mrs. Goodge declared
as she took off her hat. "I'm sorry I give everyone a
fright. I know I don't usually git out of my kitchen, but

sometimes a body's got to do what a body thinks is right.''

''Where've ya been, then?'' Wiggins asked. Relieved that she wasn't floating facedown in the Thames, he'd bounced back to his usual cheerful demeanor.

Mrs. Goodge bustled across to her stove, grabbed the kettle and put it on the boil. When they heard what she'd done, they were all going to need a cup of tea. ''Well, I've done something I thought was necessary.'' She was determined to stall for time until she could think of just the right way to put it.

''Yes, but what was it that was necessary?'' Betsy prodded. Unlike Wiggins, she was still a mite upset. It had frightened her badly when she'd seen that the cook was gone without so much as a by-your-leave. That wasn't like Mrs. Goodge. She was of the old school. Before this incident, Betsy would have bet her next quarter's wages that the cook would never leave the house without permission from the housekeeper.

''Just give us a moment to get the teapot ready.'' Mrs. Goodge started for the china hutch.

''I've already done that,'' Mrs. Jeffries said quietly. ''As a matter of fact, I've done up a tray. Smythe, will you fetch it from the dry larder, please. You must be tired after your outing, Mrs. Goodge,'' the housekeeper continued smoothly. ''Do sit down and rest your feet. Betsy and I will get the tea.''

Mrs. Goodge sat down. A few moments later the tea was ready and the rest of them had joined her at the table. Everyone gazed at her expectantly. She cleared her throat, a bit nervous at being the center of attention. ''Well, now, when you hear what I've done, I don't want any of you kickin' up a fuss, not till you hear me out.''

''I think we can all manage that,'' Mrs. Jeffries said.

"All right, then." She took a deep breath. "I wanted to make sure you were right about the killer bein' Charles Burroughs, so I went over there with my scones. Burroughs isn't the killer and neither is Eloise Hartshorn. Both of them ate every bite of them scones, walnuts and all. So despite us findin' out who Burroughs really is, someone else killed Roland Ashbury," she finished.

No one said a word. They were too surprised. Finally Mrs. Jeffries said, "But, Mrs. Goodge, maybe it was Ashbury who picked the walnuts out of his cake. Had you considered that? In which case your theory that the killer didn't like walnuts would be categorically incorrect."

"I don't understand," Wiggins interjected. "What's the killer got to do with walnuts?"

"He picked them out of the cake," Mrs. Goodge replied. "The inspector said that one of the dessert plates found at the scene of the murder had walnuts on it. That's been nigglin' at me ever since we started this investigation. I'm a cook. I know a lot about food and how people pick and choose what they'll eat. And I know our killer didn't like walnuts. He probably doesn't even realize what he did can point the finger of guilt at him, but I know it and I know that Ashbury liked walnuts," she declared gleefully. "He had to; he's the one that bought the cake. No one in their right mind buys a cake with nuts in it if they don't like them."

Everyone glanced at one another, wondering if anyone at the table would have the nerve to argue with the cook. No one did. The truth was, her idea made a sort of sense.

"What did the inspector say when you showed up?" Betsy finally asked. In her lap she crossed her fingers, hoping and praying that the cook hadn't mucked things up completely.

"He were a bit surprised," Mrs. Goodge admitted.

"But I've worked with Mrs. Jeffries long enough to understand what I need to do in a situation like that. I handled it right well, even if I do say so myself. He's got that basket of scones with him. He ought to be feeding one to Andrew Frommer anytime now."

Andrew Frommer belched loudly and scratched at the stubble on his face. His clothes were dirty and wrinkled, his hair uncombed, and he was missing one of his shoes. He sat on the settee in his drawing room, oblivious to the fact that he had two policemen staring at him suspiciously.

"Where have you been, Mr. Frommer?" Witherspoon asked. Though it really was a rather foolish question: one could tell from the smell emanating off the fellow that he'd been drinking.

"I don't think that's any of your business," he replied. "I don't have to answer your questions. I'm not under arrest."

"Not yet, sir," Barnes muttered.

"Mr. Frommer," Witherspoon began sternly, "your wife is in very serious condition. She's been shot. She's in the hospital."

"And I'm in a pretty miserable state myself," Frommer replied morosely. "What am I going to do? The bank's going to foreclose and I know that cow I'm married to won't lift a finger to help me."

Witherspoon thought he was beyond shock. "We need to know where you were last evening at seven o'clock."

"Seven o'clock?" Frommer repeated. "I don't remember. Damnation, man, how am I supposed to know where I was at any particular time yesterday? My whole life is in ruins. The party's withdrawing their support, I'm losing my home, I've no money and that tart I was sleeping with

is running off to America with that lout who used to be
my neighbor."

Barnes stuck the basket of scones in his face. "You
look like you might be a bit hungry, sir," he said. "Eat
one."

Frommer, so lost in his own misery that the incongruity
of a policeman offering his a pastry completely slipped
past him, absently reached into the basket and helped himself. "Thanks," he mumbled as he took a bite.

The inspector watched him carefully. He wasn't precisely sure how Mrs. Goodge had jumped to the conclu-
sion that he expected her to make pastries with walnuts
in them, but for some odd reason, she had. Though he did
rather think it beyond the call of duty for her to come
across town to bring them to him while he was interview-
ing suspects. But then again, his staff was quite excep-
tional. Even the constable thought so.

"Mr. Frommer," Witherspoon began again, "perhaps
you don't understand that your wife is gravely, gravely
ill."

Frommer dismissed him with a wave of his hand. "Quit
harping on that, man. She'll be all right. She's too much
like that old father of hers to go quietly out of this life.
She'll do all right now that Roland's gone. She and Henry
are both going to dance on the old bastard's grave. I tell
you, she'll not die."

He chomped away on the scone. Witherspoon wondered if it was a fair test. He was almost sure the man
was still a bit drunk. If he did dislike walnuts, perhaps all
the drink had made him forget that fact.

"But don't you think you ought to go and see her?"
The inspector tried one last time. He simply couldn't believe that the man was so callous about his wife's condition.

"Why should I?" Frommer gave an ugly bark of a laugh. "She doesn't need my company. Hospital or not, Henry will go see her today. He told me this morning that he was looking forward to it."

"You saw Mr. Alladyce this morning?" Witherspoon pressed.

Frommer stuffed the last bite into his mouth. "Yeah, he told me about MaryAnne."

"He told you your wife had been shot?" Witherspoon wanted to make absolutely sure he'd heard that correctly.

"That's what I said, man." Frommer sniffed pathetically. "I tried to get him to loan me some money now that he's got so much of it. But he cried poor, just like he always does and sent me on my way."

"What do we do now?" Betsy asked. Like everyone else at the table, she was confused. "If Charles Burroughs isn't the killer, then we're back where we started."

"Not quite," Mrs. Jeffries replied. "We do have Mrs. Goodge's idea, of course. It's actually quite an excellent one. I should have listened to you earlier," she told the cook. "If I had, we might have the killer under lock and key now." She suddenly frowned. "But if one or more of the suspects doesn't eat the scones, then what will we do? Just because they refuse to eat in the presence of the police won't necessarily mean that they don't like walnuts."

"Not to worry." The cook beamed proudly. "I thought of that already. That's why I sent out one of my sources early this morning." She glanced at the carriage clock on the hutch. "As a matter of fact, Jeremy ought to be back anytime now. He's a clever lad, he'll do well, I know it."

"Jeremy Slaven, the boy who first brung us news of

the murder?'' Wiggins asked. '' 'E's one of your sources?''

''Now he is,'' she said. She cocked her ear toward the hall as she heard the clink of the back door and then footsteps coming their way. ''Maybe that's him now.''

But it wasn't. It was Luty and Hatchet.

The staff quickly brought them up-to-date with all that had happened. When they were almost at the very end of their narrative, Jeremy Slaven finally came racing into the kitchen. He skidded to a halt as he caught sight of the entire group at the table.

''It's all right, boy,'' Mrs. Goodge said reassuringly. ''They know everything. Now, you just get on over here and have some tea while you tell us what's what.''

''Are there any of them nutty scones left?'' Jeremy demanded as he popped down in the chair next to Wiggins. ''I could do with more of them; they was right good.''

''Nary a one, boy,'' Mrs. Goodge replied. ''But if you've found out what I wanted you to, I'll bake you a batch tomorrow all your own. You'll not have to share 'em with anyone.''

''Except Sally,'' he replied promptly. ''That's my little sister. I'll share with 'er. Can't I 'ave a slice of bread? I'm hungry.''

''Certainly.'' Mrs. Jeffries shoved the plate of bread and the butter crock toward him. He grabbed a slice and slathered it with butter as the housekeeper poured him a mug of tea. ''Ta,'' he said, when she pushed it next to his plate.

''Well, go on, then,'' Mrs. Goodge encouraged. ''What did you find out?''

''Mr. Frommer's 'ome now.'' Jeremy took a huge bite out of his bread. ''Accordin' to the 'tweeny that works fer 'im, he were on a powerful drunk and come in smellin' like a pub. But she said he likes walnuts well enough. The girl said Mrs. Frommer likes 'em too. That Mr. Burroughs—none of his servants would talk to me, so I didn't find out anything. But Miss Hartshorn ain't got nothin' against 'em. I couldn't find out anything about Mr. Alladyce either. His 'ouse was locked up tight and his neighbor said he was leavin' London as soon as he got back from visitin' Mrs. Frommer in the 'ospital.''

"That doesn't tell us much more than what we already know," Smythe muttered. "Too bad this isn't like some of our other cases. All you 'ad to do then was keep yer eye on who ended up with the money.''

Mrs. Jeffries's head jerked up. "What did you say?"

Taken aback, Smythe stared at her. "When?"

"Just now. What did you say? Repeat it, please," she ordered.

"I said it's too bad this isn't like some of our other cases. All we 'ad to do then was see who ended up with the money," he repeated. "Well, you've said it many a time yourself, Mrs. Jeffries. The one who ends up with the goods at the end of the day is usually the one that did it.''

Mrs. Jeffries couldn't speak for a moment. She stared blankly at the far wall. Then she shook her head. "I've been a fool. A stupid, arrogant fool.''

"Now, Hepzibah," Luty began, "don't be so hard on yerself. We've all made mistakes. So you thought the killer was Burroughs. Based on what we knew at the time, it was a right good assumption.''

Mrs. Jeffries looked at the faces staring at her from around the table. "Do you still trust me?" she asked them. "Even after the dreadful mistake I made about this case. Are you still willing to do what I ask.''

" 'Course we are," Wiggins volunteered. "You're right smart."

"I trust you," Betsy declared. "Why? What's happening?"

"Hatchet and I always trusted ya," Luty said, speaking for the two of them. "What's wrong? Why you lookin' like a fox that just figured out the farmer's got a gun?"

"Mrs. Goodge?" The housekeeper looked at the cook.

"You know I trust you too," she said. "You've not been wrong very often."

Smythe was already getting to his feet. "What do I have to do, Mrs. J? Just tell me what ya need and I'm on my way."

CHAPTER 11

Mrs. Jeffries glanced at Jeremy. The lad was working on his second piece of bread. Mrs. Goodge, seeing the direction of the housekeeper's gaze, acted quickly.

"Jeremy, boy," she said, reaching across and patting him on the arm. "You've done a fine job. But we've a number of things to take care of now, so you'd best be off." She got up as she spoke and made her way to the pine china hutch. "Let me wrap up this loaf of bread for ya. That way, you can take some to your sister." She yanked open the top drawer and pulled out a big sheet of brown paper and a bit of string.

Jeremy slanted a quick, suspicious look around the table. He knew he was being shown the door, but there was nothing he could do about it. He was curious as to what was going on, but not so curious that he'd risk losing the bread by being overly bold. He watched as the cook deftly wrapped the bread and neatly tied the package with the string.

"Ta," he said as she handed him the wrapped loaf. "Do you want me to come by tomorrow?"

"You might as well," she replied. "We might have somethin' for you to do."

With one last look around the table, he nodded and scampered out to the back door.

They all called out their good-byes as the lad left. As soon as he was gone, Mrs. Jeffries turned to the coachman. "You've got to get to the hospital. I think Mrs. Frommer is in terrible danger."

Smythe started for the hall. "Wait," she called. "Take Hatchet with you." She turned to him. "That is, if you're willing to go."

"You need have no fear on that account." Hatchet nodded at Luty as he got up and joined the coachman.

"What do ya want us to do when we get there?" Smythe asked. "There'll be a police constable on duty. What do we tell 'im?"

"Whatever you have to, to get into Mrs. Frommer's room," Mrs. Jeffries ordered. "But hurry. We'll find the inspector and get him there as soon as possible. Don't worry; I'm sure that between the two of you, you'll think of something to get you inside. But it's imperative you stay with Mrs. Frommer until the inspector arrives."

As soon as the men had left, she turned her attention on Wiggins. "Go upstairs to my sitting room," she instructed, "and get me the cigar box from the the bottom drawer of my desk."

Wiggins was off like a shot. Sensing the rising excitement in the air, Fred bounced after him.

"Do you know where the inspector was going after he left Mr. Burroughs's?" she asked Mrs. Goodge.

''Well . . .'' The cook thought hard. ''Just as I was walkin' away I thought I heard Constable Barnes sayin' somethin' about the Frommer house, but I couldn't hear exactly what. Why? What are we goin' to do?''

''We've got to find the inspector,'' Mrs. Jeffries said, ''and we've got to get him to the hospital.''

''Knowing you, I expect you've got a plan,'' Luty said gleefully. ''Goody. I'm itchin' to git out and about.''

Wiggins dashed into the room. '' 'Ere you are,'' he said, sliding the box on the table. ''What now?''

Mrs. Jeffries flipped open the lid, reached inside and pulled out her supplies one by one. A bottle of black ink, cheap writing paper and a pen. ''I'm going to write several notes,'' she said. ''One for each of us. We don't know where the inspector might be, so we've all got to go out, so to speak, and find the fellow.''

''Even me?'' Mrs. Goodge asked.

Mrs. Jeffries stared at her for a moment. ''I thought that after this morning you might like getting out and about as the rest of us do. Don't you want to go?''

''To be perfectly honest, Mrs. Jeffries''—the cook sighed—''this mornin' was a bit of an emergency, at least to my way of thinkin'. If it's all the same to you, I'd like to stay here and keep my eye on things. Wouldn't want to start any bad habits now, would we? Out and about is good for them that likes it, but for some of us, stayin' close to our kitchens is what's important.''

Mrs. Jeffries smiled. ''I think that's a fine idea. As a matter of fact, we do need someone here. Just in case the inspector comes back. But you'll need a note all the same.''

''What are these notes goin' to say?'' Luty asked.

''They'll all say the same thing.'' She took the cap off

the ink bottle. "And naturally, I'll disguise my handwriting."

For several minutes she worked in silence, concentrating on making her handiwork as authentic as possible. Bad spelling, poor grammar and barely legible handwriting. When she finished the first one, she held it up, studying it critically.

Inspectaur Withiespon

Hurry to hospitel. Danger. Lady killed.
Hurry up or you'll be late and she'll dy.

"I think this will do nicely," she said. "Now, to make one for each of us." She pulled another sheet of cheap paper out of the box. "Each of us will have one. Betsy, you'll take yours to the station, in case he or the constable comes there."

"I'm to tell him what," Betsy asked, "that a lad showed up at the house with this note?"

"Precisely. But please, all of you, use your own judgment and take care who you show either yourselves or the note to."

"In other words, ask if the inspector's about before we bring out the paper, right?" Luty said.

"Right. It doesn't matter so much if the inspector hears that five different people from his household were looking for him. We can always say we enlisted all of you to help locate him when the note arrived." She finished writing and slipped the note across to Betsy. Then she started the next one. "But it is imperative that he doesn't hear that each of us had a note with us. I think you all get my meaning. You show the note only to Inspector Witherspoon, no one else."

"You want us to keep our mouths shut and use our 'eads, right?" Wiggins said bluntly.

"Excellent, Wiggins, I knew you'd understand precisely. We'll all meet back here later this afternoon and see how we've done."

"Hurry, man, hurry," Hatchet yelled at the coachman through the window. "A life may be at stake."

Deacon Dickson, Luty's coachman, took the butler at his word and urged the horses onward. The coach careened around the corner, cutting it close and narrowly missing a letter box.

"He's goin' pretty ruddy fast," Smythe muttered darkly. In truth, the only person he trusted to drive this fast was himself. "I'd like to get there in one piece."

"Never fear," Hatchet said calmly. "Our coachman is an expert. He's fairly useless at anything else, but at driving a coach, no one can beat him."

Smythe, looking worried, stuck his head out the window as the coach rushed past slower traffic, veering dangerously around coopers vans and hansoms. Up ahead, he could see the entrance to the Royal Free Hospital.

"We're almost there," he called, more to calm himself than to give any information to Hatchet, who was looking out the other window. Throughout the ride, he'd been trying to think of a way to get them into Mrs. Frommer's room.

A lot of the police constables knew him by sight; he'd been with the inspector often enough. But what if there was one on that didn't know him? If the inspector had left instructions that the lady wasn't to be disturbed, then how could he and Hatchet get inside? How could the killer get inside? he wondered. But he already knew the answer to that. Desperate people could be bloody resourceful and this man had murdered twice. He was ruddy desperate by now.

The coach pulled up in front of the hospital and Hatchet and Smythe leapt out before it even came to a full stop. Ignoring the startled glances of pedestrians, patients and nursing sisters, they ran for the huge double front door. Smythe reached it first. He yanked it open and they charged inside. They skidded to a halt in front of the reception desk.

The sister behind the desk studied them with a disapproving expression on her face. "Please do not run in hospital."

Hatchet stepped forward. He doffed his hat and bowed politely to the woman. "I'm terribly sorry, ma'am, we certainly didn't mean to disturb the peace of your fine establishment. But we're in rather a hurry. Would you be so kind as to direct me to the room of Mrs. Andrew Frommer? It's most urgent we get there quickly. We've message for the police constable from his superior, Inspector Witherspoon."

The sister eyed him suspiciously, apparently, still annoyed at their heathen manners. Finally she said, "Mrs. Frommer is down the hall. It's on the left at the first corridor. She's in room number twenty-nine. But please don't run. The constable's gone to get something to eat and won't be back for a half hour or so. Another policeman came along a few moments ago to relieve him."

Smythe stepped forward. "Was this copper wearin' a uniform?"

"He was in plain clothes," she replied.

Smythe spun on his heel and charged down the hall, Hatchet hot on his heels.

"I told you not to run," the sister shouted after them, but they ignored her and kept going. Smythe swung around the corner and leapt to his left to avoid crashing into a man on crutches.

"Watch we're you're goin', mate," the man snarled, and then broke off as he flattened himself against the wall to avoid the other gent that come crashing around the corner.

They hurtled down the hall. Smythe scanned the numbers on the top of the rooms as he went. Dodging gurneys, patients, doctors and instrument carts, he ran as fast as he could, oblivious to the yelps and protests coming from behind him.

Twenty-three . . . twenty-six . . . twenty-eight . . . His heart was in his throat as he finally reached number twenty-nine. Grabbing the doorknob, he yanked it open and flew into room.

Directly across from him, a cranelike man stood over MaryAnne Frommer's bed. He was holding a pillow over her face.

The man looked up, an expression of surprise on his face. Smythe leapt at him, but the man dropped the pillow and scurried to the end of the bed, only to run flat into Hatchet, who grabbed him by the arm.

"Here now, you blackguard," the butler yelled as he jerked him around to the other side of the bed. Incensed because he too had caught a glimpse of what the fiend had been doing. "You'll hang for this."

"Watch out." Smythe called out a warning, but it was too late. The bastard used his free arm to pull a derringer out of his coat pocket. "He's got a gun."

"And it's aimed right at your heart," Henry Alladyce snarled. He shoved the gun against Hatchet's chest. "Now let me go."

Hatchet released the man's arm.

"I don't know who you are," Alladyce snapped, "but get the hell out of my way."

With a fast, worried glance at the woman on the bed, Hatchet raised his hands and stepped away. Alladyce, a mad expression on his face, kept the gun leveled in the direction of the two men, backed toward the door . . .

. . . and collided straight into Constable Barnes. Who whacked him lightly on the back of his head with his policeman's baton.

Alladyce moaned, dropped the gun and fell to his knees.

Hatchet dived for the weapon as it hit the ground. Everyone breathed a sigh of relief when it didn't go off.

Smythe leaned toward Mrs. Frommer as the inspector rushed toward the bed. "Goodness, what's happened? Did he try and kill her?"

"He was smotherin' 'er with a pillow when we walked in," Smythe said. "Then he pulled a gun on us and threatened to shoot Hatchet."

The doctor, followed by a nursing sister, hurried into the room as Constable Barnes hauled Henry Alladyce to his feet.

As the doctor tended to his patient Witherspoon walked over to Alladyce. "Henry Alladyce, you're under arrest for the murder of Roland Ashbury and the attempted murder of MaryAnne Frommer."

Several hours later all of the staff plus Luty and Hatchet gathered back at Upper Edmonton Gardens. They'd discovered that none of them had had to use their notes. The inspector, in one of those strange quirks of fate, had gone back to the hospital of his own volition.

"Odd, weren't it," Betsy said as she poured herself tea, "him going back there on his own?"

"He said he had a feeling," Mrs. Jeffries said calmly, "that he ought to. I, for one, am most grateful he arrived when he did. If Constable Barnes hadn't been able to stop Alladyce—" She broke off and shuddered. "Well, we might have had several dead bodies in that hospital room."

"I don't believe he'd have actually shot me, Mrs. Jeffries," Hatchet said thoughtfully. "I think at that point he just wanted to escape. He was quite surprised to see us. But of course, as soon as we came into the room, his plan was ruined."

"I think 'e knew it were all over," Smythe added. " 'E'd failed to murder Mrs. Frommer. Weak as she was, 'e'd not been able to kill 'er."

"How did he think he'd get away with killin' her right there in hospital?" Mrs. Goodge wondered. "He must have know the nursing sister would tell everyone he'd masqueraded as a policeman, and the police constable he'd sent off to get something to eat would certainly remember him."

"I expect Alladyce's plan was quite simple," Mrs. Jeffries guessed. "I imagine he was going to say he simply wanted to see an old friend and that the only way he could get into the room was by pretending to be a policeman."

"But she'd be dead," Betsy insisted. "Surely he must have known the police would suspect him."

"They can suspect all they want," Mrs. Jeffries replied. "But they couldn't prove he'd killed her. Not if he claimed she was already dead when he entered the room."

"Is she goin' to be all right, then?" Wiggins asked.

"For the tenth time, Wiggins," Betsy said impatiently, "she'll be fine. Smythe said he overheard the doctor telling the inspector she'd be right as rain soon."

Luty looked at Hatchet and sighed heavily. "You silly

old fool, you ought to know better than to let a man like that get the drop on ya. I've told ya a dozen different times ya ought to carry a Peacemaker. It was right in the carriage too. Why didn't you take it in with ya?''

Hatchet, who could see the worry in her face despite her words, merely reached over and patted her hand. "Next time I will, madam," he promised.

"Are you going to tell us how you figured out it was Alladyce?" Betsy asked.

"It wasn't all that difficult," Mrs. Jeffries said. "We can thank Mrs. Goodge and her theory for that."

"You mean I was right?" the cook asked.

"Absolutely. One of the things I did when I was out was have a chat with Emma Hopkins. You remember her; she's the maid who was sacked. She confirmed that Alladyce hated walnuts. As a matter of fact, she told me that every time Roland Ashbury invited Alladyce for tea, he bought a cake with walnuts."

"Deliberately?" Betsy asked.

Mrs. Jeffries nodded. "I'm afraid so. He knew the man hated the nuts, but he bought it anyway, just to be mean."

Mrs. Goodge shook her head. "It's no wonder Ashbury was murdered. He was a nasty sort. But anyway, all that aside, go on, tell us how you sussed it out."

"Well, as I said," the housekeeper continued, "because your theory eliminated so many suspects, there was really not much left to choose from when Smythe happened to mention money. That's when it all clicked into place. The one person who was going to come out of all this with any advantage was Henry Alladyce. He stood to inherit a financially sound business and several very valuable buildings."

"Do you think you'd have figured it out if it hadn't been for the walnuts?" Mrs. Goodge pressed.

"Eventually," the housekeeper replied. "Even without the nuts, there were plenty of clues. First of all, the story that Emma Hopkins told the inspector should have raised a warning flag. If you'll remember, she was sacked for breaking a flowerpot. But she claimed someone had moved the pot so she'd deliberately run into it. She was exactly right too: the person who'd moved it was Henry Alladyce. He did it to raise a commotion to buy him time."

"Time for what?" Luty asked.

"Time to look in that suitcase of old letters that Emma had put by the door. She said she'd put it there for Boyd to take back upstairs. Alladyce took the letters that we found in Mrs. Frommer's carpetbag. Those letters weren't addressed to Mrs. Frommer; they were to her father. Someone had given her those letters and I'll wager that someone was Henry Alladyce. He wanted her to suffer, he wanted her to be racked by guilt, but most of all, he wanted her to be so angry at her own father that when Alladyce murdered him, she wouldn't cooperate all that much with the police. What he hadn't counted on was her desire to leave Andrew Frommer. She was going to take the letters to her solicitor. I think we'll find that she'd planned on using them to stop her father from interfering this time. Even Roland Ashbury wouldn't have wanted people to know how abominably he'd treated his own son."

"Mrs. Jeffries." Betsy's pretty face puckered in confusion. "I still don't understand."

"It's actually very simple once you see the sequence of events," Mrs. Jeffries said. "The first thing that happened was Henry Alladyce recognizing Charles Burroughs when he saw him in the garden one afternoon cleaning his gun. You'll recall that Burroughs claimed the gun was stolen. Well, I think it was—by Henry Alladyce. He recognized Burroughs as Natasha Ashbury's brother and the plan sprang into his mind. He'd murder Ashbury and Mrs. Frommer so that he could inherit the business. Charles Burroughs coming to London and taking the house next door to Andrew Frommer gave him the perfect opportunity to carry out his plan.''

''But Emma told the police that Alladyce went on and on about having seen Mr. Burroughs somewhere before,'' Wiggins said. ''If he were settin' 'im up to take the blame for this crime, why'd 'e do that?''

''To make certain that no one else recognized him,'' she replied. ''It was an integral part of his plan that it be the police and not the Frommer household who discovered Burroughs's real identity. Look what happened when the police did find out who he was; they immediately went to arrest him. It was only Alladyce's bad luck that it was our inspector on the case. Anyone else would have clapped Burroughs into jail and brought him to trial.''

''So you're sayin' that Alladyce plotted the whole thing from the time he recognized Burroughs?'' Luty clarified.

''I think he plotted it long before Burroughs arrived on the scene,'' she said. ''But Burroughs's arrival provided an opportunity he wasn't going to miss. There's still a number of details to work out and questions that need to be answered, but I think that once the inspector gets home, we'll know everything.''

''We shouldn't have to wait long,'' Wiggins murmured, his gaze on Fred, whose tail which had begun to wag. ''I think he's comin' now.''

Fred, as always, was right. A few moments later Inspector Witherspoon trudged into the kitchen. ''Oh, everyone's here.''

''But of course, sir. You know how all of us eagerly

await the latest development on your cases," Mrs. Jeffries said easily. She had her lies all ready. "Luty and Hatchet couldn't bear to leave without hearing what happened."

"Alladyce confessed," Witherspoon said as he sank into a chair. He nodded his thanks as Mrs. Goodge pushed a plate of tea cakes under his nose. "He murdered Roland Ashbury and tried to murder MaryAnne Frommer."

"How did he get Ashbury to come back to London earlier than the rest of the family?" Mrs. Jeffries asked. "You told us that none of the servants recalled Ashbury getting a telegram. Was it arranged before Ashbury went to Ascot?"

"He sent a messenger," Witherspoon replied. "A street lad. The boy waited till Ashbury came out in the garden and gave him the message that Alladyce needed to meet him in London on urgent business. Roland told the lad to tell Alladyce to be at his home at three-fifteen for tea. Alladyce came and killed him." He shook his head wearily.

"Then he tried to murder poor Mrs. Frommer?" Wiggins murmured.

"He tried, but luckily he failed. With her dead, he got the entire business." The inspector yawned widely. "He knew that Burroughs wasn't home that evening and so he waited in his garden. Remember, Alladyce had been around the Ashbury family all of his life; he knew their habits. He knew that Mrs. Frommer escaped outside every evening after dinner to get away from her husband. Alladyce hid behind the stone wall in the Burroughs garden, and when he saw Mrs. Frommer, he shot her. He used a pillow to muffle the noise. That's why no one heard the shots from either crime. Pillows. Resourceful of him, wasn't it?"

The question was rhetorical and no one replied.

"You've had a very tiring few days, sir." Mrs. Jeffries clucked her tongue sympathetically.

"Yes, indeed I have." He gave himself a small shake. "But I do want to tell all of you how very much I appreciate your efforts on my behalf."

Everyone froze. Wiggins, who'd been reaching for a bun, stopped with his hand in midair. Smythe, who'd been sneaking a quick peek at Betsy, went rigid. Hatchet and Luty went perfectly still. Mrs. Goodge swallowed nervously. Mrs. Jeffries's heart skipped a full beat.

"I don't quite understand, sir," the housekeeper finally managed to say.

"Oh, now, I don't want you pretending you don't know what I'm talking about," he said airily. "All of you do. Let's not be coy. Sometimes your devotion is a bit misplaced, but it's always, always appreciated."

"That's good to hear, sir," Mrs. Jeffries replied. He didn't appear to be angry, of that much she was certain.

"I do believe I'm the envy of the entire Yard," Witherspoon continued. "Everyone was most impressed with Mrs. Goodge and her scones."

"I'm so very glad, sir," the cook mumbled.

"They weren't just impressed with the fact that you were devoted enough to bring me food because I'd been up all night," he said eagerly. "They were amazed at my cleverness about those walnuts. Thank you, Mrs. Goodge. Naturally I told everyone that it was your cleverness in interpreting my meaning that helped in this case."

As the cook wasn't in the least sure what he was referring to, she merely smiled and nodded at her employer.

"Smythe, you and Hatchet both deserve a great deal of thanks," he continued. "Had it not been for the two of you, that poor woman would be dead. Now tell me again, why had the two of you come to the hospital?"

Smythe was ready for this one. Mrs. Jeffries had briefed him as soon as he and Hatchet had returned home.

"We was lookin' for you, sir," he said, his expression earnest. "We got this 'ere note." He pulled one of the five that had been written out of his pocket and handed it to the inspector. "Hatchet and Luty 'ad dropped by when the boy brung it, and as I didn't want to waste time, Hatchet took me to the hospital, 'opin' we'd find you. Instead, well"—he shrugged modestly—"you know what we found. Alladyce tryin' to murder poor Mrs. Frommer."

Witherspoon squinted at the spidery handwriting. "I wonder who sent this?" he muttered. He folded it and tucked it in his breast pocket. "Oh well, as we've a confession, I don't suppose it matters. But I must say, we do seem to get a jolly lot of notes sent here."

"It's probably from one of Alladyce's servants or someone else who suspected what he was going to do, sir," Mrs. Jeffries said cautiously. "You must admit your reputation has grown so that it's only natural that people would think to, well, tip you off."

"Tip me off?" Witherspoon repeated.

"Yes, sir," she replied eagerly. "That's probably why you're always getting those sort of notes on your cases. People who normally wouldn't trust the police feel very comfortable dealing with you."

Witherspoon's brows rose. "Do you think that could be it?"

"Oh, absolutely, sir," she said fervently.

The others around the table nodded in agreement.

"You've a fine reputation," she added for good measure. "You're considered one of the fairest policemen in London. You ought to be proud that people send you notes, sir. I'm sure you get information from the sort of people who normally wouldn't give the police the time of day.''

"You know, Mrs. Jeffries"—he straightened up as he spoke—"I do believe you're right. Goodness, I'm such a very lucky man. A devoted staff and people out there"—he waved his hand to indicate the rest of the world—"who trust me above all others. It's a burden, but one that I accept with the utmost humility.''

"Yes, sir," she murmured, trying to hide her amusement. "I'm sure you do.''

They talked about the case a bit longer until the inspector, yawning with fatigue, took his leave and went to bed. Luty and Hatchet quickly followed suit.

Witherspoon was up and out in the garden early the next morning. The sun shone brightly, birds warbled from the tops of the leafy trees and the air had the crisp, clean scent of a new day. The inspector took a deep breath of air and turned to look a the house at the far end of the communal garden. *Her* house.

He told himself he wanted to enjoy a few moments of sunshine before he went to the station. There would be a mountain of paperwork to get through and a long and involved interrogation. He sighed. The truth was, he'd come out here to see if he could catch a glimpse of Lady Cannonberry. He missed her dreadfully.

His stomach rumbled with hunger. Maybe he'd ask Mrs. Goodge to make more of those walnut scones; they were certainly tasty. His fingers drifted to the waistband of his trousers. Perhaps he ought to ask the housekeeper to take these to the tailor's. They were getting a bit snug around his middle.

"Good morning, Gerald." Ruth's soft voice had him spinning around on his heel. "I saw you from my bedroom window and couldn't resist the chance to see you.''

"Ruth," he exclaimed with pleasure. "I'm so glad you did. It seems ages since I've seen you."

"It's only been a few days," she replied, stepping close and taking his hand, "but it does seem a long time. How is your case going?"

"It's over," he stuttered, staring down at the hand she held so gently in hers. "How is your houseguest?"

"Morris is going to be leaving today," she replied, stroking his fingers tenderly. "He doesn't know it, but he's going to be taking the train back to Chester. Frankly I'm sick to death of him. Gerald, would you be so kind as to have dinner with me tonight?"

"I should love to, Ruth," he said fervently. "Is it a dinner party, or will it be just the two of us?"

"Just the two of us," she whispered. "I've got to go now. I'll see you this evening at seven."

Witherspoon watched her disappear through her back door. He turned and hurried into his own house.

"Good morning, sir," Mrs. Goodge called as he flew past her, heading for the backstairs. "Breakfast will be ready in a few minutes. There's bacon and eggs, porridge, toast and kippers. Will that be enough, sir?"

"Oh, don't bother with breakfast, Mrs. Goodge," he hollered over his shoulder. "I'm going to skip it today. I believe I've gained a bit of weight."